The NEBADOR series:

Book One: The Test

Book Two: Journey

Book Three: Selection

Book Four: Flight Training

Book Five: Back to the Stars

Book Six: Star Station

Book Seven: The Local Universe

Book Eight: Witness
2014

Book Nine: A Cry for Help
2015

Also by J. Z. Colby:

Standing on Your Own Two Feet:
Young Adults Surviving 2012 and Beyond

NEBADOR

*Book Seven

THE LOCAL UNIVERSE

an epic young-adult science fiction adventure

by

J. Z. Colby

and the short story

Buna's Search
by Shadow Buffalo-walker

Nebador Archives

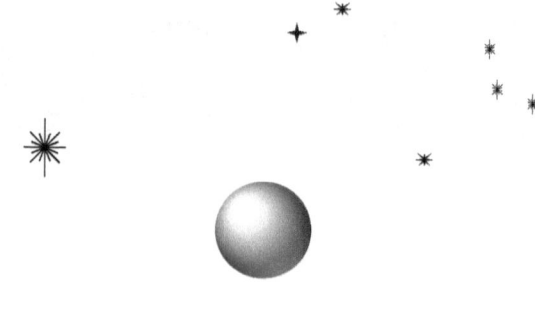

Cover art by Rachael Hedges and Sidney Oster
Illustrations by J. Z. Colby

For other print editions, ebooks, dramatic audiobooks, previews, samples, biographies, comments, questions, artwork, writing contests, Ask Kibi advice, deep learning notes, Nebador citizens, and more, please see:

www.nebador.com

Nebador Archives
Kelso, Washington, USA

Library of Congress Control Number: 2013910685
Manufactured in the USA

ISBN: 978-1-936253-69-2
NEBADOR7PBG: paperback, 6" x 9", 192 pages, global edition
  (10-point Georgia type)

Greetings, young people of planet Earth,

The previous book of the series, *NEBADOR Book Six: Star Station*, finally answered most questions about Ilika's civilization, both for the five crew members from a backward medieval world, and for us. By *Book Six*, the new crew of the deep-space response ship Manessa Kwi has been tested in many ways, gone on long journeys by land, air, and space, looked Death in the face, and come home to Satamia Star Station to heal their wounds and, of course, be tested some more. *Book Six* concluded *Trilogy Two*, and is the final book of the essential NEBADOR saga.

The book in your hands takes the story to a new level as the crew begins advanced training and real missions. No longer will they be making little supply runs here and there. Now they must work with highly-trained Nebador citizens to solve serious universe problems that involve the fates of entire civilizations.

Although our friends must continue to wrestle with physical and mental challenges, more and more they find they must understand spiritual matters. Indeed, they receive a training supervisor who is only visible when she chooses to be, and knows when to let the monkey mammals of the Manessa Kwi discover solutions for themselves.

Most people agree that *our* spiritual helpers, by whatever names we call them, also know when to leave us alone with our problems and predicaments so that we will most deeply feel the joy of standing on our own two feet.

J. Z. Colby
2013

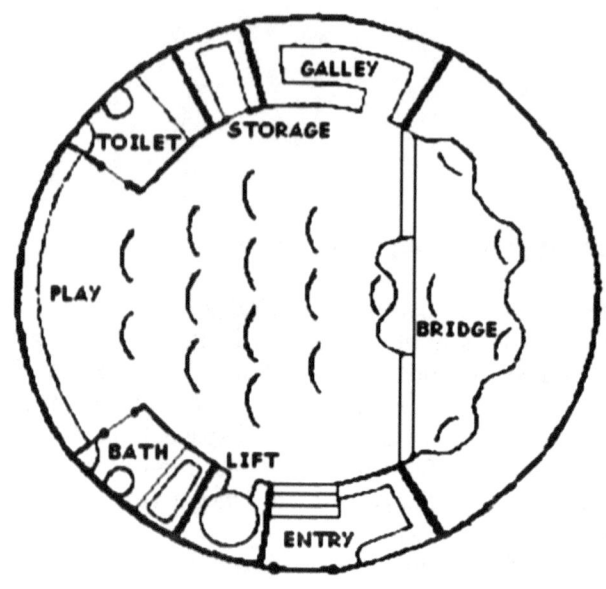

Acknowledgements

Wonderful people throughout the author's life provided unique and irreplaceable lessons and inspirations:

Juniper Russell
Vicky Ball
Linda Dezzutti
Jennifer Carolyn Gates
Rachael Bleich
Paula Wells
Sarah Satterthwaite
Ashley Riddle
Antonya Pickard

Esther Smith
Dottie Frisbie
Martha Higgins
Susanne Koller
Charleen Cox
Meredith Herzog
Patricia Sharp
Peter James

Valuable readers gave the author feedback after digging through early drafts of the book:

Karen Oster   Cecelia Harper

Excellent critiquers commented on thousands of passages, then provided reactions during in-depth interviews:

Sidney Oster, 12   Catherine "Cat" Harper, 14
Sarah Bray, 14   Dylan Oster, 14
Joshua Utter, 17   Alex Chalcraft

Careful publishing assistants, proofreaders, and technical helpers brought the final manuscript as close to perfection as possible:

Cecelia Harper

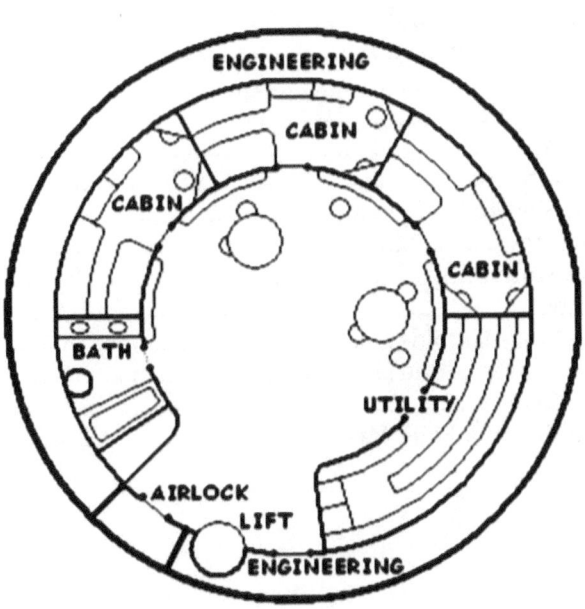

Contents

Part 2 The Center

"I have decreed it, and I will bring it to pass. My word will not return to me empty."

— Yahweh

Part 1: The Edge

Chapter 1: Deep-Space Mission

Melorania, a barely-seen blue mist, hovered near the ceiling of Satamia Star Station's main hall. People of all shapes and sizes went about their business far below, or swooped through the air in transit from balconies to corridors.

A green mist formed near her.

I want you to meet someone, Melorania said.

A small purple mist appeared nearby.

The green and purple mists touched. *Welcome, Arantiloria, to Satamia Star Station*, Kerloran said. *You have journeyed far.*

It will be an honor to supervise a response-ship crew beginning advanced training and serious missions. I applied nearly a century ago, and have been observing fully-trained crews while I awaited an assignment. These ... humans ... are unique to Nebador, I believe. We do not have any in Kalidor.

And that is best, Kerloran said, turning a slightly softer green. *They have ... many challenges.*

✳

Arantiloria decided to wander around the star station, to see what she could learn, before beginning her assignment. Many of the creature shapes were strange to her, so she remained invisible to all mortal eyes and floated down toward the activity in the main hall.

The flying creatures delighted her the most, and she quickly realized why — in Kalidor, no one had evolved feathers. Here, feathers were everywhere, sometimes floating in the air when a winged creature would shake itself, or take off from the floor with powerful strokes.

The floor ... something about the floor of the main hall called to her, so Arantiloria floated down and opened herself to its memories.

She smiled as she saw Kibi, with bucket and scrub brush, crying and trembling as the young human steeled herself to be mocked and abused, based solely on memories from her home planet. *Yes*, Arantiloria silently agreed with Kerloran, *these humans have challenges.*

The low-gravity pathways remembered Mati well, and a dishwashing room had a fond memory of Boro, struggling to get his priorities straight.

Arantiloria let herself wander, following her instincts, getting used to the mortals of Nebador, and listening to any stories that came to her. Before long, her intuition led her up to the third balcony. A little bubbling fountain in the middle of a small patio nearly reached out and grabbed her, so she went close and listened carefully.

It knew all six members of the human crew, five very recently, and the captain a few years before. Ilika had whispered his loneliness to the trickling water, sending out his hope that someday he would have a companion. It also knew of Kibi's sexual desire for another mammal, and then her shame. Sata's prayers for Boro to find his passion were clearly recorded, and Rini's joy when Mati began to walk.

After wandering for several more days and listening to countless plants, stones, tables, and the great station tree itself, Arantiloria decided it was time to meet her new charges.

*

When the call came, a day later, for the crew of the Manessa Kwi to attend a meeting in a small chamber near the Mission Assignment Room, Ilika knew no more about it than anyone else. The dimly-lit room was silent and somber as they entered and beheld three large insects studying a star chart that glowed on a low table. The crew quietly settled themselves onto benches along the outer walls.

After another minute of silence, the mantis drew himself up to full height, towering over the others. "I don't like it one bit. The numbers don't add up to the usual interstellar-probe situation. It smells of desperation. T'shlix, you have more experience with such matters."

The large, dark beetle shimmered with many iridescent colors as he twitched his mandibles. "I thought I did, but there's something way-wrong here, as you also sense. Never before, in all the records of Nebador, have ships of this size been seen. What think you, M'palta?"

The large, furry arachnid shuddered for a moment. "My food pouch is tight with worry, and I counsel against any assumptions we might be tempted to make."

A smaller insect, that the crew hadn't yet noticed, suddenly unfurled wings that moved faster than sight, leapt into the air, and hovered over the glowing chart. "It's exciting! Definitely not a routine assignment. We shall learn much, and make many new dances and songs, although some may be sad." As she bobbed in the air over the table, her delicate arms stretched out to the sides and her two tails hung down, sometimes touching the chart. "This is truly deeper than deep space. But, M'palta, I believe our ship's crew has arrived."

The spider stretched up taller on eight legs and tucked her head to look under and behind her. Her many eyes met Kibi's two. "Greetings, monkey mammals. This might be a long mission. Please consider our dietary needs."

Kibi looked around, then remembered who the steward was. "We will."

M'palta raised her head and looked back at her fellow insects. "Four days?"

The beetle shook his head. "Could take that long just to find and examine the lead ship, and there are three of them. We'd better be ready for six or eight days. Thoughts, Filia?"

The little hovering insect hopped to another part of the chart. "I feel . . . we will not *understand* until we have embraced all three ships . . . and danced upon their home planet."

The green mandibles of the tall mantis twitched nervously. "That could take . . . twenty days. I will have to find a substitute for some classes I was supposed to teach."

T'shlix nodded his iridescent head. "I, also."

M'palta ducked and looked at Kibi again. "You'd better stock for twenty days."

Kibi's mouth was dry, but she managed to speak. "Do you mean . . . twenty *Satamia* days?"

The spider's many eyes darkened slightly. "Is there another kind in use on *Satamia* Star Station?"

✳

Half an hour later, Ilika, Kibi, and Boro all had lists of extra supplies they had to stock for a mission that would push the limits of even a deep-space response ship. The four insects had gone back to discussing the glowing star chart on the table, when suddenly the smallest of them started gazing up toward one corner of the ceiling. Her wings flashed and she floated upward, an intense look of curiosity on her tiny face.

"Someone is here," she shared. "Greetings, spirit. You need not remain hidden. We welcome any wisdom you have about this difficult mission."

Arantiloria quickly made the decision to let herself be seen, and chose to take monkey-mammal shape since the crew of the Manessa Kwi were her primary charges.

To the mortal eyes in the room, a purple mist appeared, settled toward the floor, and swirled into a girl with purple hair and bright eyes. All six crew members were quickly on their feet, most gazing at her with surprise.

"You are very perceptive, little one," she said to the insect, still hovering near, as she touched it gently with one finger. "I am Arantiloria, an advanced training specialist from the local universe of Kalidor. I have the great honor of being assigned to the Manessa Kwi, and have spoken at length with the ship, but have not, until now, revealed myself to the crew. I was wondering when the right moment might be. You decided for me, little one."

The hovering insect bowed. "I am Timorafilia, linguist and mission language specialist."

"T'shlix, technology specialist," the iridescent beetle shared.

"K'storpo, mission leader," the tall mantis said, bowing low.

"M'palta, biologist and mission steward," the arachnid revealed.

Ilika was about to speak when Arantiloria put a finger to her lips. "I will speak with the crew more as time allows, but right now I do not wish to interrupt your planning session any further. I'm sorry, but I have no special knowledge concerning this mission."

K'storpo took a deep breath. "I think we would accomplish little by staring at the chart any longer today. Let us all do the research we need to do, let the crew prepare their ship, enjoy the evening party that approaches, and depart after a good sleep."

The other three mission specialists nodded their agreement, and all four left the room.

Arantiloria became purple mist, then vanished.

The six humans looked at each other, shrugged or smiled, and headed for their ship to figure out where they were going to put enough supplies for twenty long Satamia days.

✳   ✳   ✳

Chapter 2: Departure

After playing a slow, haunting ballad on her keyboard, which she knew was colored by her nervousness about the upcoming mission, M'palta closed her instrument case as some avians struck up a lively dance tune. She spotted T'shlix two balconies lower, and seeing that the ramps were crowded, climbed onto the railing, attached a thread, and lowered herself down.

The beetle clicked his four wings in greeting. "Lots of feeling in that piece you just played."

"Thanks. I'm worried about the mission. I keep trying to imagine it, but see lots of darkness and not much else."

"It *is* deep space!"

The spider looked at her friend with many eyes for a moment, then wiggled her mandibles with laughter. "Okay, you got me. Do you think the inexperienced monkey-mammal crew will be any trouble?"

"No. Next time you're at a knowledge processor, read what happened to them on Sonmatia Seven. And that high-level spirit, Aran-something, will be along. We'll be okay."

Spider and beetle listened to the music, shoulder to shoulder, until M'palta's mate arrived. The couple made their way down to the dance floor, leaving T'shlix to ponder his own worries about the upcoming mission.

✳

The next morning, station time, when the mantis K'storpo ducked his head and stepped from the boarding tunnel into the assigned deep-space response ship, he beheld the black-haired steward and the short, stocky navigator working together in the galley. All the cupboards, currently open, appeared to be full, but the two monkey mammals seemed determined to cram in more. Open boxes of food packets lined the galley counter.

To K'storpo's right, the large, muscular engineer was on the floor, reaching under the engineering console with the flexible probe of a test instrument. Boro noticed the mantis enter, and waved with his free hand.

K'storpo bowed slightly.

The small, long-haired pilot spun around in her chair, bounced up to her feet, and smiled at the tall mantis.

K'storpo quickly suppressed his fear-reaction as he remembered that such a showing of teeth was a gesture of friendship in mammals.

"Welcome to the Manessa Kwi," Mati said. "I'm supposed to take over in the galley now so Kibi can get you guys settled."

Kibi, stuffing more packets into the highest cupboard, turned her head. "Oh, yeah. Hi! I'll be right down."

Hearing sounds behind him, K'storpo stepped aside to allow T'shlix and his mate to enter the ship, followed closely by M'palta and her mate, each carrying a travel bag. At the same time, Rini appeared in the lift, Ilika came up a moment later, and for a few seconds everyone was bumping into everyone else. Kibi quickly stepped into the middle of the chaos and began pointing at passenger seats or toward the bridge. Soon, order was restored, and the new passengers immediately gained a healthy respect for the no-nonsense steward of the little ship.

Out in the boarding tunnel, the last group of passengers approached by air.

"Do they know . . . there are six of us?" Timoratamia asked shyly.

Timoradalia giggled. "We're on the passenger list!"

"They're nice," Timorafilia informed. "I've met them."

"Do little ships like this have bath tubs?" Timoradalia asked.

"Of course, silly!" Timorasimia asserted.

Last of all, Tizoromulia, feeling a bit embarrassed by the silly questions of his five mates, remained silent as they all fluttered into the ship.

Kibi spotted them, smiled, and pointed toward a passenger seat in the front row, big enough for all six with room to spare.

✳

Half an hour later, the mantis K'storpo handed Kibi a knowledge pad. "That's it. Everything we can imagine needing is on board — M'palta's portable lab, Filia's language references, and all those electronic interfaces T'shlix loves to use. But my hunch is we'll learn the most with our eyes and ears."

Kibi smiled and nodded at her fellow intuitive, even though he was a large green insect.

K'storpo took his seat, and Kibi looked over her passengers, her first group of Nebador citizens on a serious mission that had nothing to do with any of her fellow crew members. For the first time, they were just the crew of a deep-space response ship, there to run the ship, but not otherwise worry about the mission.

Turning to look down at the bridge, she saw that the rest of the crew were at or near their stations. "Loading complete," she informed her captain.

He nodded and went back to helping Sata with her new deep-space charts.

Seeing that Kibi wasn't busy, one of the small, winged females raised her tiny arms in the air. "Do we get to take baths?"

Kibi knelt down in front of the passenger seat where all six of the little insects snuggled together, tails wrapped around each other. "Yes, but it's inert liquid medium, not water."

"I know. We use it all the time in the chemistry lab where I work, and sometimes M'palta comes in to have things analyzed. She's nice."

Kibi glanced at the huge spider that would cause any girl or woman from her home planet to scream, and any man to run for a weapon. She swallowed once, then chuckled.

"Departure procedure," Ilika announced.

Kibi stood up and stepped to her console. "Manessa, is Arantiloria aboard?"

"Yes, she arrived before the rest of you."

Kibi blinked several times as her fingers began to move on her console. "Ship secure, hatch closed, docking tunnel away . . ."

*

Although the crew and passengers felt nothing unusual in the timelessness of star transit, their first leap across the vastness of Nebador was nearly eight times as far, measured in space, as any of them had experienced before, save Tizoromulia and his mates.

He and his five females, with their many skills, were often requested on challenging deep-space missions. The fact that a large part of their brains was sensitive to non-material reality, allowing them to know of Arantiloria's presence, was certainly a point in their favor.

Their problem, therefore, was finding enough time to just relax, play together in the warm waters of the star station, and do the work each of them loved.

Tizoromulia's passion was mathematics, striving to understand the mysterious relationships between matter and energy that wove their threads of meaning throughout the universe. But it was a cool passion, he knew, and not possible without the deep comfort of arms and tails touching his five beautiful mates.

Timorasimia was the emotional heart of the family, if anyone was, turning blue in empathy when any of the others was feeling deeply. She worked in the medical center, tending and comforting insects, and occasionally other creatures, as they healed.

Timorazonia would rather be flying — with her own wings, on avian-back, or in a space suit with thrusters — she didn't care. Kerloran didn't often allow her to get into a pilot's seat, as he knew well that she was reckless, and loved speed to the exclusion of all other concerns. She had eyed the brown-haired monkey mammal at the helm of this ship when they first came on board, but didn't think she was the type to easily surrender her controls.

As she loved her work in the chemistry lab, Timoradalia was much closer to her mate in skills and knowledge, and yet she was the one who embarrassed him most often. She spoke her mind, always and everywhere, without thought to the subtle timing of most social interactions. Even so, he loved her.

Timoratamia could only be described as an artist. She looked deeply into everything, but could put little into words. However, give her enough colors and she would depict the entire universe, on all levels of reality, or exhaust herself trying. Often Tizoromulia had to carry her away from her colors for nourishment or sleep. Her works glowed on many of the walls of Satamia Star Station, and several other star and planet stations.

But Timorafilia was the reason they were on this mission. She, more than anyone else in Satamia, could sense the underlying logic of a language, and untangle the grammar, even when it was barely-related to any other language. But she, and the entire mission team, knew this assignment might be especially challenging, as the language they expected to encounter probably evolved in a lone solar system, far out on the edge of the local universe.

They were, Kibi knew from her passenger list, collectively known as *Ti'ias* in the language of Nebador. Looking over their names, she could understand why.

*

Once the first star transit was complete, the rest of the crew focused on the approach to a small mining station, the farthest outpost of Nebador in this direction. Kibi stepped into the galley.

She remembered Mati and Rini talking about eating frogs with K'stimla the surgeon, and knew she had several packages, but decided they were best saved for special meals. With a knowledge pad on the galley counter, Kibi referenced her passenger list, selected *light meals during transit*, and was soon searching through her jam-packed cupboards.

With the table set a bit lower than usual, and the seat containing the Ti'ias raised a little higher, everyone looked comfortable. Having no idea how much they would eat, Kibi gave them empty trays and placed the serving packets in the middle of the table. Her passengers were soon selecting plump fruits, juicy worms, or both, as the packets were passed around and they discussed the mission.

"Final approach," Ilika said from the command chair, so Kibi stepped to the steward's station to do the other part of her job.

*   *   *

Chapter 3: Searching the Void

Ilika, Boro, and a strong reptile from the mining station quickly unloaded the cartons and canisters from the back of the passenger area. Everyone else stretched their legs or wings in the station's small common area, then waved good-bye.

Sata took longer than usual to prepare herself for star transit. She knew from her charts that they were going into deep, dark interstellar space.

*

After the star transit, the crew made sure all systems were stable, and verified that absolutely nothing was out there for several light-minutes in all directions. At K'storpo's request, everyone gathered at the large table. Ilika remained on-duty at the steward's station, and Kibi put bowls of nuts and worms on the table.

The exact location of their first destination, K'storpo explained, was not known. The huge ship had last been seen about a hundred years before, but for reasons known only to Kerloran and Melorania, a mission to investigate had not been requested until now. He picked up a worm and took it apart with his mandibles to indicate he was done speaking.

T'shlix presented what was known about the mysterious ship's speed and direction, but emphasized that the numbers were just rough guesses. He also mentioned some dark planets in the interstellar void that could have affected the ship's course. Feeling brave, he tried one of the nuts, but quickly spat it out into his claw.

Kibi smiled and handed him a towel from the galley.

Sata began squirming, so K'storpo pointed at her.

"I've looked at the dark planets on the charts, but don't know enough about the ship's course to make any calculations yet. There are three or four that could have given it a tug and sent it in a different direction . . . unless it was using engines to compensate."

"Kerloran believes it is adrift," the mantis shared, "although he did not say that about the other two ships coming along behind."

"Sata," Ilika began, "you will be in charge of the search pattern. Work with T'shlix, Boro, and Rini. Careful with fuel, and Rini has the difficult task of spotting a ship that is large, but has probably gone as dark as those interstellar planets."

"How large?" the slender, freckled lad asked.

"From what we know," T'shlix replied, "nearly the size of a star station."

Rini whistled in amazement.

*

Considering the length of the mission, Ilika allowed his passengers to use the lower deck. Kibi spread out games and toys on the tables. All six Ti'ias were soon enjoying a board game, with pieces moving almost faster than Kibi could follow. M'palta, the biologist, had no part to play in this phase of the mission, so she and the female beetle got comfortable, at a much more leisurely pace, with another game.

When she returned to the upper deck, Kibi noticed that M'palta's mate was on the long bench at the back of the passenger area, reading something on a knowledge pad.

At the big table, Sata struggled with the fact that she was in charge of the search, when everyone else was older than her, and three were long-time Nebador citizens. She quickly discovered that K'storpo, T'shlix, and Ilika would each share what they knew, but no one was going to do her job for her.

"So ... since Rini thinks we can only spot this thing within seven light-minutes," the twelve-year-old navigator began, "that means our search paths have to be sixteen light-minutes apart. I think we should make it fifteen, just to be careful." She looked up from her knowledge pad at those older and wiser.

All three nodded their acceptance. Rini smiled.

K'storpo watched as Sata the monkey-mammal navigator took on her new assignment. He knew of search patterns that were more efficient, but no one claimed to know how to find the huge, dark ship that was supposedly out there, in interstellar space, somewhere. A random hunch might work just as well as an elegant mathematical solution. He sensed that the mystery entwined in the process added an air of excitement for both crew and mission specialists.

*

Duty shifts came and went. Sata plotted search patterns. Mati approved them, then let Manessa take over and went back to reading, games, or helping in the galley.

Rini kept an eye on his sensors as they peered seven or more light-minutes into space in every direction, looking for something dark and probably lifeless in the blackness of interstellar space. He knew Manessa would announce even an interesting grain of sand, but he liked to search through his console options for any useful tools he had missed.

About once a ship-day, he, Ilika, and K'storpo conferred, but no one could think of any tricks they weren't already using.

With nothing but the ion drive sipping tiny amounts of fuel, Boro, with Ilika's blessing, disappeared into the engineering ring to take apart and put back together whichever engine caught his eye that day. Often Sata joined him, handing him tools but remembering that Boro didn't like much chatter while he worked. Sometimes T'shlix, or M'palta's mate, declared they were bored and begged to watch.

Manessa was always available when Boro couldn't remember a step, and helped him test the finished product.

✳

After two entire Satamia days had passed, the air of excitement began to wane. The entire group of six crew members, four specialists, and seven other family members, all settled into routines that had little or nothing to do with the huge object they were seeking. Entire ship-days passed when Rini was the only one who even glanced at the watch station.

M'palta and Kibi entered into a pact. Arachnid would teach human how to make meals for insects that were much more interesting than the pre-packaged stuff, and in return, Kibi would reveal how to change a pile of coarse, fibrous vegetables into something called a stew. Sata and the female beetle quickly joined.

The entire group was enjoying a meal made by Sata and M'palta when the ship's gentle voice was heard. "Large, dark object detected."

✳ ✳ ✳

Chapter 4: The Lead Ship

The huge black monstrosity towered over the little deep-space response ship long before Mati brought them close.

"Eight kilometers," Sata announced.

"Hold relative position," Ilika said, eyes glued to the big screen on the bridge.

In the passenger area, K'storpo and his specialists studied the same image on the large display over the steward's station.

"Ready ion seven," Ilika commanded.

Boro raised his eyebrows and reached for his engine control board.

"Full emergency responses, highest sensitivity."

Mati checked the setting, then nodded.

"Scan for radiation, all types, highest resolution."

Rini went to work.

"Calculate exact course and speed."

Sata turned back to her console.

Kibi checked on her passengers without blocking their view of the big screen. From behind K'storpo's seat, she gazed at the visual display. The mystery ship reminded her of a pregnant black fish that had been in too many fights.

"No radiation sources," Rini announced. "The entire thing is eleven degrees absolute and slowly dropping."

"No temperature variation *at all?*" K'storpo asked.

"No, none."

"That's about as dead as a ship gets," M'palta said. "Even spores start losing their genetic information at temperatures that low."

"The entire ship will be brittle," Timoradalia the chemist informed in her small voice, peering intently at the screen along with the other five Ti'ias. "Everything we move will just break."

"There may be knowledge crystals," T'shlix the technologist speculated.

K'storpo nodded. "We are here to learn everything we can."

"It is . . . very, very dead," Timorasimia the empath said flatly.

After a long silence, the captain spoke. "Bring us to one kilometer."

*

The four mission specialists were soon in their space suits, very different from the human-shaped suits the crew used. K'storpo added Timoradalia to the excursion team.

Timorazonia begged to go, just to fly around in space with her suit thrusters, but K'storpo shook his head and Tizoromulia wrapped his arms around her. She melted into his embrace with a chittering sound.

Kibi made sure they had gone through their checklists, then wished them well as they entered the airlock.

*

The co-mates Timorafilia and Timoradalia held hands as they activated their tiny suit thrusters and followed the large insects toward the dark, silent ship. It's plump, bulging shape clearly showed it purpose — to transport a great volume of something.

K'storpo was pretty sure he knew what, but had not spoken of it yet. The contents of the three ships had not been revealed. K'storpo knew, from experience, that if it wasn't in the mission documents, they weren't going to get it. The powers of the universe, on all levels, did not share everything they knew. On the rare occasions that Nebador citizens found out why, it was usually because they would learn more by discovering the information for themselves.

As they approached the dull-black metal hull, K'storpo focused his thoughts. "No one touches the ship. Dalia will determine the hull's integrity. T'shlix and Filia will find an access point."

The Ti'ias split up.

The little chemist approached the massive black object, pulled an instrument from a pocket of her suit, and touched its keys. After seeing the results, she made a warbling noise. "I can't believe someone thought they could build an interstellar ship out of metal. Hardly a centimeter is without asteroid pits, and it's all highly crystallized. No atmospheric integrity, little structural integrity. It's safe to touch, but will break if any force is applied."

The little language specialist joined the large beetle as they began to scan the hull for markings. Words written in paint were all but destroyed, but Timorafilia began to find symbols done with raised metal. She floated in place and peered at them, letting her mind shift into the state of consciousness that allowed her to see underlying patterns of meaning.

T'shlix had worked with her before, and several other language specialists, so he knew not to interrupt or try to hurry the process.

After several minutes, the little Ti'ia shook her head to clear it. "No connection with any language of Nebador. I'm pretty sure it's insect, but considering who was picked for this mission, that's not surprising, is it,

K'storpo?"

He chuckled. "No."

"Highly repetitive," Timorafilia continued, "lots of code, lots of negatives, probably military, or at least hive."

Beetle and Ti'ia continued to move along the hull in silence for a few minutes.

Suddenly the little language specialist stopped and stared at some markings on the hull. "That says *Danger, Do Not Open*. That would be code for *We don't want anyone else coming in this way*."

K'storpo chuckled again and came near to consider the situation.

T'shlix looked at his leader, prying tool in hand.

"Everyone else, back a hundred meters," K'storpo said. "Manessa Kwi, stand near in case of injury."

Mati quickly moved the ship just beyond the excursion team. Kibi made sure the outer airlock was open.

Seeing that everyone was ready, T'shlix approached the hatch with its dire warning. He touched the pitted metal surface for the first time, slipped his prying tool between the layers of metal, and pressed a symbol.

The hatch burst open and cracked into seven or eight pieces, all of which floated away from the dark ship. M'palta gave a puff from her suit thrusters to avoid one of them. Another bounced off the golden hull of the response ship waiting near, then slowly tumbled away into space.

When K'storpo was sure everyone was unhurt, he turned and looked at the black opening. "Manessa Kwi, any energy readings?"

"No," Rini replied. "Eight point seven six degrees absolute."

K'storpo activated a bright light, and they beheld a metal room, a half-open metal door with metal teeth along the edge, and a dark metal corridor beyond.

"I've seen things like this in museums," M'palta shared. "They're built by people who are very unhappy and constantly battling everyone, even their own kind. People like that rarely get into space at all."

"Manessa Kwi, we are going inside," the mantid leader said. "Two hours, maximum."

*

For the first hour, Ilika had difficulty getting his crew to relax. Boro, especially, looked worried.

"I never thought I'd be fretting over ... *bugs*," the engineer said, using one word from his native language, as he paced within reach of his station.

Sata smiled from her console chair. "I can tell you admire T'shlix."

Boro blushed. "I'm starting to tinker with my engines. He *understands* them."

Sata nodded. "M'palta has taught me more about cooking than even my mother, I think. Of course, back home I wasn't trying to cook for a mantis, coleopters, arachnids, and Ti'ias."

Boro snickered and Sata joined him.

Rini swiveled his chair around. "It's humbling being a servant for, you know, *bugs*."

Mati smiled at him from the helm. "I don't think we'll ever get to *do* any important missions, unless we can do our jobs when others are on missions."

At the big table, Ilika looked up from a knowledge pad. "On planets like yours, people become leaders who don't know *how* to be servants."

Rini scrunched his face. "It seems like Nebador always does things exactly opposite the way they're done on Sonmatia Three."

Ilika grinned.

✳

The second hour was drawing to a close when an alarm sounded and Manessa spoke. "Asteroid shower approaching. Decimeter scale."

Ilika flew onto the bridge. "Manessa, maximum profile and repulsion field. Mati, shield the dead ship as best you can. Rini, give her a real-time image."

"All maneuvering thrusters!" Mati ordered.

Boro's fingers moved quickly, and added full inertia canceling.

"Sata, warn the excursion team!" Ilika barked. "Inertia . . ."

The first fist-size rock arrived at nearly one-eighth the speed of light, slammed into the little ship's repulsion field, and sent both Rini and Kibi flying from their seats.

"But inertia canceling is full!" Boro yelled with a guilty tone.

"Inertia straps!" Ilika finished his thought as he checked on Rini, then went to Kibi.

"We're supposed to *avoid* this size asteroid!" Mati growled as she continued to concentrate on her screen. "It's weird letting them *hit* us. Here comes another one!"

Ilika grabbed Kibi, just getting up, and pinned her to a passenger seat as the ship lurched again.

"Okay, I can handle it now," Kibi asserted. "I need to check on my passengers."

Ilika nodded and returned to the bridge. He saw that the other four were strapped in, so he grabbed his own straps just before another asteroid struck the ship.

"They're okay, and on the way out," Sata informed.

"Tell me the moment they're outside, and tell them to approach in a straight line so Mati can protect them."

Sata nodded and turned back to her console.

Kibi quickly saw that the four Ti'ias had taken wing to avoid the shocks, and appeared to be okay. The female beetle was already strapped into a seat. That left only the male arachnid. Kibi couldn't see him anywhere.

"They're coming more often!" Mati yelled. "Three on my screen!"

Kibi held onto a passenger seat until all three asteroids had slammed into the ship, then resumed her search for the missing passenger. She had last seen him in the back of the passenger area.

"Oh, no!" Mati shrieked. "Five coming! I can't get them all!"

Kibi suddenly saw a spider's leg holding onto a passenger seat from underneath. She realized, with a shudder, that it was bent in too many places. Even with asteroids still pounding the ship, she moved in that direction, holding onto one or two seats as she moved.

"I got three!" Mati yelled. "But . . . damn!"

The entire crew, save Kibi, watched helplessly as the fourth asteroid missed the Manessa Kwi and slammed into the lifeless ship, punching a hole many times its size. A fraction of a second later, it punched a hole in the far side and continued on into space.

"I got the fifth!" Mati assured everyone.

Kibi held on while the ship jerked violently, then dropped onto the floor to find M'palta's mate under a seat, three of his legs tangled and one bleeding. Fear showed in his dozens of eyes.

Kibi struggled with her own fear and loathing for a moment. Then she heard a soft female voice she had only heard once before. "He's a Nebador citizen, Kibi, and he needs you."

Kibi looked into the spider's fearful eyes again and saw enough trust to allow her to help. She reached around his middle and spoke just as softly as the voice had spoken to her. "I've got you. Let all your legs go limp."

After a moment of hesitation, the spider did as she asked, and the pain in his broken leg was immediately reduced, allowing him to think again. "Second left leg broken, third right knee wrenched. Sometimes I wish I didn't have so many."

Kibi smiled to herself as she got him into a seat, secured his inertia straps, and worked her way toward the medical kit in the entryway.

"They're out!" Sata nearly screamed. "All five!"

"Okay, protect only their line of approach, Mati," Ilika ordered, "and close the distance. Kibi, airlock."

"Can't. Have an injured passenger."

"I'll do the airlock," the female beetle offered and popped her inertia straps.

Kibi nodded, then dashed for the medical kit.

✳   ✳   ✳

Chapter 5: Samples

"We were crossing a main corridor when the asteroid burst through the ship," K'storpo related. "Suddenly millions of metal shards came flying toward us. Everyone hit their suit thrusters at once and we were well-clear before the junk flew by."

Mati looked at her lap. "I am soooo sorry I missed that one."

Timorazonia took to the air and landed on the table in front of Mati. "I know lots of pilots," she asserted in her small voice, "and I don't know many who could have gotten *half* those rocks."

Mati reluctantly looked up, and saw that the Ti'ia had a very sincere look on her tiny face. Mati glanced around, and saw that Ilika, K'storpo, and T'shlix were all nodding agreement. "I still wish I'd gotten it," she said, holding in a slight smile.

Rini started clapping, and others quickly joined with their hands, or with insect claws tapping on the table.

Mati couldn't help but crack a tiny grin.

Boro's hand crept up, and K'storpo nodded at him.

"Is there anything I could have done to avoid all that inertia? I feel terrible about someone getting hurt."

The wounded spider, still flinching at times as M'palta adjusted his bandages, immediately spoke. "No, Boro. The energy from those rocks was far greater than anything Manessa could absorb without reaction. Every ship has limits. It would have been much worse, probably fatal for most of us, if you hadn't engaged inertia canceling when you did."

After a moment of silence, a broken voice was heard from another part of the table, and everyone looked to see trembling lips on a freckled face. "It was ... my fault. I should have ... spotted those asteroids ... much sooner. I was ... too focused on the ... the mystery ship."

Ilika nodded. "And therefore your captain shares your guilt."

Others slowly nodded.

"Forgiven," M'palta's mate said with a wave of one of his good legs. "Can we start the excursion reports? I'm *dying* of curiosity about what you found!"

The mood lightened, and K'storpo twitched his mandibles. "Good idea. Filia?"

The Ti'ia flitted about the table as she spoke. "We knew from the language glyphs and symbols that the ship was probably insect, even before we got inside. I can't read everything yet, but got hundreds of pictures, and will be studying them as we go. What I got from the glyphs matches what we've seen — a very tightly-controlled hive culture with completely centralized leadership."

K'storpo nodded. "T'shlix?"

"No luck with knowledge crystals. The ship's way too primitive. All information was stored using magnetized iron, and it's all broken and crumbling to dust. Took lots of pictures, but nothing, absolutely nothing, is in working condition."

The beetle opened a sample container. "These are already warm. I'll keep the other container at eleven absolute until we can study them at Satamia." He passed a piece of dark, broken metal around the table. Crystals of different shades of gray could be seen on its surface, and it broke in half when Boro handled it. The engineer smiled with embarrassment.

"M'palta?"

She stroked her precious mate's bandage one more time, then extended one leg onto the table for a knowledge pad. "Screen, please."

Kibi swiveled around, touched her console, and swiveled back.

"As we guessed from the shape, it was a colony hive ship." Pictures of sleeping capsules, lined up in perfect rows, hundreds wide and high, appeared on the big screen. "Extrapolating from the part of the ship we explored, it contained twenty to thirty million sleeping insects . . ." Her voice trailed off and her many eyes turned deep blue.

"Until . . ." K'storpo prompted.

M'palta took a slow breath and a little light returned to her eyes. "Until it got too cold, and they entered the deeper sleep of . . . forever."

She touched the knowledge pad and another picture appeared on the screen, the contents of one broken-open sleeping capsule, with nothing left but a crumbling husk and some dust. "Completely dead, probably not even any genetic material. I have three samples I'm keeping at eleven absolute."

K'storpo looked at her sternly. "You had another important insight."

"Oh, yeah, that. T'shlix and I agree . . . judging by the technology, the sleepers were kept cool, but not cold. So if the other two ships are in better shape . . ."

Seeing that his team member was reluctant to complete her sentence, K'storpo let a moment pass, then spoke. "They might be alive, maybe even awake."

❋   ❋   ❋

Chapter 6: The Middle Ship

During the next Satamia day, as the Manessa Kwi searched for the second ship along the course the first ship had most likely taken, many more pictures and memories were shared. Rini became very diligent, vowing to Ilika, Mati, M'palta's mate, and everyone else, that rocks larger than grains of sand were never again going to get anywhere near the ship without him knowing.

The bandaged male spider thanked him.

Tizoromulia mentioned that as soon as his mate, Timoradalia, examined the hull of the second ship, he could calculate the distance to the hive's home planet.

Sata became interested and begged to learn how.

The only tricky part, the Ti'ia explained, was measuring the asteroid pits per square meter on the two hulls. He would work from photographs, and Manessa would help.

With Sata watching, the little mathematician entered the basic formula into a knowledge pad, pointed out that *Distance 1* would be known when they found the second ship, and began touching keys until the formula was solved for *Distance 2*.

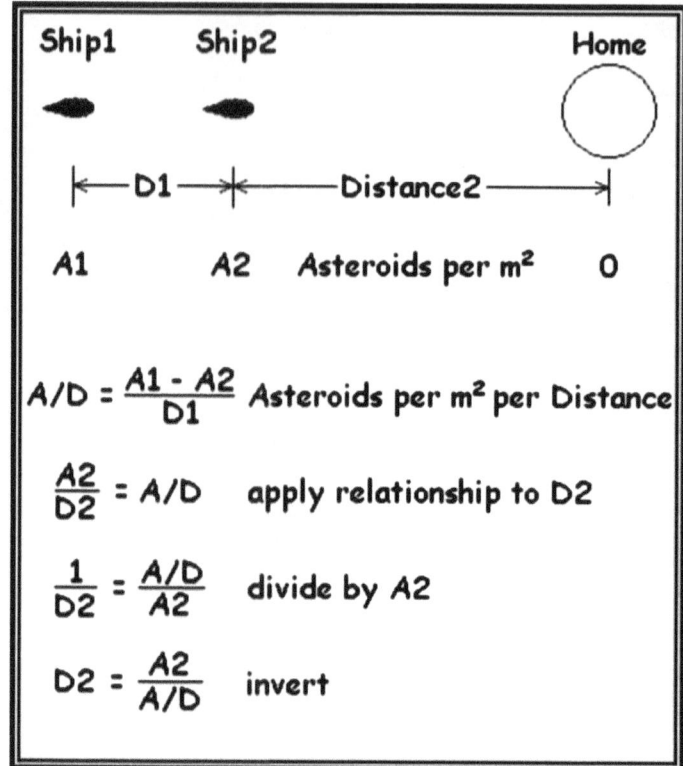

Sata took the knowledge pad and gazed at the steps until she understood. It wasn't long before Boro moved his seat close and started asking questions.

⁕

The second ship, seventeen light-hours behind the first, was much easier to find because it was still slightly warm. On nearly the same course, Manessa spotted it in a region of space sprinkled with cold gas and dust, but little else.

K'storpo speculated that the voyagers had a destination in mind, and put Sata to work examining the star charts in the direction the course would take the two ships.

At Ilika's command, Mati stopped a hundred kilometers from the second mystery ship.

Rini quickly announced that it was not all the same temperature. "Manessa sees a little room, deep in the ship, that's cold by our standards, but very hot compared to space. About four hundred degrees absolute, twenty-one below freezing."

"And look at this!" Sata announced excitedly. "From here, the stars ahead on their course aren't too exciting. But when I shifted the point of view back along their course, look what I found five light-years from here!"

The crew switched channels and Kibi routed the image to the passengers' screen.

"Oooo!" Timoratamia the artist began. *"That's* a constellation to stir the heart of any winged creature!"

"I think there were some crystallized wing structures in the remains on the first ship," M'palta said thoughtfully while gazing at the screen.

"Please identify those stars," K'storpo requested.

Sata turned back to her console.

"Ready ion seven," Ilika began, "full emergency responses. Take us to eight kilometers, Mati."

The pilot nodded and reached for her flight control.

"Rini, I want to know if that ship reacts to us in *any* way."

The slender lad turned to his console and made a new selection.

✳

The slightly-warm ship remained still and quiet, moving through space as it had been for a century or more, on the same course as its cold, dead sister ship.

As the little deep-space response ship approached, the slender monkey mammal at the watch station could make out dozens of small points of heat in the one warm room on the big ship, and those points were arranged in perfect rows.

K'storpo, the mantid mission leader, gazed at the infra-red image on the large screen over the steward's station. "That inner-most chamber must be highly insulated from the rest of the ship, judging by the extreme temperature difference. It probably contains the most important members of the hive."

"And the only ones left alive on the ship," M'palta added.

"The rest of the ship," T'shlix began, "may give us some usable knowledge records, since it's still at a hundred and thirty-five degrees absolute."

K'storpo nodded. "Let's go see what we can learn."

✳

Timoradalia the chemist hovered over the pitted hull and took pictures so her mate, back on the Manessa Kwi, could begin his distance calculations.

Timorafilia the linguist floated in space near some painted words, almost readable. After a minute, she shook her tiny head in frustration, and turned, just in time to see T'shlix inserting his prying tool on the edge of a hatch. Her tiny eyes nearly bulged out of her head as she realized what the symbols on the hatch said. "No! Not that . . ."

Before she could complete her sentence, a bright flash blinded everyone, metal fragments flew in all directions, and T'shlix screamed for a brief moment as his space suit and body were torn to shreds by the silent explosion.

K'storpo's mind raced. "Manessa, emergency pickup! I can't see . . ."

"Suit breach!" M'palta yelled. "Can't see either!"

"I'm blind too," Timorafilia said. "I should have . . ."

"Later," K'storpo commanded. "Dalia?"

"I'm okay. I was farthest away, looking at the hull. I'm heading for M'palta now. She's losing consciousness."

Just as Timoradalia reached the drifting spider, both were scooped up by Manessa's open airlock.

"Pressurize!" the little Ti'ia screamed.

Kibi had air filling the room the instant the outer door closed. She opened the inner door to find the Ti'ia trying to get the spider's suit off, but having little luck with her tiny hands. Kibi's strong mammal muscles did the trick.

Ilika and Timorasimia were quickly on the lower deck to help, and at Ilika's command, the ship raised the air pressure and temperature. Kibi cycled the airlock, and Mati maneuvered toward Timorafilia.

As the arachnid began to wake up, the helpless and sad Ti'ia in the airlock let Kibi carry her out and set her on the floor.

Mati scooped up the mission leader, and finally the body of the technologist.

At first, M'palta's mate wanted to go down to the lower deck, and started to carefully move his bandaged legs toward the lift. Then he realized that someone else needed him even more. He found the female beetle in the back of the passenger area, with her head in a corner and her wings quivering. Even though it caused him pain, he touched her trembling legs with his to share her grief as best he could.

✳   ✳   ✳

Chapter 7: Shame

The inside of the Manessa Kwi was almost as silent as the vacuum of space outside.

K'storpo sat on the floor of the lower deck feeling helpless, sometimes turning his head this way and that to determine if any of his eyes worked. He listened as M'palta regained consciousness, but could do nothing to assist.

Ilika offered to deal with the remains in the airlock, and K'storpo nodded.

A few minutes later, Boro sat down beside the mission leader. "Hi. We moved the ship back to eight kilometers. M'palta's mate and Sata are with the other beetle, and the Ti'ias are taking care of Filia. I'm gonna be your eyes, help you with anything you need."

The blind leader was silent, then managed to mumble, "Th . . . thank you."

Boro and Kibi witnessed Ilika carry a large bag from the airlock to the utility room, but didn't say anything to K'storpo and M'palta.

Eventually M'palta felt ready to join her mate in the passenger area, so Kibi guided her to the lift.

K'storpo sat for a few more minutes, then requested, in a sad voice, that Boro help him into the lift also.

✳

After everyone was comfortable at the big table, Kibi brought out frog legs, three kinds of worms, and everything else she could find that would comfort the stricken mission team. Sata remained with the grieving beetle, and Boro with K'storpo. The two spiders, one bandaged and one blind, sat together with legs touching.

"Mati, you're on duty," Ilika said. "Rini has some information to report."

Kibi took a bowl of snacks to the pilot as Rini came up to the table.

"Um . . . I analyzed the explosion. It was just light and heat, little ultra-violet, and no high-frequency gamma or x-radiation."

K'storpo nodded and whispered, "Thank you." After a long moment, the mission leader took a deep breath. "We made a big mistake. There's plenty of blame to go around, and so no reason to speak of it at this point. We will begin by getting some sleep, while the crew keeps watch over us."

Ilika sent half his crew below, and Kibi rearranged the passenger area and dimmed the lights.

*

Many hours later, warm foods and tasty drinks succeeded in somewhat lifting spirits all around the table.

During a moment of silence, Ilika spoke. "We've come a long way into deep space to find this ship, and there's another ship, and perhaps a planet, ahead that will probably tell us even more. I offer myself and my crew as your eyes and hands to complete this mission."

All five monkey-mammal crew members grinned, nodded, or both.

K'storpo's mandibles twitched. "That creates a danger."

"It does," Ilika agreed. "I will always leave someone on duty here."

K'storpo thought about it, and finally nodded.

* * *

Chapter 8: Substitutes

Rini volunteered to remain on the ship, and promised to detect asteroids in time for the rest of the crew to return.

Ilika accepted his offer, and planned to make good use of the other four crew members.

Kibi and Sata knew their job was critical. They were the first to approach the huge, silent, nearly-lifeless ship.

"You're looking for a hatch with three vertical marks under a horizontal line," Timorafilia explained over the intercom. The little Ti'ia could clearly see, in her mind's eye, the language glyph that indicated a safe entry hatch designed to look unsafe. She also remembered clearly the glyph on the hatch T'shlix had opened, the last thing she had seen with her eyes.

Sata pointed, and Kibi nodded, then spoke. "We're looking at a hatch like that, a triangle about a meter on each side."

"Triangle? What's on the right side of the glyph?"

Kibi cocked her head slightly. "A long vertical line, then two short diagonals sloping upward."

"Won't work, it's a refueling door."

The two substitute language specialists moved on. The other three followed a few meters behind. Boro carried the powerful prying tool, Ilika bore two large sample containers hooked to his suit, and Mati had four small containers.

"Okay," Sata began, "we've got a square hatch, two meters, same basic glyph, but no vertical on the right, instead three short horizontals close together."

"That's the one," Timorafilia assured. "Paint or raised metal?"

"Metal."

"Yes. They wanted that bit of dis-information to be durable."

Sata chuckled.

Ilika insisted Kibi describe the entire language glyph to Timorafilia once more, just to be sure. The two girls, one human and one Ti'ia, discussed every line and dot, and concluded they had the right hatch.

Boro approached with the prying tool, but Ilika stopped him. "I can't ask you to do this . . . after what happened yesterday."

Boro scrunched his face in thought, then swallowed. "Neither can I become a Nebador citizen if I'm not willing to take my share of the risks. I'm the ship's engineer. This is my job. And . . . I was starting to feel close to T'shlix, and would be proud to finish what he started."

Captain and engineer looked at each other silently for a moment. Eventually Ilika nodded.

Sata made a tiny whimpering sound, and hoped no one heard.

*

Unlike the hatch on the first ship, cold and brittle, this hatch reluctantly swung open on hinges that would have creaked and groaned loudly if any air had been present. Boro had to use the tool's power continuously until the hatch was wide open.

"Reaction from the ship, Rini?" Ilika asked.

"Nothing I can see."

"Are we going to rescue the ones who are still alive?" Mati asked from the back of the group, her voice colored with sympathy.

"That's a possibility," K'storpo said from the ship.

Sata chuckled. "We've done that once already. We found a girl stranded on an ice continent. The only bad part was that we had to rescue her idiot father, too!"

The entire crew of the Manessa Kwi burst into laughter.

"I'd love to hear about *that* mission," M'palta said through the intercom.

"Okay," Ilika began when the laughter died down, "I'm first, Kibi and Sata next, then Mati, and Boro brings up the rear. No one touches *anything* without my permission."

With the memory fresh in their minds of T'shlix being torn to pieces by an explosion, no one argued.

*

Ilika led them along dark metal corridors toward the front of the ship where they could see, from the outside, the bridge was located. Three times along the way, they had to stop and let Boro pry open metal doors. The first two slid open vertically. The last, just before stepping onto the bridge, slid horizontally, with metal teeth along both sides. Boro let the prying tool push it all the way to the walls, two meters apart.

Nearly everything on the bridge was made of metal. The few glass display screens were small and dark. Unlike the Manessa Kwi, no colors or textures interrupted the shades of black and gray, except some harsh lettering in faded yellow.

Kibi worked with her bracelet, and announced that the air was nitrogen and oxygen, but much too thin to breathe.

Sata began describing language glyphs to Timorafilia.

Mati, assigned to maintain a broad overview and watch for dangers, floated among the stations. She was soon gazing down at the strange helm, located in the exact center of the room, with so many control levers that it must have needed a pilot with six arms. After frowning at the cold metal seat, she opened her bracelet and took a picture.

With tiny bursts from his suit thrusters, Boro slowly made his way around the ugly room, and soon found what he thought was the engineering station. "Ilika, I found the . . . um . . . the engineer."

Ilika was quickly at his side, looking down at the dried husk of an insect who once sported proud wings and a sharp stinger, but had died in his metal seat long ago. The remains were completely hollow and brittle, and two legs had already broken off, one still floating nearby.

"He must have been the last one on the bridge," Ilika speculated, "ordered to do his job until the bitter end."

"After . . . you know . . . Sonmatia Seven, I know how that feels," Boro said, blinking thoughtfully.

They described the scene to K'storpo, who approved the collection of a bio-sample. Boro called Mati over.

The pilot of the Manessa Kwi, after tearing her eyes away from the strange and uncomfortable helm, floated that way, glancing at the three-quarter-open entrance door as she passed.

✳

Rini spent most of this time at his station, searching for ways to spot asteroids smaller and farther away, and making very sure an alarm would sound if so much as a grain of sand got near. But occasionally, he had to focus his eyes on something other than his console, stretch his legs, and ask if anyone needed anything.

Seeing the bandages on the male spider's legs made him search his mind for anything else he could do to protect his ship and the excursion team. But, he had to admit to himself with a sigh, no other precautions appeared to be possible. Through their mental link, Mati reassured him.

After setting out a fresh supply of fruit and worms, Rini wandered back to the bridge, taking a moment to look at the forward view on the main screen, still showing the half-open hatch through which his friends had gone.

✳

At a console not far from the deceased engineer, Boro and Ilika found the information storage machine, and spent an hour describing language glyphs to Timorafilia. With the help of their bracelets, they determined that no energy was present, but the magnetic patterns of stored information remained.

K'storpo, M'palta, and several of the Ti'ias, all contributed ideas as Ilika and Boro carefully took the machine apart. Although no one said it aloud, they all wished T'shlix could help.

After getting some samples that K'storpo requested, Mati floated over to the one-third-open door, turned back to the bridge of the massive ship, and imagined it buzzing with insects as it carried its precious cargo of life from somewhere they no longer wanted to be, to somewhere far away among the stars.

*

Rini went from task to task, listening to the on-going conversation between the mission specialists and his friends, and occasionally adding an idea of his own. He checked each station every few minutes, and asked Manessa if she had anything to report. Finally, he touched Mati's mind, and she assured him that all was well.

From Manessa's point of view, the little warm room, deep inside the ship, always looked the same. The bridge showed five very warm monkey mammals moving about. The image on Manessa's main bridge display was still and silent, a massive metal colony ship, with a hatch one-quarter open, adrift in deep space.

* * *

Chapter 9: Too Slow to Notice

After lending an extra hand as Ilika and Boro extracted the data module, Mati returned to the almost-closed door. She could see Sata, floating upside down while looking under a console, and could hear her describing a glyph to Timorafilia.

Mati's suit happened to be touching the door when she felt a slight vibration, as if two pieces of metal had come into contact.

She turned and frowned at the door. "Um . . . Ilika? The door just closed all the way. I think it's been slowly closing ever since we opened it."

Boro, holding a large sample container for Ilika, looked up. "I can just pry it open again."

"I felt a click, and have a bad feeling about it. Would you try it, as soon as you're done there?"

Boro nodded, then focused on holding the container while Ilika slid the precious data module in.

❋

"Kinetic energy detected," Manessa said with her gentle voice. "The hatch, through which the excursion team entered the colony ship, just closed, and a nearby mechanism changed state."

Rini was quickly at his station, requesting magnified images, and asking the ship to pinpoint the mechanism that moved. With his screen and his eyes focused on that area, just to the side of the now-closed hatch, Rini could see a small red triangle that he didn't remember seeing before.

"Manessa, show me the same place on the ship before the hatch closed, same magnification."

Rini could see the small triangle, but before the hatch had closed, it was yellow.

Just then he became aware of Mati's worry about the doors to the bridge.

❋

Boro inserted the prying tool between the teeth of the only door out of the bridge, and pressed the activation symbol. The status light became yellow, and the gap widened a millimeter or two, but no farther. Kibi could see the doors vibrating, and Boro could feel his tool doing the same.

The status light became red, and eventually purple.

"Ilika ... we have a problem," the engineer said as calmly as he could, even though his stomach had just clenched itself into a knot.

Ilika tore himself away from the dark control panel he was studying. When he took in the situation of closed metal door and overloaded prying tool, he frowned. "Power levels two and three have delays so you can get away in case things go flying. Everyone else, get behind something."

Kibi, Sata, and Mati took cover.

Boro switched the device to level two, entered a delay of eight seconds, glanced behind him, and touched the activation symbol.

He and Ilika quickly found cover.

The halves of the door separated several more millimeters, and started to dent slightly on both sides. The prying tool's status took longer to change to red, and finally purple, as it gave up the attempt.

*

"Ilika?" Rini's shaking voice came through the intercom. "This is embarrassing. The hatch you went through ... it closed so slowly I didn't notice, and now ... I have a hunch ... it's locked."

As Ilika and Boro looked down at the prying tool that had failed at level two, and the three girls peeked over their shoulders, the captain of the Manessa Kwi felt a feeling of dread rise up inside himself, the same feeling he had last felt when his little ship visited the icy core of gas giant Sonmatia Seven.

"We ... have a similar problem here, Rini. And I wouldn't be surprised if the other two hatches we opened along the way are now closed and locked also."

"There's ... level three ..." Boro suggested with questioning brows.

Ilika nodded. "We'll give the prying tool another try, then talk again, Rini. You may not, under any circumstances, leave the ship."

Boro prepared the tool as everyone else took cover. With a twenty-second delay, he slowly floated behind the console where Sata crouched.

As Kibi peeked out from her hiding place, she could see the door shaking violently, and the gap between the teeth widening to about a centimeter, maybe a little more, then closing back to a few millimeters as the powerful little machine gave up and relaxed.

"Rini ..." the captain began with hesitation. "It looks like ... we're trapped."

*

After the entire crew talked, and decided there was no better tool on board the Manessa Kwi, the five crew members on the mystery ship took a few minutes to search for any way off the bridge they hadn't noticed. Everything that would, was opened, as they looked for a crawl space or an air duct. A few conduits were discovered that might allow passage for a very small mouse.

After Rini heard the results of their search, he spent a few minutes sitting silently at his station, tears threatening to come. His mind wandered back to Satamia Star Station, and his recent wedding to the pilot of the ship, a girl who had known slavery, just as he had, and who had journeyed with him all around the kingdom, then all over the planet, and finally to most of the planets of their solar system.

The strong touch of her mind brought him back to the present. After a few deep breaths for courage, he wiped his eyes, stood, and stepped into the passenger area. "I need a crew."

❋ ❋ ❋

Chapter 10: The Crew

About half an hour after realizing there was no other way off the bridge of the dark metal ship, Ilika and most of his crew were floating about, trying to think of a solution to their problem, when suddenly the entire room shook violently.

Mati smiled.

Ilika glanced around to make sure everyone was okay. "Rini, we just experienced a severe jolt. Any idea what caused it?"

"Uh huh. And there's gonna be another one in a moment. You said I couldn't leave the ship. I'm bringing the ship to you."

Mati grinned.

Boro nodded as he imagined exactly what Rini was doing.

Kibi and Sata both clapped their space-suited hands.

"The door to the bridge has a vertical seam," Ilika explained. "Give us warning so we can get behind things."

"Will do. We're at the second door. I have to talk to my crew. Get ready."

Ilika raised his eyebrows at Rini's mention of his crew, then looked around at the real crew. "Everyone floating?"

They all nodded, and continued smiling with pride, knowing that Rini was coming to their rescue.

The ship lurched again, more violently than the first time.

"There's one more horizontal door like that one," Ilika said.

"Manessa sees it. Now I understand why Boro loves his space thruster fuel."

Boro laughed. "Good stuff, but use it wisely!"

"Yes, Master."

Boro laughed again.

Soon the room shook for the third time, so violently that a few loose pieces of metal started floating around.

"Look out!" Kibi yelled. "Junk coming your way, Sata."

The navigator twisted to the side.

"Everyone okay?" Rini asked.

"Yes," Ilika said, "but give us a minute to secure some junk before you do the last door. We took the room apart looking for a way out."

They all re-attached or wedged the loose items as best they could, then got behind the consoles again.

"Ready," Ilika declared. "You have about five meters of clear space inside the door before you'll hit a console."

"Okay. We might have to use a little thrust to stop."

"We're clear."

A moment later the room shook like a wild beast, and some of the wedged junk came loose. A golden spike pierced the door, both halves crumpled like foil, and the body of the little ship lurched into the room. A burst of blue flame brought it to a sudden stop, and completely incinerated the console in its path.

Mati and Boro both had to duck or twist to avoid floating debris.

A moment later everything came to rest, and the golden ship changed into a ball about two meters across. It rotated, and the airlock hatch appeared and opened.

"Anyone want a ride?" Rini's voice asked.

"Yes, please!" Mati declared.

Sata nodded. "We are *done* with this place!"

*

After space suits were stowed and sample containers secured in the utility room, Ilika and Kibi shared the lift. When they stepped onto the upper deck, they beheld two Ti'ias at the steward's station, a bandaged spider at engineering, another pair of Ti'ias at the watch station, a large beetle at navigation, and Timorazonia with her little hands on a tiny flight control at the helm.

Rini spun around in the command chair. "Like my crew?"

* * *

Chapter 11: The Third Ship

Ilika smiled as he asked the substitute crew of the Manessa Kwi to take them back out, and bring the ship to a relative stop eight kilometers from the huge colony ship.

Timorazonia did several handsprings for joy in mid-air before taking the tiny flight control again. But before Rini could give any commands, Mati slipped into her seat with a wrinkled brow.

The little Ti'ia ceased her antics and looked at the real pilot with a mixture of humility and pride on her tiny face.

Mati looked back sternly. "Just remember, if you don't listen to your commander, or you do anything unsafe on purpose, you'll get to ride in a sample container instead . . . with the lid closed."

Timorazonia cringed for a moment, then collected herself and bowed deeply.

"Okay, you have the helm, little pilot."

The female beetle at navigation smiled, and sent the floor plan of the huge ship, to the extent it was known, to all stations.

✳

"I feel bad that we had to trash the ship," Kibi said after everyone got comfortable at the big table.

"That ship is as good as dead," K'storpo assured her. "When the temperature drops a little more, those in that inner-most chamber will go to sleep forever. How long, M'palta?"

The biologist twitched her mandibles for a moment. "Rough guess . . . six or eight years."

"They had it coming," Boro said. "If you're gonna lock people in, you have to expect them to try to get out."

"And that might tell us something about their culture," M'palta added. "They probably collect food by trapping. We might learn more if we can find their planet."

"We know almost exactly where it is," Tizoromulia the mathematician said in his tiny male voice, "and it roughly matches Sata's calculation of where that constellation looks most impressive."

"We have another ship to examine first," K'storpo declared, "but I have a hunch we'll just be looking at it from a distance."

✳

Another Satamia day passed on the Manessa Kwi as Rini peered deep into nearly-empty space on all sides of their flight path, looking for the third ship, or anything else of concern. Many memories were shared about the explosion that had killed one specialist and blinded three, the excursion by the crew to the bridge of the colony ship, and their rescue by Rini and his substitute crew.

M'palta removed most of the bandages from her mate about halfway through that day, and he began to carefully stretch his legs. The female beetle continued to deal with her grief, and Sata or M'palta sat with her often to listen to anything she wanted to say.

Timorazonia was obviously determined to earn Mati's trust, and when allowed to be at the pilot's station, was very careful to follow the commander's orders to the letter. Mati always watched. Even though still fairly new, she was suddenly the senior pilot, and, Ilika reminded her, responsible for all flight maneuvers.

Near the end of that Satamia day, K'storpo and M'palta did a dance of joy when they discovered a little bit of their sight returning. Kibi selected some music to go with the occasion, and Sata grabbed Boro to join in the dance.

Timorafilia was not so lucky with her eyes, and let her handsome mate hold her in his arms while she listened to the dancers.

✳

The third ship was not adrift. Many windows gleamed, and marker lights flashed at numerous points on the hull. Searchlights swung back and forth, attempting to pierce the blackness of space. Smoking thrusters occasionally made minor course corrections.

The Manessa Kwi, currently absorbing all forms of energy, drifted in the same direction a hundred kilometers away. Although the little ship was as invisible as any material object could be, Mati selected an irregular shape that made them look like a black rock, just in case anyone spotted them.

K'storpo, M'palta, and Timorafilia listened as others described what they could see, and what Manessa's sensors told them about the many kinds of energy radiating from the giant colony ship.

"Even though the fuel tanks on that ship are massive," K'storpo began as his mandibles twitched nervously, "they should be conserving every calorie. With all those lights, and that hull practically glowing with heat . . . how could they expect to survive interplanetary travel?"

M'palta mulled over the words of her mission leader and the others for several minutes before speaking. "My hunch is . . . they don't know what they're doing. They don't know how far it is to . . . anything. They don't know what's happened to the other two ships, and if we told them, they wouldn't believe us."

A long silence followed. Timorasimia the empath eventually spoke softly. "Very . . . very . . . sad."

Timoratamia the artist, currently sitting in Rini's lap, had a stronger reaction. "That's STUPID! I have a color just for *stupid* in my box, and that's the color they'll get when I paint them."

K'storpo smiled.

"Then that's the color my people should get too," M'palta said flatly.

Timoratamia squirmed with embarrassment.

"And they would deserve it," M'palta continued, looking at the little artist. "They have this bad habit of starting wars just because they're angry, not because they need to defend themselves, or even because they want to win. And since they do it so half-cocked, they usually lose!"

The grin formed by the spider's mandibles caused those who could see to laugh, and the rest quickly joined in.

Sata wore a serious face as the laughter died down. "So . . . there's no way to help them?"

"No," K'storpo answered. "This is interstellar space, the void that cannot be crossed by mortal beings in home-made ships. As I remember, you have oceans on Sonmatia Three . . ."

Sata nodded.

"Imagine trying to cross an ocean in a tiny rowboat."

"Suicide!" Sata declared without hesitation.

"Would you rescue someone who insisted on trying it?"

"Um . . . *maybe* . . ."

Boro jumped in. "People that stupid would just find other ways to kill themselves, seems to me."

After a moment of thought, Sata reluctantly nodded agreement.

"That's how Nebador sees this situation," K'storpo continued. "All the information was there for those insects to see — distances to other stars, temperature of space, everything. To build a ship like that, you have to be capable of mathematics. If you are, then you can calculate that interstellar travel is not possible by any act of will. If M'palta is right, and they really are clueless, than Tamia is going to need lots of that special color of hers."

The passenger area of the little deep-space response ship became thoughtfully quiet as the huge colony ship, visible on every display screen, continued to desperately search the darkness of interstellar space for its destination.

✳   ✳   ✳

Chapter 12: Home

The Manessa Kwi stayed near the third colony ship for almost half a Satamia day, studying it in every way they could, describing what they saw to those with little or no vision, and discussing the findings.

Eventually nothing remained to be learned without prying open a hatch and creeping down the corridors. They all laughed and agreed that if they tried that on this ship, doors that closed behind them would be the least of their worries.

With course and hull-pitting information from three different ships, Tizoromulia worked with Sata to refine his calculations and determine, as closely as anyone could, the point of origin. Rini watched and nodded. Boro, Kibi, and Mati watched, sometimes nodding, and sometimes frowning.

After a light meal, all the passengers and crew got comfortable for star transit. Mati let Timorazonia issue the final command that activated the star drive.

＊

They found themselves in the outskirts of a solar system far from any other, which had a number on Sata's charts, but no name. It didn't take long to determine that the seventh, sixth, and fifth planets were all gas giants with no insect life.

The fourth planet slowly grew larger on their screens. Although mostly white, a couple of small oceans still glimmered deep blue at their centers.

"High equatorial orbit," Ilika ordered.

As soon as Sata sent the orbit calculations, Mati reached up to rearrange her display. "You ready for this, Zonia?"

"I've never . . . piloted anything into . . . orbit."

"See the altitude and speed graphs? Just follow those with your flight control and your ion drive level."

"B-both at once?"

"Yep."

"Won't that take . . . two brains?"

Mati smiled. "Want me to do speed so you can concentrate on direction?"

"Um . . . please. I only have one brain."

The senior pilot didn't mention the fact that humans had three.

*

"It's bitter cold even on the equator," Rini reported. "Three hundred sixty-four degrees absolute. Thirty-five below freezing. Poles are even colder."

"This couldn't be the home-world of hive insects!" M'palta declared from the passenger area.

"Any warm spots at all, even around geothermal vents or in heated buildings?" Ilika asked, looking over Rini's shoulder.

Rini increased the magnification of his infra-red display and entered a search request. "Not in this hemisphere."

Ilika stepped back to the command chair. "Finish an orbit, Mati, and then if Rini doesn't see anywhere sapient insects could have lived, we'll go look at the third planet."

The pilot nodded, and continued to keep one eye on her orbit profile.

*

Finding nowhere above freezing, the Manessa Kwi departed for the third planet of the lonely solar system.

It turned out to be bone dry, airless, and lifeless, and had clearly been that way for millions of years.

Just to be sure, they peeked at the second planet. Volcanic activity covered nearly the entire surface, and no higher life forms were detected.

Ilika was at the big table with the mission team, wondering what to do next, when Rini suddenly started bouncing up and down in his chair.

"We were looking for the wrong thing! There was nowhere and nothing warm on the fourth planet, but I was bored so I started looking at the pictures under highest magnification, and look what I found! Buildings! Huge buildings mostly covered by ice and snow!"

Ilika was quickly at the watch station, and a moment later several Ti'ias hovered nearby, chittering with curiosity. Timorafilia, still without sight, whimpered from her chair.

"Some of them," Rini continued, "are big enough to . . . you know . . . assemble space ships."

"Okay," Ilika said with renewed hope, "pick out the most visible, and send them to Kibi's big screen." Ilika looked around the bridge. "Boro, you have command. Low orbit, fourth planet."

The engineer's eyes grew large, and he had to swallow several times before he could find the courage to move to the command chair.

Sata, who already had the necessary charts on the main bridge screen, glanced at him and grinned with pride. Mati turned and looked at him with reassuring eyes and a slight nod.

Timorazonia, not knowing what a huge moment this was for Boro, did flips in the air above the pilot's console.

*   *   *

Chapter 13: The Story Unfolds

While Boro, with advice from his pilot and navigator, commanded the return trip to the cold fourth planet, Ilika and Kibi sat with the mission team as those who could see took turns describing the images on the screen.

"That's an aircraft or spacecraft hanger," M'palta's mate assured. "Not nearly big enough for the huge colony ships, but they were probably assembled in orbit."

Kibi touched a knowledge pad to change the image.

"Some kind of fuel conversion plant," Timoradalia the chemist offered. "Those lumps to the south look like mine tailings, so it was probably something they dug up in solid form, then purified, or converted to liquid."

Silence lingered, so Kibi changed the picture.

The female beetle's mandibles started twitching. "I've seen something like that before. Those snow-covered piles of twisted metal could have been transmission towers. Yes, I think it was some kind of power generating plant."

Tizoromulia the mathematician nodded agreement.

"I'm starting to get a picture of what happened here," K'storpo said, "but I want to know more."

Kibi moved on to the next image.

The male Ti'ia leapt into the air and hovered. "Another generating plant. And right beside it, if I'm not mistaken, was a reverse-combustion plant where they changed electricity into solid or liquid fuel."

"For their colony ships," Kibi mumbled.

Timoradalia nodded while gazing at the screen.

After a moment of silence, the picture changed.

"Another spacecraft hanger," M'palta's mate shared, "with a vertical launch pad and a landing strip . . ."

After they had discussed more than a hundred pictures from the icy surface of the fourth planet, and a moment of silence had passed, Kibi timidly raised her hand.

"Kibi wishes to speak," Ilika said.

K'storpo nodded.

"If they made those big space ships because their planet was growing cold . . . and those ships aren't going to make it to . . . anywhere . . . doesn't that mean we should rescue them . . . or at least . . . some of them?"

"Exactly what the rest of us are thinking," M'palta said. "It looks like they got off their planet just in time, as it was, and still is, rapidly plunging into an ice age."

K'storpo drew himself up to full height. "You are completely correct, Kibi. Under these circumstances, Nebador will find them a new home, just as some of your crewmates helped to do recently for that little group of jungle lizards."

Kibi smiled.

✳

Boro wiped the sweat from his brow when Sata verified that the Manessa Kwi was in a stable low orbit over the icy fourth planet.

"Thank you, Boro," Ilika said, stepping beside the command chair.

"Can I . . ." the engineer began, pointing toward his station.

The captain smiled and nodded.

"Because of the nippy weather down there . . ." Ilika began, taking his seat, "we're going to do as much exploring as possible with the ship, but a few excursions will probably be necessary. Sata, you have Rini's list?"

She tapped at her display selector. "Yep."

"We're starting at location thirty-four, but beyond that, it will depend on what we find. Prepare to de-orbit."

Rini produced a weather chart, Sata defined an elliptical curve, Boro warmed up anti-mass and ion drives, and Mati arranged it all on her screen. As soon as Kibi declared her passengers ready, the pilot turned and looked at her captain.

He nodded.

"Shall we let Manessa do this one?" Mati asked Timorazonia, currently perched on the pilot's shoulder.

"That'll be fast, right?"

"So fast your head will spin."

"Okay!"

✳

Timorazonia's little eyes nearly bugged out of her head as the Manessa Kwi swooped toward the cold planet at ion three, coming to a sudden stop four thousand meters above the snowy ground.

Kibi had to close her eyes.

Mati and Sata exchanged grins.

K'storpo, M'palta, and Timorafilia wished they could have seen it. Fuzzy light and dark patches were starting to come to them, but no focused images.

Under Mati's watchful eye, Timorazonia took Manessa's smallest flight control and guided the ship over the ice and snow. Ilika or Kibi described the scenes to those without vision, and K'storpo made choices about what they should explore.

After finding a large metal door that had collapsed inward from decades of snow, the little ship lurked about in a huge aircraft assembly building. The bodies of faithful security guards, still seated in front of monitors that had gone dark long ago, proved that this was once the home of the same insect species that was attempting to cross the vast interstellar void.

*

After Rini declared the air a bit thin but breathable, he, Sata, and Tizoromulia put on harsh-environment suits and explored a building near a shuttle launch pad. The mathematician could not fly in the insulated suit, so he rode on Sata's shoulder, or jumped down to explore tables and shelves. He found plenty of star charts and astronomical calculations.

"They certainly had enough brains to figure out how far away things are in space," the male Ti'ia began back in the Manessa Kwi. "But I see no sign that they had the wisdom to realize they couldn't do it, they couldn't build a ship that would survive for hundreds or thousands of years. Pride always trumps intelligence, especially in any large group."

"Maybe they were getting desperate," Timorasimia the empath suggested. "Their home planet was dying. Desperate creatures usually don't think clearly."

Rini nodded with a thoughtful, far-away look in his eyes.

*

A few hundred kilometers to the west, the ship hovered beside an ice-covered surface-to-orbit shuttle plane that had skidded off the landing strip and crashed into a small building. Boro stepped through the airlock onto a small platform that Manessa provided. With his favorite prying tool, the one T'shlix had used when he made his fatal mistake, Boro wedged off chunks of ice until he could look inside the shuttle's command cabin.

"Pilot's all smashed into his console, probably when they landed. Same winged bugs . . . I mean insects. Door to the inner cabin is open, and I can see others who died just sitting in their seats — but they weren't smashed or anything — just sitting there like they couldn't think of anything else to do. All the panels are dark and covered with years of frost."

*

With everyone at the table sharing a hearty meal, K'storpo began to speak after taking a few bites. "The evidence seems to be telling us that the three colony ships got away in the nick of time. From the ice samples Dalia took, it looks like the temperature was dropping very quickly when they left."

"Another year, I think," the little chemist added, "and they wouldn't have made it."

"It's sad," Boro began. "The shuttles and their crews, after building and supplying the big ships, returned to their home bases, but had no further purpose . . . other than to . . . you know . . . die from the cold."

Kibi nodded in sympathy.

"That's the nature of a hive society," M'palta began. "With the leaders at the top commanding some effort, it's almost unstoppable. With the leaders gone on the colony ships, nothing, almost literally nothing, gets done in any collective, organized way."

*

The Manessa Kwi perched on a wind-swept field of ice as everyone got comfortable for sleep. The crew members all took short walks in the bitter-cold air, in pairs. Kibi asked her passengers if any of them wanted to stretch their wings or legs, but K'storpo explained that insect bodies didn't work at that temperature. Kibi apologized.

"No need to be sorry," Timorasimia the empath, hovering, assured the steward. "We can work and play at temperatures so high you'd be on the floor drenched in sweat."

Kibi grinned and gave the little Ti'ia a friendly poke, who chittered and fluttered into the seat where her family awaited.

A few minutes later M'palta, still able to see little, asked for Kibi's help with her mate's bandages. The two arachnids agreed that one bandage could come off, leaving only the one on the broken leg. Kibi worked very slowly, carefully unhooking the stretchy material from the sharp spikes on the spider's leg.

That done, Kibi stood and looked around the passenger area, her passenger area. Suddenly a warm feeling welled up inside her. As a slave, she had never been able to take pride in her work, never able to trust anyone or be trusted by anyone. Now, at least with Nebador citizens, it was all about trust.

At K'storpo's seat, he and Ilika finished talking about what they hoped to accomplish the following day. Kibi watched as the captain of the ship, her sweet lover, strolled around the bridge to check each station, then waved with a shy smile and stepped into the lift.

After leaving a bowl of plump fruits on the galley counter, and checking the supplies in the toilet rooms, Kibi dimmed the lights and slipped into an unused seat at the back, where she soon drifted into a light sleep.

* * *

Chapter 14: More Information

The following day, the little ship poked around in a huge concrete building that the team agreed was a power generating station. The Ti'ia mathematician and chemist peered intently at the display screen, and got opinions from the other Nebador citizens who could see. Timorafilia listened to the others describe language glyphs, then did her best to translate. K'storpo and M'palta asked questions, and the entire team, plus Ilika, discussed possible answers. The five crew members from a medieval world felt completely lost.

A huge machine, sporting countless pipes and wires that snaked away in all directions, towered over them as they talked about its purpose. Soon a tense silence came over the entire mission team.

Timoradalia broke the spell by saying, "Uh . . . oh."

"What?" Kibi questioned from her station.

Several others looked up from the bridge.

"Too soon to tell for sure," K'storpo replied before anyone else could speak.

✳

Hours later, after exploring the interior of another power generating plant, those who could see stared with wide eyes at a huge shaft that went straight down into the planet. It would have been big enough for the Manessa Kwi, if it wasn't for the many ice-covered pipes that plunged into the shaft's darkness.

Kibi immediately noticed the same tension that had come over the mission team at the last power plant.

"Bad news," Timoradalia whispered.

Kibi looked at all her passengers, but could see that they weren't yet ready to talk about it.

"We need to get into a city and look at some cultural expressions,"

K'storpo declared. "Tamia, you up for an excursion or two?"

"Sure!" the little artist replied. "I can *almost* see how I'm going to color them, but not quite."

✳

The city was a massive hive. Although it was constructed of concrete, steel, and glass, it was nonetheless completely hive-like in its look, feel, and layout. The little ship slowly explored large, round corridors, from which smaller tunnels branched, each lined with many round holes that led to individual rooms.

Dried, frozen husks littered the floor, all that remained of the winged creatures who did not leave in the three colony ships. M'palta asked a few questions about the scene, then fell silent.

Timorafilia translated language glyphs as others described them. After a while, K'storpo interrupted and reminded everyone that they were looking for graphic cultural expressions. They were looking for art.

The Manessa Kwi moved on, and soon found the art they were seeking in many places, from dining halls to toilet rooms.

Most of the paint was faded, usually just yellows and oranges, but the themes were clear. Scenes of battle and war showed the many other creatures who had once shared the planet, only to be proudly and methodically hunted to extinction. The death and destruction was usually carried out with high-technology weapons from aircraft, but occasionally the murals actually showed the winged insects stinging their prey to death.

From his station, Rini looked at the faces of the mission specialists, trying to judge their reaction. They didn't seem too surprised, and even talked about similar times in the histories of their own peoples.

But then another mural was discovered, in a large assembly hall with places for thousands of insects to perch on metal rails. It was much more recent, judging by the brighter colors. A swarm of the insects, here painted unnaturally large and powerful, were stinging their planet to death. In the background, they could be seen moving on to other planets, treating them the same way, then heading off toward the stars.

A deathly quiet came over the entire mission team.

Mati noticed and whispered to Timorazonia, "Landing struts. I think we might be here awhile."

✳

Timoratamia the artist was in and out of the ship many times as the same theme was found in the newest art works all over the hive city, then in five other cities, scattered around the planet, that Rini picked at random.

At K'storpo's request, the Manessa Kwi explored three more massive power plants, all with a shaft that plunged deep into the planet. After studying their tell-tale shape and entering a new search query, Rini announced that there were hundreds more like them.

Ilika, Sata, and Timoradalia crept about in another fuel conversion plant, again right next to a power plant, and the chemist verified that the former residents were indeed making huge amounts of crude space thruster fuel.

*

K'storpo remained silent as they found a level place to land and quietly shared a solemn meal. To everyone's surprise, Arantiloria appeared, took on her purple-haired human form, and appeared to sit on the galley counter.

Kibi grinned at the mysterious seventh member of the crew, but a brief moment of eye contact nearly made the steward's head spin, and she was forced to close her eyes and grab the sides of her seat, as if she had just looked into something deeper and more mysterious than she could imagine.

Sensing a presence, the mission leader turned his head in that direction for a moment, then twitched his mandibles to collect his thoughts. "I think I begin to see why Melorania was not in any hurry for this mission to take place . . ."

"As a point of training," Arantiloria interrupted, "I think we should let the new monkey mammal crew evaluate the situation."

Mati and Sata looked at each other with wide eyes. Timorazonia, perched on the back of Mati's seat, snickered.

Boro swallowed. "Are they . . . maybe . . . too *bad* to be rescued?"

Timoradalia flopped back in her seat and rolled her many eyes. Tizoromulia chittered at her with a scolding tone.

Boro smiled at the bickering pair of Ti'ias.

Sata took a deep breath. "Isn't . . . every kind of people . . . bad . . . in some ways? My people would kill all the wolves and mountain lions . . . you know, canines and felines . . . if they could. They just haven't figured out how yet."

"Canines and felines on our planet eat people's farm animals," Mati explained to everyone. "I think you're right, Sata. Every kind of people has to fight other creatures for food. If they didn't, they would have . . . um . . . died out a long time ago."

Rini could see M'palta nodding slightly.

Kibi dared to glance at Arantiloria again, but didn't try to make eye contact. At the same time, a memory came to her, and she let her mind drift back to the medieval capital city, to Rumble Town, to the house of Doti the healer. "Ilika taught us something about this once . . . about the difference between . . ."

Sata's hand shot up. "The difference between bad and . . ." Suddenly she stopped and scrunched her face as she searched for a word, but only found it in her native language. "Evil."

Kibi translated the word for the mission team.

K'storpo's mandibles twitched with large open movements that meant, they all knew, he was laughing.

Arantiloria smiled.

*

After a break for dessert, one kind for insects and another for humans, Ilika could sense Arantiloria looking at him. He stood and organized his thoughts.

"A few worlds have open contact with Nebador, but most do not. A few individuals qualify for the Nebador Services, but most do not. We have seen, on this mission, a good example of one of the things that separates the two. As you guessed, all of our peoples could be called *bad* in some ways . . . maybe many ways . . ."

Boro suddenly thrust his arm into the air. "But the question is, what do they do when they discover they're powerful enough to do *evil?*"

Ilika nodded. "And I think Kibi has remembered the difference . . ."

She grinned. "Evil is when you *know* it's bad."

Timoradalia was jumping up and down, ready to explode. Her mate, from behind, slipped his arms around her, and she relaxed.

Mati glanced at the Ti'ias, smiled, and spoke. "So . . ." she began, looking at Rini for inspiration, "something about trying to kill your planet is way, way worse than just killing other creatures. Right?"

Ilika knew who could best put the answer into words, so he looked at her, even though he knew it might make his head spin.

Arantiloria accepted the challenge. "The universe is so arranged that the power to destroy the climate and/or ecosystem of your home planet only comes when you also have the intelligence to know that doing so is a fatal error. Therefore, any species that does that is, by its nature, suicidal, and will probably not qualify for any kind of help, from the powers of the universe, with fixing that mistake."

✳ ✳ ✳

Chapter 15: The Report

The Manessa Kwi, with its crew and mission team, stayed on the icy fourth planet of the nameless, lone solar system for nearly another Satamia day. Arantiloria no longer appeared.

In between the exploration of large buildings from the comfort of the ship, or small ones with harsh-environment suits, K'storpo gave a more complete explanation of the story they were seeing. The dominant sapient species, the winged insects, had learned how to remove heat energy from both the atmosphere and the core of the planet. They probably did it on a small scale for many years, without any noticeable effect, before deciding to conquer the universe.

Tizoromulia explained that the energy needed for the three huge colony ships was not available from normal mining operations. They needed much more. In a very real sense, it required the insects to kill their planet, just as they could be seen doing in their recent works of art.

M'palta's mate finished the train of thought. By aggressively tapping into the energy of both the air and the land, an ice age was triggered. The winged creatures were not fleeing from a planet entering a *natural* ice age. They had caused one by their efforts to get into space.

A sense of completeness came over the crew. They now knew the whole story, as sad as it was, and they understood why there would probably be no rescue of the foolish creatures currently making their way slowly through interstellar space.

But ship-day after ship-day, whenever Kibi wondered aloud if it was time to prepare the Manessa Kwi for the return journey, she would find the mission specialists deep in thought, or gazing at scenes from the planet on the large display, or just fluttering about as if looking for something they couldn't find.

The final mission report, needless to say, remained unfinished.

Kibi, who used to think of herself as quite intuitive, struggled to understand what they were sensing and feeling. She couldn't think of any angle they had not fully explored. She looked at Ilika, K'storpo, and M'palta, and could see in their eyes that they were mostly acting on faith, faith in something they could not yet see, and that Kibi could not yet imagine.

*

With the help of those who could see, the mission team continued to review hundreds of images. Excursion teams of a crew member or two, a Ti'ia, and sometimes the female beetle, poked around in the smaller rooms of the insect cities, or the tighter places in the power generating plants.

Between excursions, they worked on the parts of the mission report they could, and wished aloud for Arantiloria, or anyone, to give them some idea of what else to look for.

The training supervisor remained absent, or at least invisible and silent.

The ship-days passed slowly, with everyone becoming more and more frustrated, and requesting to go on excursions just for something to do.

*

Boro, Mati, and Timorasimia, all in harsh-environment suits, sat silently on a frosty concrete slab in an aircraft assembly building. A cone-shaped pile of ice and snow, from a broken window high above, lay nearby. The three had just fruitlessly explored another record-keeping room, and found nothing of interest.

Boro was about to suggest they head back to the ship when the little empath on his shoulder cocked her head, listening. She quickly hopped down to Boro's knee and looked toward the pile of ice and snow.

The engineer and pilot remained silent, straining to hear or see what their little friend had sensed.

After several minutes of silence, a tiny rustling sound was faintly heard, a scraping noise, as if metal upon ice. The three remained still.

After many more minutes, a tiny hole appeared in the ice pile, and a thin metal tool poked through.

The three visitors waited.

The hole was carefully enlarged, and Boro recognized a drill bit, like the ones the former insect inhabitants used, but it was not turning, just being used as a poker.

Timorasimia turned her head slowly to glance at Mati, then returned to watching the drama. Mati received a thought from Rini, on the ship, and tapped a code into her mission bracelet.

As the ice hole became larger, tiny, furry hands could be seen gripping the drill bit, furry arms followed, and finally, when the hole was large enough, a brown creature, not much bigger than Boro's fist, rolled out onto the floor. Another furry ball followed, seemingly just as comfortable rolling as walking.

The two little creatures uncurled themselves, made a sound that might have been laughter, then exchanged a stream of complex sounds. Suddenly they realized their mistake, looked up at the two humans and one Ti'ia not far away, and vanished into their icy tunnel with a single leap, not bothering to take the drill bit.

"Get all that?" Mati asked after a moment of silence.

"Got it," Rini replied through the intercom. "Filia is already working on the language, and is very glad to have a task she can do with her ears."

"I wonder if this is what we've been missing . . ." Timorasimia pondered aloud from Boro's knee.

Boro smiled as he placed the Ti'ia back on his shoulder and stood up. "I think we'll soon find out."

✳

Back on the ship, Mati and Boro listened as the blind Ti'ia used Rini's station to play the seven seconds of conversation between the two little mammals, again and again. Often she would slow it down, sometimes speed it up. She applied noise filters, canceled various amounts of high or low tones, eliminated harmonics, or completely reshaped the sounds. Eventually those watching wandered away to get a snack, and Kibi set a bowl of small worms beside the laboring linguist.

At the big table, K'storpo and M'palta listened as Boro and Mati described every detail of what they had seen, while others watched the video from Mati's bracelet. Timorafilia would sometimes pause her playback to listen to the conversation, then return to her work.

✳

More than an hour later, with a burst of excitement, Timorafilia took wing and fluttered high above Rini's station, declaring, "Of course! Why didn't I think of it sooner?"

Those words were hardly out of her tiny mouth before the blind Ti'ia began wobbling in flight and reaching out in panic with her small arms and two tails to find somewhere to land. Luckily, Timorasimia the empath quickly realized the problem and joined her co-mate in the air to guide her safely back down.

Kibi used the intercom to call everyone to the table. Ilika and Boro came up the lift a moment later.

The little linguist perched on the edge of the table near her family's chair, her excited wings moving almost enough to make her airborne. "I cannot translate the small amount of speech we captured, and can never do so without a much larger sample. It is, just like the insect language, unrelated to any other language of Nebador. But I discovered something that I think will tell us a lot, and I am embarrassed to have not seen it sooner."

K'storpo's mandibles moved in laughter. "You are forgiven, Filia."

The Ti'ia on the edge of the table collected herself. "Even though I cannot give you the words, I am quite sure that the little mammals' language is structured almost exactly the same as the insect's language. Either one was derived from the other, or they are literally the same language."

K'storpo sat thoughtfully for a long moment. Boro raised his hand, and the mission leader had just enough sight to make out the shape. "Whoever has an arm in the air, please speak."

"Um ... I was just remembering the data module from the second ship. Maybe there's some bug ... insect speech in it."

K'storpo nodded. "We'll give it to the technicians as soon as we return to Satamia, and Filia will be the first to get whatever language, audible or otherwise, they find."

The linguist bounced up and down on the table for a moment, then stopped to steady herself and get her bearings.

"I have a theory," M'palta began thoughtfully.

K'storpo and everyone else looked in her direction.

"From everything we've seen, it's very unlikely the insects willingly *shared* the planet with anyone. I think it's more likely the little mammals were pets, or perhaps even slaves. They were sapient, learned the language of their masters, and adapted it to their own needs and speaking abilities. The insects were just too arrogant to notice."

Laughter rolled around the table for a long time.

✳

Another ship-day saw the mission report quickly assembled from narratives, pictures, videos, charts, and Timorafilia's one audio analysis. The five crew members from a medieval planet were surprised that their experiences were also needed for the report, and haltingly spoke about what they had seen, heard, and felt.

Just as the report was completed, Arantiloria appeared, and obviously knew what was in it.

"Every civilization comes to this point," she explained, floating around the room as she looked at each of them in turn, then gesturing toward the large display screen over Kibi's station where the mural could be seen of the insects stinging their planet to death. "Most of them poke around in their home solar systems and learn many things. Some do great damage to their planets before growing up. A few can't resist the temptation to expand their spheres of influence beyond their home solar systems ... in other words, to become gods."

Timoradalia leapt into the air and spread her little arms wide. "These insects did it all!"

Arantiloria laughed. "Well said, little one."

Rini's hand slowly came up, and K'storpo nodded toward him. "Um ... what about the sapient mammals? Are they going to be okay with the planet getting colder and colder?"

Everyone deferred to Arantiloria.

"As M'palta recommended in your report, we will be watching that closely. We might do some things to stabilize the climate, or we might move them, but in either case, we had to wait until a certain ... other species ..."

Chuckles and twitching mandibles encircled the table.

"... had left the planet, or perished ... completely and permanently. That has now occurred. That was one of the reasons this mission did not take place until now."

Rini smiled and nodded.

"All of you," Arantiloria continued, "will probably be involved in those decisions and missions, as you now understand both species — the former dominant insects, and the future dominant mammals — better than any other mortals."

Both the female beetle and the male spider noticed Arantiloria looking at them, as well as the others, as she spoke.

"Is there nothing that can be done for the winged insects?" Mati asked with slight sadness in her voice.

"No. Every species is an experiment, Mati. Those still alive can live out their lives, in space where they chose to be. The universe has no place for creatures who foul their nest and then set out on a journey they cannot survive."

✳   ✳   ✳

Chapter 16: The End of a Long Mission

The Manessa Kwi perched on an ice-covered runway that would never again welcome aircraft or spacecraft. Kibi and the female beetle cooked and served a final meal from the best of the ship's remaining food stocks.

The mission team and the crew were now completely mixed in their seating places. Either Kibi or Sata, sometimes both, were always beside the beetle who had grieved over her mate earlier in the mission. Boro often grabbed a chair next to K'storpo, whom he was beginning to admire greatly, especially after the mission leader lost his sight. Most of the Ti'ias spread themselves around, with Timorazonia usually on Mati's shoulder, and Timorasimia the empath often with Rini.

Everyone was in a light-hearted mood, joking about the frustrating ups and downs of the mission, and laughing about how many times they thought they knew the whole story, only to discover a completely new angle not much later.

Toward the end of the meal, M'palta's mate noticed Rini pop a juicy worm into his mouth. The spider's mandibles twitched thoughtfully for a moment. "Could I try one of those orange things . . . what do you call them?"

"Stewed carrots," Rini replied, and spooned a small one onto the spider's tray.

Several others watched as the spider tried valiantly to suck the juice out of the cooked vegetable, but eventually gave up. Laughter rippled around the table, and whispers informed those who had not been able to see the funny sight for themselves.

*

After a good night's sleep, a hearty breakfast, and plenty of time for baths for both passengers and crew, Ilika stood near the steward's station and looked around.

Timorazonia hovered over the pilot's console while Mati toweled her wet hair.

Boro leaned back in his station chair, looking over the results of a diagnostic.

Rini was in the galley putting away the last of the breakfast dishes.

Kibi stood up after helping M'palta check the mostly-healed break in her mate's leg.

Ilika caught her eye. "Does anyone need any more time here?"

Kibi looked around. At that moment, Sata and Timoradalia appeared in the lift. "I don't think so . . ."

K'storpo listened to the voices around him, then shook his head.

Tizoromulia visually located all his mates, then looked at Ilika and also shook his head.

"Steward, you have command. Please take us home."

Kibi smiled and stepped to her console. "Navigator, high equatorial orbit. All passengers, please begin preparations for star transit."

Rini and Sata sat down at their stations and began making selections.

Timorazonia quickly landed near the flight control and looked at Mati with dozens of tiny insect eyes.

The pilot glanced at her little student with fondness. "Think you can handle all aspects of the vector this time?"

At that moment, the orbital insertion diagram flashed onto Mati's screen. The Ti'ia turned her head and looked it over. "Um . . . yes . . . if you'll watch in case I make a mistake . . ."

Mati smiled and nodded.

✳

The Manessa Kwi returned to Satamia Star Station in one long star transit, and Mati took back her helm for the complex journey past navigation markers, into the docking tunnel, through hull sterilization, and finally into the awaiting fingers of quarantine dock C five. Timorazonia watched from her shoulder.

Several hours later, they were all released from quarantine, but Arantiloria appeared and asked the crew to remain a little longer. After words and touches of friendship, the mission team departed.

"There will be a memorial service for T'shlix in the near future. His mate is grateful for all the support you gave her as she grieved."

Boro took a moment to wipe at some moisture that had somehow gotten into his eyes.

"I have recommendations for additional training for most of you."

Everyone pulled their chairs closer to the round table in the middle of the room.

"I think it would be very good for Mati and Boro to switch positions . . . immediately."

Both jaws dropped. They had each begun some cross-training, but not with each other. Neither had ever imagined doing the other's job. They both looked at Ilika.

He looked surprised, but forced himself to smile. "It will not be an easy transition, but I think you can both do it."

Mati struggled to find words. "I . . . um . . . I'm just glad . . . I got my knee fixed first!"

Others laughed, and Arantiloria smiled.

"Kibi," the floating purple-haired lady began once the laughter died down, "your intuition, as you know, has served you well in mortal life. On the mission you just completed, you saw its limits. I will now recommend that your Psychic Development training enter a new phase to prepare you to sense spiritual realities."

Kibi forced out a smile, but obviously wasn't sure what to think.

Arantiloria looked at Ilika, then at Sata. "Melorania has already told me about a mission she would like the Manessa Kwi to handle. A little planet deep in the heart of Nebador needs some help getting their priorities straight. It will require two of you to become mission specialists, one on the ground under pretense of being a citizen of the planet, one on the ship. I'm recommending Ilika for the under-cover position, and Sata for the ship. That will put you in command of the mission most of the time, Sata, which is different than being in command of the ship."

Sata swallowed and nodded slowly.

"The mission will require you to learn the local language," the floating spirit said, looking at both of them. "Are you up to it?"

"That'll be my third language!" Sata said with pride, grinning.

Kibi stuck out her lower lip for a second. "Teach me later?"

Arantiloria laughed. "After you see how mixed up this planet is, I don't think you'll *want* to know it!"

Several crew members chuckled nervously.

Finally, Arantiloria looked at Rini. "I do not have any training recommendations for you right now, Rini."

After a moment, Rini smiled weakly.

Mati noticed that his eyes lacked their usual sparkle.

"Okay," Ilika began after Arantiloria faded from sight, "let's go enjoy our beautiful star station and the party that's only about a ship-day away. I don't know about the rest of you, but I've *missed* the place!"

"Me too!" they all added as they hopped up and pointed their feet toward the quarantine room door.

*   *   *

Part 2: The Center

Chapter 17: Liberty

Snowflakes fell slowly through the thin early-winter daylight outside the barn. In the large indoor stall, the three brown horses worked intently on their feed boxes, newly stocked with alfalfa and grain. Liberty's long black hair bobbed among the horses, sometimes behind, sometimes between two of them, the brush in her hand working over their shaggy coats.

Two of the horses suddenly moved closer together. The girl's elbows quickly went into action, and her feet danced to avoid their hooves. "Move over, ya big lunks!"

A few minutes later, the door to the barn opened and in stepped a gray-haired man, dressed and groomed as formally as possible while doing outdoor chores.

"Hi, Harold! Pfew, I'm glad I'm not allergic to horse hair!"

"Miss Liberty, I am amazed at how tidy you are keeping the barn and what good care the horses are receiving."

"Keeps me from getting too bored. No, Chelsea! I like my hair the length it is, thank you!"

The man couldn't suppress a chuckle.

"There, you guys are brushed, and I'm *not* going to do it every time you see me! Hand me that can of salve, please, Harold. Penny's got a scratch."

"Hmm. We'll have to walk the fences as soon as the weather improves a bit, and look for loose wire."

"Yeah. Doesn't look like anything bigger than fence wire."

"By the way, I've got the mail. Would you like to do the honors?"

Climbing over the stall fence and hanging up her brush, Liberty replied with routine excitement, "Sure! And I'm starved! What's cooking?"

"You don't want to go back to hay and grain?"

She snickered. "You're going to remind me about that for the rest of my life, aren't you Harold? I only did it for three days!"

"Actually, I don't think I'll need to remind you. I have a hunch that every time you start losing perspective, you'll remember those days of sleeping in the barn, running barefoot in the snow, and nearly starving to death while chewing on alfalfa. I've got a meatloaf in the oven and some potatoes baking."

They both pulled up their hoods and trudged through the snow toward the stately three-story house. Inside, Liberty plopped down on the couch and began looking at the envelopes. She selected a small one and ripped it open.

With a sarcastic voice, she read aloud, "*Dear Mr. Neils. I'm sorry to inform you that we do not accept delinquents into our nationally-acclaimed program ...*" She grabbed another and opened it. "*Dear Mr. Neils. In order to determine if we can provide psychiatric services for Miss Liberty Buchanan, we must have a five-axis diagnosis ...*"

"Any luck?" the man called from the kitchen.

"Negative, unless dad wants to send me to a funny farm. I'll add them to the pile." She placed the letters and envelopes on an already-thick stack, and looked at the mail again. A large blue envelope caught her eye and a wrinkle of curiosity appeared on her face. "For me?" She pulled a letter and a large bound book, a hundred pages or more, out of the envelope, leaned back, and began to read to herself.

Dear Liberty,

I am addressing this directly to you because Lyceum does not accept applications from third parties. I have read the brief description of your background that Mr. Neils sent, and find you an interesting person. I have enclosed a book that describes our facilities and services in detail. If you find yourself interested in membership, please write back, answering the questions on the second page of this letter.

Sincerely,
Sister Nancy

"*Sister* Nancy? I'm not going to some lousy convent!" she said with disgust and tossed everything onto the table. When it landed, the letter slid off the book and allowed her to see its cover, an aerial view of numerous ultra-modern buildings, plazas, gardens, play fields, and even some corrals and pastures. "Hmm. Sure doesn't look like a convent ..." She picked up the book and opened the cover to the first page.

✳

The snow had stopped and midnight was approaching as Liberty sat at the little desk in her room, and by the light of a small lamp, finished reading the last page of the book. She was silent and thoughtful for several minutes. Finally, she turned to her computer and started typing.

Dear Sister Nancy,
*   I read the book you sent me, cover to cover.   Lyceum sounds pretty*
interesting.   Actually, it sounds very interesting!

Liberty smiled, wondering if Sister Nancy really was fat and wore nun's clothes, like she imagined.   Not yet sure what else to say, she looked at the questions on the second page of the letter.   A number of expressions visited her face as she considered the first question.   Finally, with a mental deep breath, she began to type.

I would be happy if I had people to talk to about all the things I learn on my own.   School is always so boring because everyone else is struggling to learn things I knew years before.   Mr. Neils wrote to lots of places for gifted kids, but they won't take me because . . . sometimes I do things that get me in trouble.

Liberty answered several more easy questions, then nearly bristled when she read the last one.   She breathed for several minutes, debating with herself how to approach it.

I have friends in the city who have a lot less than me of everything, and I've always tried to be kind to them . . . but I have to admit I don't always succeed.   I'm very kind to animals, all the time.   The only people I don't know how to be nice to are people who are trying to force me to be like them for no good reason.
*   Please let me know if I'm the kind of person you might consider for membership at Lyceum.*

Sincerely,
Liberty Buchanan

✳

After another month of light snows that usually melted quickly, a day came when the flakes fell rapidly and promised deep drifts.   Liberty dashed in the front door, wearing only a sweater and clutching a bundle of mail to her chest.

"How deep does it get, anyway?" she asked while trying to brush the snow from the knees of her pants.

At the large desk in the corner of the room, Mr. Neils glanced up from his work.   "Two or three feet."

Liberty whistled.   "What do the horses do when the snow's that deep?"

"Same as you — pace.   But as soon as it stops, they'll have the corral packed flat in no time."

"I'll sort the mail," she said, sitting down on the couch.

"Anything from that school up north that looked promising?" he asked without turning around.

"I'll see."   She began making piles of mail.   "Dad, dad, you, dad, junk, you, dad, bill, dad . . ." Then she held up the last envelope, large and blue. "And another one for me! Several things for you, Harold, but nothing from that school. I'm gonna look at the magazines and stuff." She skipped across the living room to a cozy chair, curled up and ripped open the one piece of mail addressed to her.

Dear Liberty,

It has been such a pleasure getting to know you, that I was very happy to receive your request for more information about membership.

Your question about world-class standards is right on the mark. In order for Lyceum to be of service to a wide variety of people, organizations, and governments who are involved in important work, we have to keep our standards at an extremely high level.

I could really relate to the thoughts you shared about your changing values. I think you and I are very much alike. I too once prowled the back streets of a major city, until one day I realized it wasn't taking me where I wanted to go.

Sincerely,
Sister Nancy

A few minutes later, she joined Mr. Neils at the couch and pretended to pay attention as he described a reform school that looked like it might accept her, but for several reasons, Liberty just couldn't get excited about it.

To begin with, she didn't feel she needed *reforming*. And equally as important, she no longer felt the desperate need to find a school, any school, that would take her. She had gotten used to life at the Buchanan country house, and no longer dreaded the thought of just reading books and taking care of the horses. And besides, someone in the world already believed in her.

Dear Sister Nancy,

The more I learn about all the things you people do there, and the ways you do them, the more I can picture myself being there. And the longer I'm out here in the country, the farther away the city streets are starting to seem . . .

✳

Liberty gazed out one of the large front windows at a light spring rain. She was almost sad that the last patches of snow were beginning to melt. But it had been a long winter and she welcomed the coming of warmer weather and the new shades of green that were emerging everywhere.

"Here's something for you. A magazine, I think," Mr. Neils said from the couch where he was going through the mail.

With a dreamy, far-away look in her eyes, Liberty received the large blue envelope and sat down in a chair by the window.

She tore it open and extracted the contents. There it was, in her hands, just as she had requested in her last letter to Sister Nancy. After quickly reading the letter, Liberty clutched the membership application forms to her chest like a valuable treasure as she gazed out the window at the falling rain.

*

Three days later, she sat in her dormer window reading a book and waiting for her father to arrive. Outside, mottled late afternoon sunshine warmed the grasses and buds that were appearing everywhere. Tiny patches of snow only lingered in the places of deepest shade. All three horses roamed the pasture, happily nibbling at the new shoots of grass. The long white car, a little muddy along the bottom edge, crunched through the gravel just about when it was expected.

For as long as Liberty could remember, the most important events in her life could not be shared with any adult — especially her father. Now, for the first time, she was anxious to tell him what she was considering.

She hopped out of the dormer and paced nervously, wondering what to wear for the occasion. When she finally decided, quickly dressed, and pranced downstairs, Mr. Neils was about to serve dinner and her father was sitting at the dining table, sipping tea and talking. She quietly sat down and listened.

"... so the hearings on the nuclear weapons treaty will probably go through summer, and then we should be able to bring it up for a vote. It's going to be the issue of the decade, and there are powerful forces on all sides."

"I'm glad *you're* the senator, and *I'm* the caretaker!" Mr. Neils said, taking a covered roasting pan out of the oven.

Senator Buchanan smiled. "But now that Liberty's here, let's talk about the project you two have been wrestling with. What kind of luck have you had?"

As Mr. Neils brought out serving dishes brimming with baked ham, buttered mashed potatoes, and a vegetable medley with hollandaise sauce, he began to list, as best he could from memory, the many places he had written to, and the kinds of responses they had received. As father and daughter served themselves, he got his notes so he could give a more complete accounting. Finally, he sat down at his place and served himself while summarizing.

"So as you can see, there have been many negative responses for a variety of reasons. And there were a few fringe operations that had placed misleading ads, which I was able to spot as soon as their literature arrived. Liberty has grown immensely in patience and perseverance. The best outlook so far is that reform school that can evaluate her next summer, with the girls' school up north a contingency plan for the following year." He fell silent and began to eat.

"Wow, I didn't realize we'd come up with such a short list!" Senator Buchanan said.

Liberty gathered her courage, and then spoke without looking at the adults. "Except there's a place I've been writing to that's invited us to come and visit, and they have an evaluation week in early summer."

Both of the men looked at Liberty with confusion for a long moment.

"This is news to me!" Mr. Neils declared.

"They don't take applications from third parties," Liberty explained, "so I had to be the one to write to them. Sorry. At first I didn't think it would come to anything, and then I just got used to writing to them myself. But they do have the history sheet about me that Mr. Neils sent everyone."

"Let me guess," Mr. Neils began, "those blue envelopes that kept arriving for you?"

Liberty grinned sheepishly. "They sent me detailed information, and I've read every page of it, most of it twice. It sounds really good." She looked at her father for a reaction.

He finished chewing a bite of food, wiped his mouth slowly with his napkin, and gave her a long look. "Well ... I presume you still have everything they sent you?"

"Yep."

"Okay. Stack it all up, and I'll take a look at it tonight."

"Thanks, Daddy!"

During the remainder of the meal, Mr. Neils described the reform school and a couple of other remote possibilities. Then the discussion turned to springtime chores around the estate and other light topics.

Right after dinner, Liberty delivered the entire pile of books and letters to her father in his bedroom, where he was already at work at his big roll-top desk. Her stomach was tied in knots as she headed for the barn to do her evening chores. She busied herself for almost two hours, knowing she would just pace in her bedroom otherwise.

* * *

The following morning, Senator Buchanan finished reading everything Liberty had given him, then leaned back in his chair and closed his eyes for several minutes.

As soon as he sat up, he tapped a number into the telephone. "Good morning, this is Senator Michael Buchanan. I'd like to speak to Senator Giles ... Yes, I'd like to speak *directly* to the senator ... Thank you."

While waiting, he organized the Lyceum materials on his desk.

"Bill! This is Michael Buchanan! How are things out west? ... Good to hear it! You still with me on the nuclear weapons treaty? ... Good, good, and you've got me in your pocket on that timber bill, you know, and all those I can drag along ... Excellent! I'm calling because I need a reference about a place in your neck of the woods. It's called Lyceum, and its address is in a little town ... You've heard of it? Wonderful! ... Well, that's even better! Fifteen or twenty times? Tell me about it, please."

Senator Buchanan listened to his colleague for a couple of minutes. "Wow, it sounds almost too good to be true. No skeletons in the closet *at all?*"

At that moment, Mr. Neils poked his head into the bedroom, and motioned that he would come back later, but the senator waved him on in, and punched the speaker button on the telephone.

". . . only thing I can think of that even approaches weird is that they're very strict about confidentiality — for their own people, and all visitors. Reporters go out to scrape up a story about some famous person who's been spotted there. They grab the nearest staff member, and can get any general question answered. But the only name they can ever get is Brother John or Sister Jane or whatever, and never a whisper about the person they're trying to write about."

"Well, that sounds pretty nice from my point of view."

"That's why I like getting out there fairly often. I know that if I don't spread who I am, no one else will either. And they've got places you can go to get *totally* out of the public eye."

"Well, thanks, Bill. If there's nothing else you can think of, I'll let you get back to work."

"Their literature is totally up front. Have you got it?"

"Yes. My daughter wants to go out for a visit."

"I see. She'll love it! See you next week, Michael!"

"Yes, see you then. Bye!"

The senator looked at Mr. Neils. "Did you find out anything?"

"They do indeed have an office in every major city . . . in the entire *world*."

"Interesting. Thanks, Harold."

The caretaker left and the senator sat for a minute thinking. Then he grabbed a note pad and began jotting down thoughts as they came to him.

Father and daughter, wearing warm sweaters and windbreaks, walked side by side as they neared the top of a grassy hill that was just beginning to turn light green with new spring growth. Both wore serious faces.

"This place is not your usual private school, like the ones you're familiar with, I hope you realize," he said.

"I know, Daddy."

"So . . . tell me what about it attracts you."

"Well . . . from everything I can tell, it would really challenge me to be grown up and do my best."

"Uh huh . . ."

"And remember that world-class feeling I've always liked? This place has it."

"I can see that." He walked in silence for a moment. "Part of being a member is being assigned work and projects. At your age, I believe it was sixteen hours per week. Whatever you're told to do. No back talk, no sneaking off. Can you handle that?"

She thought for a moment. "I think so . . . if I like the place. I wanna try."

"I'm sure you've noticed that they call each other *Brother* and *Sister* there. Know why that is?"

"N . . . not really."

"The basic economic and social arrangement of the place, as far as the members are concerned, is most similar to a religious monastery."

"Doesn't seem like one when you look at the pictures, does it?"

"No . . . it doesn't. And yet, it's designed to provide its members with a contemplative, service-oriented life. That doesn't sound like you, Liberty."

"I know." She looked at the ground for a while as they walked. "But you know how I love to read and learn new things. And look how happy I've been out here, once I started taking care of the horses!"

They walked in silence for another minute. "I don't know exactly why this place feels right. I just know it does. If it doesn't work out, I'll go and be evaluated at that reform school, I guess."

They walked through a short patch of woods without speaking.

"So . . ." Senator Buchanan said, "see if you can coordinate a visit with the senate's spring vacation. We'll fly out together, spend a day there, and if I like what I see, I'll go on alone."

She stopped and wrapped her arms around him. "Oh, thank you, Daddy!"

✳   ✳   ✳

Chapter 18: Shawn

In late spring, the Reverend Tommy Mitchell's only son turned eighteen. Shawn's church youth group put on a party for him, even though Shawn was two years older than anyone else in the group. He tried to enjoy himself, but was aware that the other boys wanted to get away to a baseball game, and the girls just giggled among themselves about their boyfriends. He didn't know exactly what he wanted out of his eighteenth birthday, but he knew he wasn't getting it.

During the weeks that followed, Shawn busied himself with school so his final grades, just before graduation, would be as high as possible. He continued to visit at least one other church each week by pretending to take a long walk on the way home from his family's regular church. He didn't like telling a lie, but neither did he feel the strength to openly defy his father. Not yet.

He did, however, enjoy his graduation ceremonies. He had worked hard, and had good grades to show for it. He even surprised himself by managing to have fun at the graduation dance that evening.

❋

Two days later, Shawn was sitting in the living room of his family's spacious suburban home on the west side of town when his father, with obvious purpose, sat down beside him.

"Well, son, perhaps it's time to make some plans for the future. Have you had a chance to look at the literature about our seminary?"

"Yes, father, I've read it. It sounds like a very good seminary."

"They're reserving a space for you, but they won't be able to hold it forever. They'll be getting lots of applications now that school is out."

I wonder why they're reserving a space for me? Shawn asked himself, even though he already knew the answer. "I'm not sure that's the right place for me, father. If it's okay with you, I'd like to consider some other options."

The reverend took a moment to recover. "Well, um ... there are some other good seminaries in the country, I guess. Um ... I could get their literature for you."

"Thank you, father. That would be great."

*

A few days later, Shawn had packets containing the literature of five other seminaries around the country, all identical to the one operated by his family's church, at least as far as religious doctrine was concerned. He read the information out of respect for whomever had mailed the packets. As much as he dreaded the thought of defying his father, he also knew that somewhere inside himself was a line he couldn't cross.

That line, and its exact location somewhere between his own will, and his father's, had often occupied Shawn's thoughts during the last couple of years. That line had been coming into clearer focus in recent months, and now Shawn seemed to be face to face with it. Signing up for a multi-year course of study, one he knew wasn't right for him, was somewhere on the other side of that line.

A few days after the packets arrived, his father must have decided that Shawn had had enough time to read them, as he again joined his son on the couch.

The reverend went through the brochures and letters on the coffee table, organizing them to his preference. "As I understand it, these three are the best, but this place has a fairly good reputation also."

"Yes, father, they all sound like good places where I could learn a lot about the Good Book."

"So, which one do you prefer? Remember that *our* church's seminary might still be an option if we act quickly."

Shawn swallowed once. "Actually, father, I'm not sure a seminary is the best place for me right now. I think it might be an important part of my education someday, but I think there are many other things I need to learn first."

"Um ... well, perhaps some courses at the local college would be a good idea. Or ... did you have another good college in mind?"

"To tell you the truth, father, I've already found a place where I think I can learn some things that are interesting to me, even some things about the Good Book."

"Where's that, son?" the reverend said in a dry, suspicious tone.

Shawn steeled himself. "It's an international service organization called *Lyceum.* Maybe you've heard of it ..."

"YES I've heard of it!" the Reverend Tommy Mitchell stood up and immediately began yelling. "And it will be a cold day in HELL before any son of MINE goes to that place to learn about the GOOD BOOK and the Lord's teachings! That place is doing NOTHING but the Devil's work, and has NO place in the education of any true minister of God!"

The angry man stood in the middle of the living room, glaring at his son and waving his hands. Shawn just sat on the couch looking at him, his heart in his throat.

The reverend had always been good at improvised speeches, and today was no exception. "... and if YOU think that I paid for all those church CAMPS, all those RETREATS, and that tour of the HOLY LAND just so YOU could tell me you're going off to some place that has NOTHING to do with OUR church, you are DEAD WRONG!"

Shawn held onto the line deep inside himself. It was the most painful hour of his life, but he knew there was no way to avoid it. As he listened to his father go on and on, he knew there was nothing he could say now. The corner had been turned. He was no longer a child, and he had decided what he was going to do. But he also knew he had to respectfully hear his father out, if for no other reason than because his father had paid for all those things.

"... and starting right now, TODAY, you are forbidden to have ANY contact with Lyceum or ANY other place where the Devil's work is done! And you shall have NO further access to the resources of this family until you get your VALUES and your PRIORITIES straight!"

Shawn realized that his father had just saved him the trouble of working up the courage to leave home. If he had no further access to the resources of the family, then he had better not be taking up a bedroom and eating the family's food. He had never dreamed it could be so easy.

"... and NOW I want you to go to your ROOM so that you can think about what I've SAID to you, and get all this NONSENSE out of your head!"

The silence was deafening. Shawn waited a few seconds as his father continued to glare at him with wide eyes. Finally, when he felt sure the lecture had ended, he whispered, "Yes, father," and dashed for his room.

After Shawn stepped into his bedroom, he closed the door ever so softly, sat down on his bed, and listened to his heart pounding in his chest. His father's words still echoed in his mind, but their literal meaning no longer mattered, as they all boiled down to one simple message. Shawn was legally an adult now, and yet, in his father's eyes, he did not have the right to make any decisions about his life.

As Shawn began to cool off, he became aware of the clock on his desk. It was almost four o'clock. His mother would serve dinner at five. If he was no longer entitled to use family resources, he should be gone by then.

He moved around his room, tossing things he wanted onto his bed. Shirts, a sweater, a jacket, and a duffel bag. From his desk came his wallet, journal, and a Lyceum booklet. As he zipped his duffle bag closed, another problem dawned on him. He was ready to walk down the street to whatever awaited him, but he wasn't sure how to get to that street.

After a minute of thought, he looked out his window into the back yard. The screen wasn't hard to unlatch, and his duffel bag hardly made a sound as it landed behind a bush.

Ever so slowly, he opened his bedroom door, to discover by listening that his mother had returned from the grocery store and was making dinner, and his father was taking a shower. He stepped out into the hallway, closed his door without a sound, and crept toward the back door, his heart again pounding in his chest.

"Shawn, Honey, we're having baked cod for dinner," his mother's voice said, causing him to freeze as he neared the back door. She walked right past him and turned into the pantry.

"Uh . . . g . . . great, Mom. Um . . . I'll be in the . . . the back yard."

"Okay, Honey."

Soon he found himself outside, with only a lawn between himself and the freedom of the alley. He collected his duffel bag, walked to the back gate, and slipped through, all without daring to look back. Then he froze and listened.

Nothing.

He began to walk down the alley, and as he did so, the throbbing of his heart slowly began to relax. After he had gone past a few back yards, all well-fenced so that no one could see his passing, he dared to glance behind him.

Still nothing.

His long legs put several more blocks of the alley behind him. He began to swing his duffel bag as he walked along, and his footsteps lightened until he was almost skipping.

As he moved toward the center of town, the houses along the alley became poorer, and he began to see children playing in the yards. A little colored girl looked up from her toys in a yard without grass, and waved shyly. Shawn waved back. An ancient man with white hair tending a tiny garden peered up at him. Shawn smiled and waved.

He began to feel a sense of purpose as he walked along, a sense of being guided by unseen forces to exactly where he needed to be, in order to learn and do . . . whatever it was God wanted him to learn and do. And he wondered why it had taken him so long to get out into the world and see what it was like.

✳

Shawn Mitchell spend the first few nights of his adult life under a loading ramp in the railroad yard, and the days in between in the park, a working-class diner near the train station, or the library. He learned many lessons about taking care of himself, and the money in his bank account allowed him to get clothing and equipment better suited to the task, including a small backpack and a light sleeping bag.

Eventually he was drawn to the rescue mission, also near the railroad yard, for a hot shower, companionship, and perhaps some clues about his path in life. It felt safe because he knew it was run by a church his father didn't like.

✳

The man at the front desk advised Shawn to keep his belongings with him at all times.

Shawn didn't realize how literally he should take that warning. He found the bunk room and selected a free bed. While he took a lukewarm shower in the slimy shower stall, his water bottle disappeared. While he was at dinner, reminding himself that he should be thankful for even instant mashed potatoes, his jacket walked away. That was all it took. His pack came with him to the church service, and he noticed that the other men had their belongings with them also.

The service, to Shawn's surprise, was a one-man show. Reverend Walker preached, prayed, and sang. Shawn added his voice when he knew the hymns, to the obvious delight of the preacher.

When Reverend Walker asked for all those who had accepted the Lord into their lives to come up, Shawn did not hesitate. One old man joined them. Shawn genuinely felt for the preacher as he tried to coax others to accept the Lord. One timid hand went up, and then another, out of about thirty men. As they came up to the front, Shawn and the old man made them feel as welcome as they could, but the rest of the audience was getting bored, and the preacher soon had to wrap up the service.

As Shawn thoughtfully headed back toward the bunk room, the old man began to walk along beside him. "You would find your jacket in the short colored man's bag, and your canteen in the long-haired man's pack, but I hope you are secure enough in the love of the Lord to let those things go, and know that they will be put to good use."

Shawn thought for a moment. "Yes, I think they need them more than I do."

"Maybe, maybe not. But getting them back could get ugly."

"I see what you mean," Shawn said.

"I sense that you are not new to the Kingdom, but very new to missions."

"You're right. My father's a preacher."

"Your faith is not just because of your father," he said.

"No. In fact I'm going against my father's wishes right now."

"But not against the wishes of your father in Heaven?"

Shawn thought about that question as they entered the bunk room. "I don't pretend to know much about God's will for me yet. I seem to be drawn toward a place with lots of religious people, but they are from many different faiths. My father wanted me to go to the seminary run by our church." Shawn sat down on his bed, and the old man sat on the adjacent one.

"Different faiths? Is there more than one Kingdom of God?"

Shawn thought. "No, I don't think so. To my father, the place I might go does the Devil's work."

"Ah! *The Devil's Work.* Many good things are so labeled. Many bad things go unnoticed. Beware of labels."

Shawn was thoughtful for a moment. "I've . . . seen my father label too many things . . . and too many people."

The old man fell silent, and soon the mission staff announced quiet time and lights out.

* * *

During the following week, Shawn became very comfortable at the rescue mission. He asked for a scrub brush, and made it his personal project to keep the showers clean and tidy. He added his singing voice to the church service every day. By the fourth day, he was helping to serve meals, and by the end of the week, he could stay all day, any time he wanted, to assist the staff with their work. He did so about every other day, but also began to search the library with a wrinkled brow for clues about the direction his life should take.

About two weeks later, Shawn was deep in the library shelves when a large man appeared beside him, pretending to look for a book.

"Your father wants you to come home now, Shawn," the man said.

Shawn's face became hot and his heart started to pound. "I'm busy," he said, and walked away.

As soon as he turned the first corner in the stacks, he sensed that the man was right behind him. Shawn started walking as fast as he could.

Shawn was angry, but didn't want to cause a scene. He was long-legged and fast, and knew the layout of the library by heart. The large man was still following him, but the distance between them was growing.

Suddenly Shawn realized that *two* men were after him. Every time Shawn turned a corner, one of them would follow him, and the other would go a different way.

A plan popped into Shawn's mind. He strode toward the reference area with its long row of study tables. He selected a point near the middle where no one was sitting, and skidded to a stop. As soon as the large man turned a corner and saw him standing there, he slowly walked toward Shawn. The other man did the same from the opposite direction. When they were only a few steps away, Shawn dropped to the floor, crawled under the tables, and dashed for the door.

Shawn never knew if the men attempted to crawl under the tables, or went the long way around. He didn't care. After he ran around a corner, down an alley, across two streets, and onto a weedy bicycle path, no one was following him. He slowed to a walk, and after collecting his thoughts, planned a route back to the mission that no one would guess.

* * *

Shawn didn't encounter any of his father's messengers for three days after the incident in the library, and he began to relax, thinking his show of resistance had make them stop.

But his spirits were low, as he reluctantly decided that clues about his future were not going to be easy to find, in the library or anywhere else.

He rose early the next morning to help cook and serve breakfast. An unusually large number of mission guests lined up in the dining room, and it was nearly nine o'clock by the time they were all fed. The work had helped Shawn clear his mind, and he wanted to browse in the religious bookstore.

But when he reached the front door, he froze. Outside, standing on the sidewalk talking, he could see three men — the mission's Reverend Walker, the large man from the library, and Shawn's father. He veered into the day room, and made his way back to the kitchen.

"Brother Shawn, you look like you seen a ghost!" Charlie the cook said.

"I did. Two of them. Brother Charlie, in about five seconds, I'm going out that back door. You can shut off the power to the alarm system if you want to, or you can just let it ring. Either way, I'm going out."

"Now hold on, Brother Shawn. That don't do no good. It got batteries. But what I can do is hold in this here reset button while you slips out the door, nice and quiet like. Anything you want me to tell the ghosts, if they get this far?"

"Tell them . . . tell them, *The Lord be with you.*"

"Okay, I say that for you. You ready?"

"Yes. Take care, Charlie."

Shawn slipped out the back door, shut it firmly, and wound his way through alleys and back streets until he came to the railroad yard. He wasn't sure why he had gone in that direction . . . perhaps just because it was the last place in town his father would ever go. The yard was busy at that hour, so he headed for the little working-class diner, ordered pie, and tried to collect his thoughts.

✳

After two pieces of pie, a glass of milk, and finally a roast beef sandwich, Shawn pushed his plate away and laid his head down on his arms.

I hope to meet you someday, Shawn!
Brother Jacob

He could clearly see in his mind the end of the last letter from his contact person at Lyceum. He suddenly wanted more than anything to talk to someone who had nothing to do with his father or their church.

Standing up, he pulled both money and a Lyceum card from his wallet. He was still shaking as he paid his bill, but made himself breathe as he walked to the public telephone near the restrooms.

A female voice greeted him and identified herself as Sister Larissa.

"Hi, uh . . . I'm Shawn Mitchell. I was wondering if Brother Jacob was anywhere around . . . Yes, he's been my contact for more than a year now . . . Teaching a class? Oh, okay . . ."

Larissa could hear the fear in Shawn's voice, and feel his despair and frustration. She continued listening as she touched several keys on her computer console, and Jacob was there a minute later.

"Shawn, hang on. Brother Jacob just took a break from his class, and he's here." She touched a button. "He's in some kind of trouble, and he's scared, and doesn't know what to do."

Jacob took the phone. "Hello Shawn! How are you? . . . Uh huh . . . Uh huh . . . And what's your plan now? . . . Uh huh . . . I sense you're having some trouble with that . . ."

Soon Jacob knew what Shawn was dealing with. He handed the phone back to Larissa and rolled his chair to another computer. Within moments, he knew that Lyceum had a member about fifteen miles away from Shawn's location. He touched some keys and picked up a telephone.

"Brother Joseph, this is Brother Jacob! I have a mission for you . . ."

*

Shawn could hardly believe his luck as he hung up the telephone. He had a ride out of town, and all the way to Lyceum if he wanted, in just twenty minutes. He would soon be gone from this town that had become nothing but a trap. He decided to use those twenty minutes to get some snacks to share with his rescuer.

Nearly prancing with excitement, he entered the little store two blocks away, and headed for the snack aisle. Chips, nuts, and chocolate quickly filled his basket. The moment he stepped out of the snack aisle, he came to a sudden stop almost face to face with the large man from the library.

He dropped the basket, turned, and ran, just as the man recognized him and ran after. Turning and running along the meat counter, Shawn spotted another man ahead of him, so he turned into another aisle.

He got to the end of that aisle and started down another, but skidded to a stop when he saw the large man in front of him. He turned, but the other man blocked his escape. He was trapped, and they were closing in on him.

Suddenly the store manager and two employees entered the aisle, pushed past the men, and surrounded Shawn.

"WHAT is going on here?" the manager demanded. "WHY are you chasing this fellow?"

"He's a run-away. We're helping his father find him," the large man said.

"I'm an ADULT, and I can PROVE it!" Shawn screamed, red faced and out of breath.

The manager thought for a moment. "Are you with the police?" he asked the men.

They said nothing.

"Do you have any legal authority over this young man?"

Still no answer.

"Okay, kid, you're out of here."

Shawn slipped by the large man and dashed for the front of the store.

"Don't EVER do that in my store again!" the manager warned the two men before they left.

Shawn ran back to the diner as fast as he could. When he arrived, nearly out of breath, a car was stopped in front, motor still running, with a stout man of about forty leaning on it. Shawn ran up to him and saw a small Lyceum symbol on his jacket. "I'm . . . Shawn!" he gasped out.

"I'm Brother Joseph, Shawn. You need a ride?"

Just as Shawn got in and closed the passenger door, the two men ran up and abruptly stopped about ten feet from the car. Brother Joseph looked at them. "It's a different game now. Good time to call it a day and go home."

As the car moved onto the street and left the two men standing there, Shawn, listening to his throbbing heart, watched the streets of his home town become green countryside, and wondered what sort of life path he had just stepped onto.

✳   ✳   ✳

Chapter 19: Ashley

When Ashley arrived at school the day after taking first place in the National Gymnastics Championships, little work got done in her sixth-grade classroom for the rest of the day. All her classmates made it clear to the teacher that they were *not* going to concentrate on lessons until they had heard the entire story directly from Ashley, with all their questions answered.

When Ashley arrived at the gym that afternoon, the coaches had the same problem. But since gymnastics lessons were expensive, and some of the parents were always watching, a different solution was called for.

"It's four o'clock," the coach announced, stepping out of the office. "Ashley, please warm up the class."

It was the first time he had asked one of his students to lead the warm-up. It was also the first time he had had a national champion in his gym. Ashley, a bit embarrassed, stepped to the front of the class of fourteen gymnasts, and had to stand there grinning for a moment before she could remember what to do.

"Let me see ... oh, yeah. Running in place." The gymnasts spread out and began to follow her instructions. "Add left arm circles ... add right arm circles ..."

The warm-up continued, and Ashley eventually remembered everything the coaches did, although the other gymnasts let her know with giggles and rolled eyes when she did them in the wrong order.

Both coaches worked with individual gymnasts as Ashley led the class. An unusual number of parents looked on from the visitors' gallery, and they seemed pleased that Ashley was being honored in some way.

At the end of the warm-up, the coach stepped beside Ashley. "Okay, we're going to use no more than one minute each day to answer a question put to *our* champion."

Everyone clapped at his recognition of their champion.

"And I want you to let Sue or Gina answer questions whenever they can, since they were at the championships also. So, what is today's question?"

About ten hands shot into the air. "Kathy," the coach picked.

"What was the most important moment of the whole meet for you?"

"This may sound funny, but it was when I thought Cheryl Adams was winning for sure, and all of a sudden I just felt free, like a kid going out to play, because I didn't have to worry about winning anymore. That was just before my beam routine when I got the nine point nine . . ."

＊

That weekend, Ashley had plenty of time to look at her gymnastics books and videos. She knew that the level-seven compulsory skills were a good start, but they wouldn't be enough for the World Championships. Above the compulsories, most of the moves were named after the first gymnast to perform them in competition. She gazed at pictures of the great gymnasts who had come before, and then turned her mind to which of those new skills she wanted to learn first.

On Monday at four o'clock, she warmed up the class, handed the day's question to Sue, and looked at her books again to get clear in her mind what she wanted to learn.

All that day and the next, she worked on the skills that were needed for the new moves. They were similar enough to the regular level-seven work that no one noticed she was doing anything different.

But on Wednesday, she was trying a new dismount from the beam and a new release move on the bars. When everyone was going home at eight o'clock, she heard the coach call her name.

"Ashley, I need to talk to you for a moment."

She sat down near him on the mat. "Hi, coach!"

"Ashley, you know we don't have an elite optionals program here."

"Yeah, I know. That's okay. I can teach myself, from books and videos and stuff."

"Well, it's not that simple. You see, whatever we do here, we have to have insurance that covers it, and our insurance is limited to beginner through level seven compulsory skills."

Ashley looked at her coach a moment longer, then at the vaulting horse in the far corner as she began to feel the impact of what he was saying.

"But if it's any consolation, we've decided you can use the gym for free from now on, as long as what you're doing is covered by our insurance, of course."

Ashley felt her throat begin to close and her eyes begin to water. "You mean . . . you mean I can't get ready for the World Championships . . . here at the gym?"

"Yeah, I'm afraid that's right. Nothing that requires elite skills."

Ashley looked at the exercise floor for a long moment. She knew it better than her own living room floor. She looked at the uneven parallel bars, and they were more familiar than any of the climbing trees in her yard. She looked at the balance beam, where she was as comfortable as most people on a sidewalk. And she glanced at the vaulting horse. Her hands had touched its leather surface more often than the handle bars of her bicycle.

She couldn't think of anything to say, and she didn't have the courage to look at her coach again. She tossed her hair band into her gym bag, stood up, and left the gym, not looking back or pausing for anything until she had walked the six blocks home, burst through the front door, and thrown herself onto her bed crying.

✳

Ashley didn't go back to the gym. She moped for three days, then began to picture the difficulty she faced as a huge boulder in her path. And boulders, she knew, could be moved, or at least chipped at, in a variety of ways.

By the time warm weather was causing new leaves to appear on all the trees, Ashley had worked with her mother, and a pile of gymnastics magazines from the library, to write letters to every gym that advertised a residential training program.

One evening, after Ashley and her parents had eaten a pleasant dinner, she decided the time was right.

"Hey Dad, can I show you the stuff I've been getting from gyms? I've gotten them all now, except for one that closed and I got my own letter back."

"Sure, Ashley. Let's take a look."

Ashley ran to her bedroom and dashed back with a shoe box full of envelopes and papers.

"Oh, boy, where do we start?" her father said. "Why don't you first show me the one you like best?"

"Okay! It's this one." She handed him an envelope with a letter and a thick color brochure.

"Hmm. Fancy place ... beginners through world-class elite. Pictures of their champions — nationals, even world. Now lets take a look at the bottom line. Room, board, and supervision, with elite optionals program, five thousand a month."

"What do you think?" the eleven-year-old asked excitedly.

"Very nice. And I truly wish we could consider it, but we can't. So now let's take a look at the lowest-priced one, shall we?"

"I know which one that is, too."

"Smart girl. Hmm ... smaller, no names of champions to flash ... four-student dorm room, basic board, clothing and spending money not included, one thousand a month."

He leaned back in his comfortable chair and closed his eyes for a long moment. Finally he hunched down to Ashley's level. "Ashley, dear child, when we adopted you, we knew there would be expenses, especially as you got older. We thought about it long and hard, and decided we would do it with glad hearts. You told us clearly that we could only have you if you could have gymnastics lessons. Over the years, those lessons have gone from fifty to three hundred a month, and we have paid for them gladly, knowing how important they were to you. We want you to know that we'd do this for you if we could." His voice became very quiet. "I'm sorry, but we can't."

*

Ashley retreated into her daily routine. School filled her weekdays, and homework, if done very slowly, helped the evenings to pass. On Saturdays, she continued to volunteer at the local nursing home. The old people loved having stories read to them, but Ashley always saved an hour for Jenny, the one young resident, and Ashley knew where to find her.

Jenny stopped playing her penny whistle as Ashley pushed open the door to the little porch. With difficulty, the ten-year-old turned her head and strained to look over the top of her wheel chair. "Hi, Ashley! What'd he say?"

"Too expensive," Ashley began as she pulled a plastic chair next to Jenny. "I guess . . . I was afraid that was going to happen. I think they've really had to scrape to keep paying for my lessons as long as they did. But . . . for an orphan . . . I guess I've been pretty lucky."

"Hey, try dying of cancer at ten! About once a week, some new nurse's aide tries to take away my penny whistle, my only joy."

Although the meaning of Jenny's statement nearly made Ashley cry, the goofy grin on her friend's face forced her to chuckle instead. "What were you playing?"

"Second bridge in Voice Four, minor adagio to major allegro. I think I've nailed it. Want to hear?"

"Yeah!"

Ashley listened with deep respect and near-amazement as the dying girl played a small part of one voice of her musical symphony. Even with the simple penny whistle, the transitions in both tempo and key were smooth and satisfying. Jenny ended with a few bars of the verse after the transition, which Ashley had heard before.

"Amazing . . ." Ashley breathed.

"So were your routines at the National Championships! I watched it *live*, and the nursing home's getting the video."

Ashley grinned, but said nothing.

"So what are you going to do now?" Jenny asked.

"Um . . . don't know. Seems like I just . . . you know . . . retired from gymnastics."

"Have you put ads on all the gymnastics bulletin boards on the internet?"

"Um . . . no. I've never been very good with the net."

Jenny rolled her eyes and sighed.

*

During the following week, Ashley's mom helped her draft the ad. The eleven-year-old didn't sleep much on Friday night, going over and over the ad in her mind, wondering if she had said each thing in the best possible way.

When the sun finally rose Saturday morning, she could vaguely remember one dream in which she was sweeping floors in a huge gym, and another in which she was teaching beginning gymnasts. As she hopped out of bed, her mind was set on making those dreams come true.

        *

At the computer that any nursing home resident could use, but few ever did, Jenny typed in the ad, and she and Ashley both checked it over for mistakes.

Champion Seeks Elite Training

I'm Ashley Riddle, the current national gymnastics champion. I'm 11 years old. I lost my parents when I was 6, and the people who adopted me can't afford the cost of a residential training program in another city. I'm ready to begin elite training for next year's World Championships, but our gym doesn't have an elite program. I would like to do chores, lead warm-ups, teach beginners, and things like that to pay for my room and board at a gym that has an elite program. I get good grades and don't get in any kind of trouble. Thank you!

"How long will it take to get responses?" Ashley asked her wheelchair-bound friend.

"Someone could respond in five minutes, I suppose. In a week or two, most people will have seen it who're going to."

Every Saturday, Jenny showed Ashley the responses. They were all variations on *I'm sorry, but we get hundreds of requests for scholarships every year, only offer five, and those are filled for both this year and next year. We wish you luck in your search for elite training.*

The responses trailed off after the second week, as Jenny had predicted. By the third week, Ashley quit asking about new responses to her ad, and the two friends went back to talking about school, boys, and Jenny's music.

On the fourth Saturday after placing the ad, when Ashley opened the door to Jenny's little porch, the ten-year-old said nothing but was obviously about to explode with happiness as she handed Ashley a piece of paper.

Dear Ashley Riddle,

I know of a place that has a small gymnastics program that might fit your needs. It's not a typical gym, and you will have to decide for yourself if it's the kind of place you would like. When you call, ask for information for new members.

                        Best wishes,
                        Sister Claudia

        *   *   *

Chapter 20: Sub Rosa

The crew of the Manessa Kwi gathered at the eating place Kibi had chosen, on the second balcony of Blue Hall, at the requested time. Mati selected a table while Rini went up to the counter for a big tray of food. Ilika and Sata arrived a few minutes later, practicing their new language as they walked.

Kibi, the acting captain of a deep-space response ship of Nebador, looked around. "Anyone know where Boro is?"

"Riding a horse," Rini informed as he slid the tray onto the table.

Kibi raised her eyebrows.

"He's felt so uncomfortable in the pilot's seat," Mati explained, "that he's trying what I did, you know, learning to ride first. But there's no donkey on the star station, or anywhere else, that's strong enough to carry him . . ."

"Here he comes!" Sata noticed.

The massive stallion, pale orange with long hair that completely covered his feet, caused several mouths to open in wonder.

"Everyone," Boro announced proudly from atop the huge equine, "this is Malika-Terno, the only horse on the station who would let me ride. And I think it's really gonna help my piloting."

"Just don't forget," the huge horse began, "an hour of brushing my coat and massaging my sore muscles for every hour you ride."

Boro grinned with embarrassment as he dismounted, and all his friends chuckled.

"You're welcome to eat with us, Malika-Terno," Kibi said.

The horse looked askance at the food tray. "There's a place not far along the balcony with things I can digest. See you in an hour, Boro. We still need to work on your center of gravity during vector changes."

With a slight cringe, Boro nodded.

"Okay," Kibi began as the horse walked away, "while we eat, let's talk about the mission."

Sata swallowed a bite. "They brought in a native speaker, and Ilika and I are meeting with her several hours a day. That language is *weird*, patched together from three or four older languages, and from what we've heard, the people who live there are actually *proud* of how hard it is to learn, and refuse to do *anything* to make it easier. Then they wonder why all their children hate school."

Ilika smiled and nodded his agreement. "I think we'll be as ready as we can be in another Satamia day."

"How does that fit with your training, Boro?" the acting captain asked.

"Good. Mati's taught me everything she can, I just need to get the *feel* of it."

"That'll come slowly, over months and years," Ilika said. "For Mati, it was almost natural. *You'll* have to work at it, like I once did."

Kibi waited a moment to see if that conversation had run its course. "Mati?"

"As you know, it's been a real challenge for me to be constantly *listening* for what the pilot needs, instead of giving flight commands. Boro's teaching me to think ahead, you know, anticipate what he'll need. We're tinkering with something in the engineering ring almost every day."

Kibi nodded. "Rini?"

He sighed. "Bored, I guess. There's nothing I need to do for the mission, and every time I try to take a class, they say that's not what I should be doing right now, that I should wait until after we get back."

"Wanna help me stock the ship?" Kibi asked.

"Sure!"

❋

The four ship-days before the next Satamia evening party passed quickly — for everyone but Rini.

Sata declared she was starting to dream in the new language she was learning.

Kibi continued to study the lesson materials every ship captain was expected to know, and practice the mental exercises, with three others at her level, aimed at expanding her intuition into the realm of spirit.

Mati wondered how she was going to keep herself from reaching over and grabbing Boro's flight control during difficult maneuvers. In training simulations, as the ship jerked and lurched, she practiced breathing deeply and keeping her eyes on her engine control board.

Ilika studied the new language with Sata, and smiled with pride as his crew took steps, large and small, toward becoming citizens of Nebador.

❋

At the party, several new people were introduced by Kerloran, having just survived breath-taking adventures and heart-pounding dangers to escape their home planets. Rini and Mati looked at each other knowingly.

Three avians, scientists from a planet where science was forbidden, tried to express their deep wonder at the sights and sounds of a star station, but mostly just clucked with delight. Boro smiled, remembering his own initial feelings of wonder not so long before.

Two furry mammals, almost but not quite ursine, declared themselves Seekers of Spirit, and mumbled their amazement at a place where they could actually see and talk to non-material beings. Kibi, who had just come from a class led by a glowing blue light, held in a grin.

A reptilian artist stood alone, but her eyes sparkled as she noticed the many beautiful artworks that adorned the star station's main hall. Kerloran described the punishments for being an artist on her planet, and visible scars among the newcomer's scales bore witness.

＊

The next morning, on a balcony overlooking Violet Hall, over slices of fresh fruit and grilled seed cakes, each member of the crew declared that they were ready for the mission, but pointed out that they had no idea what it was.

Arantiloria appeared, settled into her purple-haired human form, and pulled up a chair. "The planet you are about to visit has more than its share of myths. One they rarely talk about, but which has great power over them, is that any mistakes they make, any damage they do to each other or their world, will be fixed, before it's too late, by someone else."

"That's pretty childish!" Mati declared.

Several of the others remembered Buna's tendency to blurt out her thoughts.

Arantiloria just nodded. "Some of them think it will be *gods* who save them, some think *aliens*, and many trust that their own *scientists* will invent something new in the nick of time. The effect is the same. Taking responsibility for themselves is just *not* a value among those people."

"So . . . what's the mission?" Boro asked.

Arantiloria smiled slightly. "Because of this tendency of theirs, they have great trouble with priorities. All of you, even though you are just beginning your advanced training, have a much better sense of what's important, and what's not, than even the highest leaders on that planet."

Boro opened his mouth at the pause in Arantiloria's talk, but closed it before any sound came out.

She pretended not to notice. "They *will*, I guarantee, try to suck you into every little problem they have, no matter how trivial, how personal, or how much they could have avoided it with a little forethought."

The crew members looked at each other, but since Boro hadn't had any luck, no one else dared ask what they were all still wondering.

After a long silence, the training specialist spoke again. "As for the mission, you will know it when you find it. It is the only thing on that planet, with enduring value for the universe, that would be lost without your help."

＊

After a stop at a supply dome on an uninhabited planet to leave some cases of food and canisters of fuel, the Manessa Kwi popped back into space and time not far from a planet that almost looked like Sonmatia Three from a distance.

"Very similar," Ilika said as he looked over a planetary summary at the steward's station. "Slightly more ocean area, but less volcanic activity. The humans are the only dominant race, although several other sapient species are lying low because the humans are technologically advanced, and very dangerous to everything and everybody at this point in their history."

"So . . ." Boro began after locking his controls and spinning around, "our planet was only . . . safe for other creatures . . . because we weren't very good at killing them yet?"

Rini and Sata laughed nervously.

Kibi grinned.

After a moment, Ilika nodded.

✳

Mati noticed that Boro was still closing his eyes during de-orbit with ion drive. "It's only scary the first time you watch," she said softly.

"I'm trying to work up the courage," he mumbled.

"Even though it's almost night, take us down below the hills," Kibi ordered, "before they see us with . . . what was it called, Ilika?"

"Radar. Radio detection and ranging."

With some hesitation, Boro guided the ship from four thousand meters to treetop level. "Real-time high-res topo, Rini."

"Channel four. No weather to worry about. It's a beautiful late-spring evening down there."

"Where are we going, Sata?" the commander asked.

"Chart on channel five, Ilika's drop-point is about twenty kilometers from here, one valley to the northeast."

Boro studied the chart as he crested a rise so close to the trees that Manessa could feel their leaves brush her hull.

"Everyone remember the important aspect of the drop-off?" Ilika asked the entire bridge.

"Slow, silent, and invisible for the last few kilometers," Boro repeated from memory, "and the same on the way out."

Ilika nodded. "These people would tear someone apart whom they thought was cooperating with . . . what was the term Arantiloria used? Oh, yes, *an alien invasion force.*"

Chuckles rolled around the bridge.

"Oh, no!" Mati gasped dramatically at the engineer's station without turning around. "We might . . . we might . . . put them to sleep!"

Boro howled with laughter.

"Hey!" Mati continued with sudden realization, looking at her console. "I've got those controls right here!"

Ilika laughed. "And you might need them before this mission's over."

As soon as the laughter faded, Boro cleared his throat. "Okay, we're getting close. Quiet on the bridge, please."

Everyone got serious.

"Hull matches the sky," Boro said to himself, "tallest trees are thirty meters . . . there's the river . . . a light in a house, I see it on the chart but it's not the right house . . . a dirt road . . ."

As soon as Boro passed another group of trees, a clearing came into view, and in its center, a circular area paved with flat stones and ringed with dim lights.

"Bingo," Sata said softly. "Matches the coordinates."

"You ready, Ilika?" Kibi asked.

As Boro lowered the ship, Ilika shouldered his bag, stepped onto the bridge to give Kibi a quick but serious kiss, then opened the hatch.

A tall man stood on the edge of the circular area holding a lantern.

As soon as Ilika descended the ramp, it vanished and the hatch closed. A moment later, the Manessa Kwi silently rose into the still night air and floated away among the treetops.

"This is all happening exactly as I saw it in my dreams," the tall man said in his native language.

＊

Mati noticed a smile creep onto Boro's face as he guided the ship through the darkness just above the treetops. After curving around a hill, many glowing lines on his topographic display suddenly blocked the ship's path and Boro pulled back sharply on his flight control. "Whoa! What're those?"

Everyone looked.

"Wires," Sata informed. "Manessa color-codes them bright cyan."

Boro swallowed. "Oh, yeah, blue-green. Um . . . thank you, Manessa."

"You are welcome, Boro. Thank you for piloting with ever-increasing skill."

Boro grinned sheepishly.

"And *those* wires are carrying electromagnetic *energy*," Rini added.

"We still want to avoid . . . radar," Kibi reminded them, now commanding from the steward's station.

Boro moved the ship this way and that. "I'll try to squeeze under. Minimum vertical profile, Manessa."

"Disc, two meters vertical," the ship replied.

Just as the little ship passed underneath the wires, several small beams of light shined onto the hull.

"Uh oh," Rini said. "We've been discovered." He sent a down-angle view to all stations.

Kibi looked at her display and saw four children with hand-held lights gazing up with open mouths. After a moment, they all started running toward a house in the distance.

She chuckled. "*They'll* have a story to tell!"

"I doubt anyone will believe them," Sata said. "*I* wouldn't."

"Clear of the wires and resuming treetop flight," Boro said. "Where are we going?"

"The only place on the planet," Sata began, "where people won't think we're ... an alien invasion force ... and I think we're close enough to communicate. They use radio waves here. Luckily, Manessa knows how." She turned and looked at Kibi.

"If you remember what to say, and how to say it, go ahead."

Sata nodded and made some selections on her console. She cleared her throat and spoke in her newest language. "Lost Forest Heliport, zulu one-three-seven, ten miles north, inbound for landing on Pad Three."

An anxious female voice replied in the same language. "Zulu one-three-seven, did you say ... um ... Pad *Three?*"

"I thought *I* was nervous," Sata mumbled in the language of Nebador. "Yes, Lost Forest Heliport, Pad Three."

"Um ... zulu one-three-seven ... I've never done this before ... there's instructions around here somewhere ... here they are ... okay, just send the code you should know on the frequency you should know, and the hanger door will open."

Sata touched a symbol.

"Wow, it's opening," the female voice said. "Um ... zulu one-three-seven, do you need landing pad lights?"

"Do we need lights?" Sata asked, looking at Boro, then Kibi, both of whom shook their heads.

"Lost Forest Heliport, no need for lights. We'll be inside in a minute."

"Wow ... okay, zulu one-three-seven, I'll ... um ... see you soon. We keep some extra equipment in there, but the middle of the floor is always free."

Sata closed the connection, and everyone was quiet as the ship covered the last few kilometers.

"Going to slow, silent, and invisible," Boro said, studying his chart. "The trees are taller here ... a road cuts through with lights along it ... a big open space with all shapes and sizes of metal carriages and wagons ... gardens with little lights on the paths ... buildings that almost look like parts of a star station ... and way in the back, I see two lighted landing pads."

"Those would be Pads One and Two," Sata said. "Pad Three should be completely dark."

Boro took a moment to bring the ship directly over the proper coordinates. "Yep, there's a circular landing pad right under us, and a big square building beside it."

"Down and in, pilot," Kibi said. "We don't want to be outside any longer than necessary."

With white knuckles, Boro lowered the ship until his display showed one meter of altitude. "Whew!" he said, changing hands and flexing his fingers. "This is intense!"

Mati chuckled in sympathy. "Remember, you can let Manessa handle the altitude now."

"Oh, yeah. Manessa, maintain one meter altitude. Mati, minimum maneuvering thrusters."

She touched her control board.

Boro slowly nudged the deep-space response ship into the hanger building, and sighed with relief when he was finally able to extend landing struts. "Whew! Finished with engines."

With a mission bracelet on her arm, Kibi opened the hatch. By the light from inside the ship, she saw a tall, blond woman standing nervously to one side of the dark hanger, between an engine hoist and a stack of boxes.

"I have *no* idea how you made that landing, at night, without lights, into a hanger under power," she began in her native language, "but welcome to Lyceum. I'm Sister Nancy."

✳ ✳ ✳

Chapter 21: A Shadow of Nebador

As Sata walked beside Boro along the carpeted corridor, she was aware that she, at not quite thirteen years of age, would be the primary representative for Nebador to these people. Ilika would not be arriving for several days, and even then, he would seem to be just another citizen of the planet.

Kibi was the acting captain of the Manessa Kwi, but they were no longer on the ship, and she didn't yet speak more than a few words of the local language.

Sata was the mission leader. She was absolutely sure that Arantiloria, and possibly Melorania herself, would be listening to every word she said. She could feel herself shaking inside, and hoped it didn't show.

Sister Nancy entered a small conference room, switched on the lights, and gestured for her guests to make themselves comfortable. "There's a small team trained to handle these rare visits, they're on their way, and will bring refreshments."

Sata translated as she tried to take a seat off to one side, but Boro poked her until she moved to the head of the table. She frowned at him for a second, and he smiled. At that moment, five more people entered the room.

An elderly woman moved slowly, helped along by a slightly younger man. Her eyes sparkled with experience and curiosity as she took the seat at the other end of the table.

The man, graying but still in his prime, received trays from those who came behind and spread them out on the big conference table. Rini and Mati leaned forward to look over the goodies.

The remaining three people, all not much older than Kibi, tried to find places to hide in the corners of the room, but the man motioned for them to take seats at the table.

Once the door was closed and everyone was settled, a long moment of silence passed.

Sata looked at Kibi, and Kibi looked back and said *You!* with her eyes.

After another moment, Sata took a slow breath. "Hello. My . . . my name is Sata. I am the . . . leader of this mission, and the . . . navigator of our ship."

"I am Sister Rebecca," the elderly woman began, her eyes moving from Sata to Kibi, her face showing slight confusion. Eventually her eyes settled on Sata. "You are welcome in this humble place, Sata and her companions. I must remind all Lyceum members present that *everything* about this visitation is strictly confidential . . . no, strictly *secret*. It is a great honor to have contact with people from . . . outside . . . and we will lose that honor if we do not handle it with complete discretion and wisdom."

She made searching eye contact with each of her people, then continued. "This is Brother Jacob, also highly trained in these matters. Sister Nancy and these three young ones are our pilots, and must be trained for these events in order to run the Lost Forest Heliport."

Sata nodded, and noticed that Kibi seemed to be following the emotional tone of the conversation, if not the words.

Sister Rebecca looked at Sata again. "How may Lyceum be of service to you?"

"We . . . do not know. We are here to help with . . . something very important, maybe save someone . . . or something. We are supposed to know it when we find it . . ."

*

Sister Rebecca placed a thin bracelet on each visitor's right wrist that would open any door or buy anything for sale. The crew of the Manessa Kwi followed Brother Jacob and Sister Nancy out of the conference room.

At first, Kibi had a worried look on her face, glancing back and forth from their simple and comfortable flight clothes, to the complicated suits and dresses the Lyceum people wore.

But as soon as the corridor brought them to the first large room, she relaxed, seeing a wide variety of clothing among the people waiting on couches, or standing in little groups talking.

"The heliport lobby isn't always so busy," Sister Nancy explained, "but a flight is about to depart for the international airport."

While Sata translated, Mati and Boro pressed their faces against a glass wall that looked outside. A couple of children were doing the same from the floor nearby. A large pale-green helicopter sat on the landing pad, its silver rotor gleaming in the bright lights. As they watched, two people with clipboards finished their inspections and waved to someone in the cockpit. A moment later, twin jet engines on top of the aircraft roared to life.

"Wow," Boro said. "Manessa's not *that* loud even with space thrusters going!"

Mati chuckled. "I wonder how it flies?"

"I think those silver blades turn and beat on the air."

"How would it . . . get into orbit?"

"I don't think it can."

Mati became aware that the children were looking at them. "What language is *that?*" the boy asked.

Mati and Boro just smiled.

✳

Ambling along behind their guides, the five newcomers made their way down a glass-lined corridor with lighted ornamental gardens on both sides. In one, water trickled from pond to pond as ferns dripped and orchids opened their colors to the late evening sky. In another, roses climbed wooden trellises around neatly-trimmed lawns with stepping stones and benches.

It's almost like, Rini began a thought, *they've had a glimpse of a star station.*

Maybe they have, Mati silently replied. *Maybe they visit us, just like we're visiting them.*

Entering a round room even larger than the heliport lobby, the guides waited for their visitors to gather. "This the is recreation center," Brother Jacob began, "with a gymnasium, ball courts, a pool, and a performance arena. Those doors lead to outdoor play fields."

But this isn't like Satamia Two and Ubalora Three, where we visit each other openly, Rini continued their silent conversation. *This is hush-hush. Arantiloria said that if anyone else on this planet found out, they'd burn this place to the ground.*

That's sad, Mati replied. *And I bet their religions pretend to worship the powers of the universe.*

✳

After walking along another glass-walled passageway, the group emerged into a huge indoor space under a high ceiling supported by soaring wooden beams. Archways led to other corridors, or directly outside, in six other directions. An elaborate metal sculpture, roughly spherical in shape, towered five or six meters high in the center of the room. Arrangements of couches and potted plants contained several small groups of people.

"The main lobby," Sister Nancy announced. "The green arch, you should notice, leads back to the recreation center and the heliport."

Sata made sure her shipmates memorized the color of their arch.

"The red arch goes to the gift shop and clinic," Brother Jacob added. "Gold leads to the cafeteria and dining room."

Boro turned in a slow circle. "No cyan arch," he mumbled to Sata.

"Maybe they can't see that color," she speculated. "Remember, we didn't know about it until Satamia. All the avians love it."

Kibi approached the center of the room and gazed up at the sculpture. When she tilted her head one way, the globe seemed to be made of intertwined tools and instruments, like a scientist would use. Leaning the other direction, candles, scrolls, and fancy goblets came into view, things more suited to churches.

Turning back to the group, she noticed Sata and Sister Nancy chatting in the local language, so she scanned the room.

One group clearly included a king, or some other high leader, judging by his clothes and manners. Kibi was pretty sure she could tell who his trusted advisors were, and which of the three women was his wife, or at least his favorite. The remaining men were probably guards.

She continued scanning. A group of five men in black suits, all pretending to have nothing to do with the king's group, were his *real* guards. Occasionally one of them would say a word or two into his shirt sleeve.

Her eyes kept moving, not wanting anyone to think she was staring.

Two women and a man conversed about something technical, not paying attention to anyone else in the room.

The next group Kibi spotted almost made her shiver. Four men in casual clothes were acting very nonchalant, but glancing up just often enough to reveal, to her deeply-intuitive mind, that they were keeping an eye on the king's group. The signs were too subtle, she judged, to be noticed by the king's guards.

She glanced at two other small groups, didn't sense any connections with anyone else, and walked toward Sata.

"The garden walkway lights stay on all night," Brother Jacob was saying.

Sata translated.

"I think we could all use some fresh air," Kibi said assertively.

Sata noticed the implied command in her acting captain's voice. The other three also heard Kibi's tone and gathered quickly.

As they walked with their guides toward the white archway that led to the outdoor plaza, Kibi glanced at Rini. From the way he moved his eyes, she knew that he, too, was aware of the many things going on in Lyceum's main lobby.

*

After describing the seven gardens, each based on a different continent or culture, the two Lyceum people said good-night and left the visitors alone to explore.

Lots of sevens, Rini shared with Mati. *It must be a sacred number to them.*

The helicopter had five blades, she pondered silently. *Maybe they like all the odd numbers.*

The pair wandered into one of the gardens, as close to tropical as could survive the temperate climate. They passed three men in suits, at different points on the wide path, all pacing and looking quite bored.

When they came to an open area, Mati knelt down to examine some stone sculptures that reminded her of something in the tropics of Sonmatia Three during their basic flight training. Rini noticed a faint animal track that led into the trees, and crept along it to see where it went.

He soon came upon a small clearing at the end of a path of stepping stones, where an old man sat on a bench with his eyes closed. Only one walkway light illuminated the space.

Rini immediately sensed the man was a religious leader of some kind, and judging by his robes, a respected one.

Even though Rini had approached as silently as anyone but a mouse could, the old man opened his eyes.

Rini bowed his apologies and started to back away, but the old leader motioned for the lad to sit beside him on the bench.

Rini smiled and came forward.

"It is not often that my protectors let someone get this close without being searched and background-checked," he said in a kindly tone.

Rini shook his head and shrugged.

The old man tried four other languages, but Rini responded the same way each time.

"Well, you *are* from somewhere far away!"

Suddenly, all three men in suits burst through the trees with guns drawn.

Rini's heart pounded, but he remained seated beside the important religious leader.

It took Mati about two seconds to understand the situation and stride down the faint track Rini had followed. *Put them to sleep?*

No, wait.

"Put those away!" the leader ordered. "Can't you tell an innocent lad from a dangerous terrorist?"

"But Your Grace, we're supposed to . . ."

"Yes, I know, you're supposed to keep me from meeting anyone who hasn't been processed to death. Our Lord Himself couldn't pass your background checks. Now put those away before his friend teaches you a lesson."

The three men did as they were told, but also began looking around with guilty expressions for the person they hadn't seen.

Mati waited until the men in suits left the clearing, then crept forward.

So you could put them to sleep, could you? the religious leader asked with his mind.

Rini turned and looked at him with wide eyes of surprise.

Mati nodded, her eyes also wide.

How interesting, he continued. *You, who speak no language of this world, would put them to sleep. They, who work for the spiritual leader of half the people of the planet, would riddle your bodies with bullets.*

Mati and Rini both shrugged, understanding the old man's thoughts, but not knowing how to respond.

*

Eventually the crew of the Manessa Kwi gathered back at the outdoor plaza and returned to Lyceum's main lobby. Only one small group was relaxing on the couches, talking quietly in a language Sata didn't know.

With midnight at hand, the five visitors found the cafeteria, selected some things that looked familiar, and showed their Lyceum bracelets to the cashier.

The recreation center was very quiet at that hour, with soft music playing, one attendant on duty, and a couple of men in shorts emerging from a ball court.

No one waited in the Lost Forest Heliport, and a sign on the desk announced, Sata figured out, that the next flight would be early the following morning.

Kibi's new bracelet opened the locked door to the hanger beside Pad Three, but it wasn't until they were safely inside the ship, with the hatch closed, that everyone started talking at once, eager to share what they had seen, heard, sensed, and experienced in this mysterious place called Lyceum.

✳ ✳ ✳

Chapter 22: Evaluation

The early summer days brought gentle sunshine, light rain, or a mixture of the two, as the crew of the Manessa Kwi got more and more comfortable with the location of their assignment. Somewhat to their surprise, knowledge of the golden ship in the hanger of Pad Three did not go beyond the six Lyceum members who had greeted them.

Sata taught the other crew members a hundred or so words to help them get around, and Kibi bought some clothes from the gift shop to help them fit in. Beyond that, their only task was to keep their eyes and ears open, looking for the only person or thing that was of great value to the universe, and which, in some way, needed their help.

※

As evening approached on a pleasant early summer day, Brother Randy, a slender man of about forty, hovered near the door to a conference room, greeting the potential new members with handshakes and gestures to the books and papers on one table, and the platter of cookies and bowl of fruit on another. After sharing a few words with a new arrival, he glanced over at the tall black-haired teenage girl who had come early. She was still browsing through the shelf of books about Lyceum, reading the jackets and peering at the tables of contents.

Just then a short, small girl, even younger, dashed in.

"Welcome!" he said.

"Hi," she said with a little hesitation. "I'm . . . Ashley."

"Come in, Ashley. Take one from each stack on that table, and help yourself to a snack if you'd like."

She smiled, already feeling comfortable with the Lyceum evaluation process.

Brother Randy had to turn his attention to a new arrival, so Ashley got herself the books, papers, and an apple. As she sat down in an empty seat near the back, she noticed a boy coming in. He looked about seventeen and fairly cute. She overheard him tell someone his name was Shawn. After a minute, she tore her eyes away and opened a book to see what was inside.

A few minutes later, Brother Randy closed the door and stood in front of the assembled group. "Good evening, everyone, and welcome to this place called *Lyceum*. My helper for this session is Sister Joan . . ."

The curly-haired blond girl of about sixteen, sitting near him, rose and acted a bit embarrassed. Shawn smiled at her, but she didn't seem to notice.

Ashley's hand went up.

"Yes?" Randy asked.

"Is Sister Claudia okay? She was my contact person, but I can't find her anywhere."

"As far as I know, she's in good health, but she's on another continent right now helping with a political crisis that's threatening to become a civil war. You've probably seen it in the news."

Ashley nodded. "Thanks."

"Well, well," Randy said, looking at his list. "I have a whopping nine people in my group, which I think is a record. Sometimes we have only two or three. And all but one of you are here on time."

At that moment, a girl of about nine years, with straight blond hair, slipped in the door and handed a note to Joan.

"Thanks, Sarah," the sixteen-year-old said. "Randy, I think we just found our missing person. "She was on an airplane that had engine trouble and had to land east of the mountains, and she can't get a bus until tomorrow."

"Hmm," Randy considered. "Sounds like something you can handle, Sister Joan."

The girl's eyes opened wide, but were sparkling. "She'd miss orientation tonight, and the service tomorrow. That's too much. Do you think it's worth a flight?"

"You decide, but there are several groups on campus tonight, and I bet you could fill the extra seats with people who'd love to see the mountains at sunset."

Joan looked at the note again. All of the candidates watched and listened with interest. "She *did* make a very good effort to get here. I think we should do it."

"You have as much authority to make that decision as I do," Randy said.

Liberty's mouth fell open.

"I'll go set it up," the teenage member said.

As soon as she left the room, Randy addressed the group. "The situation you just witnessed illustrates one of Lyceum's unique qualities. You will study and discuss that quality in more detail on . . . let me see . . . day after tomorrow. But since it happened before your eyes, I'm sure you're curious how a sixteen-year-old could make a decision that will cost us thousands, utilizing a vehicle worth millions. It's simple — she used her intelligence to realize that a good member is worth far more than one little helicopter flight, and if we don't stand beside that person now, in her moment of need, we'll probably lose her."

One lady in the room seemed offended by what had happened, and began to argue, saying something about standard operating procedures and accounting controls. Liberty wasn't really listening. She was remembering things she had discussed with Sister Nancy in letters, and now, seeing an example, it was all starting to make sense.

"Even though Lyceum is changing all the time," Brother Randy said in an attempt to conclude the argument, "you are going to have to make your decision based on Lyceum as it is today."

"Well, that's the most un-democratic attitude I've ever heard!" the lady said, and quickly walked out of the room.

Randy let the silence linger for a minute, then spoke slowly and solemnly. "The only valid reason for becoming a member of Lyceum is to be of service to humanity, in the many ways that Lyceum does that. If your purpose is to impose your will upon Lyceum, then you have come to the wrong place."

The situation was striking a very personal nerve for Shawn. He suddenly realized that his father, the famous Reverend Tommy Mitchell, imposed his will on everything and everyone. Shawn swallowed hard, and hoped that for him, at least, the will of God would come first.

Soon Sister Joan returned to the conference room and shared with Randy that the flight had been nearly filled by a group of executives, and would be lifting off in a few minutes. The stranded person had made arrangements to get to the nearest heliport. A murmur of compliments came from the evaluation group. Joan blushed.

Next, Randy went over the schedule for the week, then sat down.

Joan rose nervously. "Now it's time to share a little about yourselves," she said, "including your first name, your favorite hobby, and something you like about Lyceum."

After a minute of silence, a clean-cut man of about thirty stood.

"I'm Dario, and I love sailing, so if I become a member, you'll find me on the river on my days off. The thing I like about Lyceum ... if you're willing and able to contribute, you can, without getting caught up in petty political stuff."

Everyone clapped.

"Hi, everyone! I'm Ashley. My life is all about gymnastics, and I'm the national champion right now. I like Lyceum because it'll let you do things that sometimes you can't do in other places."

Again, applause.

"I am Ilika. I was the ... captain of a small ... ship, and so my hobby was keeping her in good ... condition. I like Lyceum's quality of ... honoring higher values, instead of just ... human values. The ... situation earlier was a good ... example."

The quiet young man, who spoke the language slowly and carefully, received a hearty applause, and a very friendly smile from Liberty.

"I'm Shawn. I like volunteering at rescue missions, and reading the Good

Book. I like Lyceum because its people are there when you need them. They had to shuttle me all the way across the country!"

He received applause and sounds of surprise.

Liberty frowned slightly at Shawn's hobbies. After another person had taken his turn, she gathered her courage.

"Hello, I'm Liberty. I've done lots of things, but most recently I've been caring for horses. I like Lyceum because it doesn't pay much attention to what you've done in the past, or who the other members of your family might be."

A hearty applause, and some noises of agreement, filled the room.

After the remaining candidates had introduced themselves, the session leader stood. "My name is Randy, and I dearly love singing in the choir. One thing I like about Lyceum is how it manages to surprise anyone who comes here with assumptions."

Everyone clapped.

"Now it's my turn, I guess," the sixteen-year-old said nervously, standing back up. "I'm Joan. Um ... oh yeah ... my favorite hobby is fantasy role-playing games. And I like Lyceum because it lets me use my brains. Sixteen-year-olds don't get to do that many other places. Whew!"

Everyone applauded and several chuckled at her nervousness.

Liberty was grinning from ear to ear.

*

After a break and a long question-and-answer session, the nine-year-old entered with a lady at her side. The session leaders greeted her.

"I'm Sapphire, and I was *so* touched when this sweet little girl stepped out of the helicopter, looked over all the people at the heliport, and walked right up to me.

Sarah rolled her eyes. "I've already told her most of the stuff she missed."

"Thank you, Sarah," Randy said.

The orientation session continued, and both leaders took turns going over the remaining topics, from meals to health care, lodging to recreation.

With the formal talks over, everyone mingled and chatted. Several borrowed a book from the book shelf. Liberty took three, and wandered out of the room, already reading.

Two teenage girls in leotards appeared at the door, and Ashley was quickly whisked away to the gymnasium.

Shawn entered into a deep conversation with Dario on some religious topic, and they left together, anxious to see the shrines and chapels, even if they couldn't get into the Lyceum Temple until the following day.

Brother Randy and Sister Joan made sure Sapphire was fully briefed on all the topics they had covered before she arrived.

Ilika lingered and entered into several short, light conversations, but kept his eyes and ears open for any hint about the reason he and his crew were there.

*   *   *

Chapter 23: Religion

Over breakfast, Sata and Kibi agreed on a plan. They would look for the object of their mission in teams of two or three. Kibi would improve her language skills as quickly as possible, then she or Sata would be with each team. Knowing there was at least one telepathic person nearby, possibly more, Mati and Rini would split up.

The entire crew would meet in the cafeteria mid-morning and mid-afternoon, when few other people were around, then back at the ship, where they could speak more freely, in the evening.

"How will we know if Arantiloria likes what we're doing?" Boro asked, glancing around.

Kibi smiled. "I think we can trust her to jump down our throats if she *doesn't* like something. As long as we don't see her, we're not screwing up *too* badly."

Rini laughed.

Sata and Mati smiled.

✳

Shawn remembered his first glimpse inside the Lyceum Temple for the rest of his life. As he stepped in, the vast interior opened out to his left and right, and the main walkway completely encircled the interior, connecting with three other entrances. The ceiling rose to dizzying heights, where he could see at least two balconies and many hanging banners. Rows and rows of seats, quickly filling with people, extended above and even behind him. Finally he noticed that more seats, already full of people, dropped down to a large circular floor below.

An usher led the evaluation group to a section of reserved seats.

The service was simply entitled *Fruits*, and the drama began with the humble work of the farmer harvesting the produce of the soil, giving it to his family and selling it to other people, who enjoyed its goodness in homes and restaurants. The choir sang country tunes, and a narrator read passages from folk literature.

Shawn soon realized that the theme had changed, as he watched scientists, researchers, and diplomats pulling new ideas and new devices from their flasks, books, and computers. Dancers looked on with dramatic curiosity.

Slowly, the story moved to yet another level, as the farmer, the scientist, and the diplomat, joined by ministers and monks from several different faiths, knelt at little shrines that the dancers brought out, some containing an elaborate statue and altar, others as simple as a small piece of rug. They prayed or chanted fervently, and an air of excitement filled the Temple.

Suddenly the lighting changed, and the faces and clothing of the actors became radiant. The choir began a lively, happy tune, and an abstract holographic image formed in the air and began to move upward, an image in which each viewer saw something a little different.

The dancers returned, bringing baskets of fruit and tasty vegetables up the aisles to all the rows of people — plums, cherries, and strawberries, sweet peppers, little carrots, and mild radishes. The evaluation group members, along with many other first-time visitors to Lyceum, were surprised by the bounty. They were used to religious services in which baskets were passed for a different purpose.

When the service ended, many people left for a late breakfast, but some lingered, pondering what they had seen, listening to the choir, watching the dancers, or talking softly among themselves.

Fruits of the soil, fruits of the mind, fruits of the spirit, Shawn thought. *Sorry, Dad, but the Devil would have a hard time busting into this place.*

✳

At lunch in the cafeteria, the youngest three from the evaluation group took a table that would hold four. Liberty glanced at the empty seat, then stood up and looked around. Her eyes quickly found the young man from a foreign country who was just emerging from the cafeteria line. She strode in his direction.

"You're young and cool. Join us?"

Ilika nodded and followed the tall, black-haired girl.

"Has *anyone* ever seen anything *so* inspiring?" Shawn asked with excitement.

Between bites, Ashley shared that her church did things like that all the time.

Shawn lost some of his excitement.

Liberty admitted she'd never really been in a church before.

Shawn's face fell a little further.

Ilika's eyes darted from person to person, quickly taking in each one's temperament and cultural background as quickly as he could. "You must be used to . . . churches that don't do . . . dramatic plays, Shawn."

The younger lad shrugged. "Yeah. My church . . . I mean my dad's church . . . was pretty . . . um . . . boring."

With prompting by both Liberty and Ilika, the conversation turned to other subjects, but Shawn rolled over and over in his mind the sights, sounds, and words of the religious service he had just witnessed as he nibbled on his roast chicken, cheese, and tomato sandwich.

✳

"How many of you have a concept of god?" a Lyceum member, Sister Maria, asked as the evaluation group began their afternoon session.

Shawn, Ashley, Ilika, and Dario raised their hands.

"How many of you are convinced of the *correctness* of your concept of god?"

Only Shawn's hand remained in the air, but it quickly fell when he noticed he was alone.

"One of the fundamental purposes of Lyceum is to run an all-faith religious services center. Notice that I did not say *run a religion*. The two are very different. The members of Lyceum are here to create, maintain, and operate this place, a place where any religion can come. There is no *Lyceum Religion*. There never will be."

Shawn released his breath after holding it a little too long.

"One of our deepest fears is of people with different beliefs and assumptions about life. Being a different religion, even a different sect, often means very different beliefs. So in our civilization, we keep our religions separate, and when we must come together in the workplace or the grocery store, we avoid religious topics."

Ashley listened closely, occasionally nodding.

"The visitors to Lyceum can easily avoid religions and cultures with which they are not comfortable, and our public worship services, like the one you saw this morning, are designed to be very general and all-inclusive."

Sister Maria looked into the faces of the candidates before going on. "Members do not have that luxury. Among us, just about every possible religion is represented, and we must sit at table, work, and play together."

She looked around the room at the discomfort she saw in some of the faces. "If you are not convinced of the essential *validity* of every single person's religious experience, *for them* . . . then you would have a hard time being a member of Lyceum."

Shawn struggled for several minutes to swallow the lump in his dry throat.

Ilika noticed Ashley's easy acceptance and Shawn's discomfort. But he also noticed that Liberty appeared to be thinking deeply about something she had never thought about before. And he noticed that she was, quite often, looking at him.

✳

That evening was free time for the evaluation group, so Ashley spent an hour in the gym, then went to find Liberty in the swimming pool.

"Hi," she said as the tall girl finished a lap. "Want to spend some time?"

"Sure! You must have been doing gymnastics . . ."

Ashley glanced down at her old practice leotard. "Yeah. Just enough to loosen up."

"Teach me some if we become members?"

"Sure. But you have to teach me how to swim!"

"Deal!"

After Liberty toweled dry at her locker, the two girls wandered out into the warm evening air and the orange glow of a sunset not long past.

"So ..." Liberty began as they strolled along winding paths in a flower garden, "... quiz me. What should I have gotten from today?"

"Okay ... what do you do if someone's a different religion than you? (A) convert them, (B) call the cops, or (C) kill them."

Liberty burst out laughing. "You and me aren't the ones who'll have trouble with that. Did you see Shawn sweating?"

"Yeah! His church must be one of those that thinks it knows everything. But I have a hunch he's about to let go of that."

Liberty looked thoughtful as they came to a sign that said *Cemetery*, and without hesitation, walked on in. "Next question?"

"You like that foreign guy, don't you?"

"I think so. He's sweet ... and mysterious. About twenty-four, I think. So, what *is* the deal with religions, anyway? Why do people go to church?"

Ashley thought about the question as they wandered along the lighted walkways among the headstones. "You know how everyone has things they can't figure out by themselves?"

"Yeah ..."

"When I go to church, all those big, confusing questions just seem to go away. I'm part of something bigger, and there's a purpose to it all, even though I don't understand it yet. See what I mean?"

Liberty thought about it as they gazed up at a large, fancy grave marker. "You mean ... there might be some kind of good reason my mom left my dad when I was three?"

"Yeah. But ... your mom may not even know it."

Liberty was silent for another minute. "Okay. I can buy that. But what does religion have to do with it?"

Ashley stopped dead in her tracks. "That's what religion is! Religion is people trying to figure out all those things they can't figure out any other way!"

Liberty pondered the idea in silence.

"There!" Ashley said, pointing at a gravestone near a walkway light.

Liberty looked at it. "Eight years old."

"Why did she die?" Ashley asked.

Liberty sat down on the edge of the path in front of the grave. "I don't know. Car accident maybe?"

Ashley sat down beside her, then looked up at the star-studded sky. "I have a ten-year-old friend who's dying of cancer and is writing a symphony. She says the stars teach her to play."

Liberty took a slow breath. "I'm ... sorry."

"No need," Ashley said, looking back down at the headstone. "She's the happiest person I know."

Liberty was silent for a long time, but eventually her face lit up with an idea. "How's this sound? Lyceum does both science and religion, right? Both are looking for the truth, but science is looking for the part we *can* see ... or, you know, measure somehow ... and religion is looking for the part we *can't* see."

Ashley looked at Liberty and smiled.

Eventually the two girls said good-bye to the eight-year-old and wandered back to the recreation center. They could have talked for hours more, but they also knew that the next meeting of the evaluation group was at three o'clock the following morning.

*

Ilika and Kibi met that evening, far from the gardens and buildings. Hoods up against the cool air, they found a little grove of trees and settled onto a fallen log. Once bracelet lights were off, no one but the wild creatures could see them.

"Missed you!" Ilika assured before pulling her close and kissing her deeply.

"Mmmm ..." Kibi breathed when they finally parted. "That was almost worth the wait. Almost."

Ilika chuckled. "How are the others?"

"Sata's growing into her new role, and I'm letting her, even though I'm getting pretty good at the language. The rest have learned a couple of hundred words, enough to get by. Boro likes the pool and the physics labs. Mati and Rini discovered another person they can talk to, you know, mentally."

"That'll be good for them, as there are others on the star station, but they haven't noticed yet. There are seven other people in my evaluation group, and the three younger than me have let me into their social group. All three are strong and deep — they wouldn't have gotten this far in the process otherwise. One has a father who, in the lad's opinion, would like to rule the world ..."

Kibi snickered.

"Another has a father who's something important, but she hasn't told us much yet. I can tell she's worried about him."

"Any sign of the ... you know ... the mission?"

"No, not yet, You?"

"I'm ... not really sure how to look for it."

"You can trust the universe to lead you to it. This is a Nebador mission, and we will always have all the help we need. Follow the clues, no matter how subtle, or even how silly, they might seem."

Kibi nodded and snuggled close to Ilika.

Two squirrels, an owl, and a deer all took good looks at the pair of dark silhouettes seated on the old log. None of them sensed any danger.

* * *

Chapter 24: Work

Sister Rachael walked through the Lyceum Lodge, at a few minutes before three o'clock in the morning, and knocked on each door where a candidate was staying. At all but one door, she heard a groggy voice saying they were almost ready.

Ashley quickly dressed and washed her face, stepped into the corridor, and found Shawn emerging from his room. They slapped hands, then both yawned at once. A minute later, Liberty and Ilika approached, each from a different direction.

Liberty looked at Ilika with admiring eyes. "*You* look wide awake."

"I'm used to it. On a ship, you can be called to the . . . bridge at any time of the day or night."

Ashley smiled, noticing how Liberty's gaze lingered on the mysterious young man.

As the group began to follow Sister Rachael, Shawn kept looking back toward the lodge. "Will the guy who didn't wake up be kicked out?"

Sister Rachael squinted. "Of the evaluation group? Naa. Only extremely bad behavior would cause that." The middle-aged lady poked into her little tin of tobacco as they walked.

"But . . . he won't be accepted, will he?"

Rachael considered her answer as they crossed the main lobby. "Service doesn't always happen at the convenience of the servant. If a person is sick or injured at one o'clock in the morning, would the healer go? If an eclipse was happening during the lunch hour, would the astronomer come out to watch?"

Shawn twisted his face in thought. "I see what you mean. It just doesn't seem fair that sleeping in once would ruin someone's chances."

"I sleep in sometimes too. But not when people are counting on me. Lyceum's not for everyone."

A hint of dawn light already colored the sky as they crossed the empty plaza and entered one of the gardens. Shawn kept looking back, but finally had to give up his concern, lest he too be left behind.

✳

They followed the Lyceum member into an open area that contained a number of grotesque stone statues. It was Ashley's first glimpse of this garden, and she felt quite small among the ten-foot-high stone faces.

Sister Rachael sat on a large stone block and began to roll a cigarette. "Learn what you can in this place," was her response when anyone asked why they were here. After hearing it twice, Shawn didn't bother to ask.

The more Ashley saw of the stone carvings of strange gods and serpents, and murals of trade and warfare between primitive peoples, the more uneasy she became.

"Sister Rachael?" she asked, stepping up to the Lyceum member.

The older lady exhaled the smoke she was enjoying. "Yes?"

"Didn't these people practice human sacrifice? Why would Lyceum create gardens and shrines to remember such evil?"

Rachael contemplated the glowing end of her cigarette for a moment. "Very little is known about these people. Even the question of human sacrifice is not well established, but let's assume it for the sake of discussion."

Three others gathered to listen.

"It's a fact that every religion has, at times and places, engaged in practices that today we would call *evil*. Sacrifice, war, torture, genocide, corruption . . . you name it." She glanced at Ashley.

The young gymnast was gazing off across the open area. "I guess I see what you mean. If we left out all religions with skeletons in the closet, we wouldn't have any!"

"Exactly, but not entirely. The skeletons are part of our heritage, part of who we are. We cannot successfully move into the future without repeating our mistakes — our *evils*, if you will — unless we know where we've been, who we've been, and what mistakes we've made."

Ashley thanked Sister Rachael, and took a deep breath before turning back to the grotesque stone faces.

Ilika, who had been discretely watching and listening, smiled slightly.

✳

The sun rose shortly after five o'clock, and the group arrived at a picnic area at the same time as a food cart bearing a simple but hearty breakfast. Sister Rachael said nothing when the sleepy man joined the group.

So many people entered into discussions with the lady who smoked that it was almost seven o'clock when she finally began to explain their next activity.

"It's not easy, but we manage to let an odd corner of the campus get weedy for the use of each evaluation group. We even assign our young members to scatter some trash so it will look like an empty lot in whatever city you'd like to name."

Several people chuckled.

As soon as they saw the space in question, the man who had slept in, and a woman, began to argue with Sister Rachael about this use of their time. She assured them that no one was forcing them to do anything.

Instead of listening to the argument, Ilika and Ashley set to work surveying the area of berry vines, weeds, and trash, and looking over the available tools and materials. Shawn and Liberty noticed and quickly joined.

"I think it should just be a berry-picking garden," Ashley asserted. "Look at all this fruit that's gonna ripen in a few weeks!"

"Yeah," Shawn agreed, "we could trim all the long vines — they don't have berries on them anyway."

"We've got wood chips for the ground," Liberty began, "and we can make benches out of these boards!"

"Good ideas," Ilika said as he handed out work gloves.

Sapphire and Dario joined them and settled into the task. They were soon chatting about their favorite parts of the Lyceum campus as they worked. As noon approached, they stood back to admire the finished product.

"This is going to be the youngest group of new members we've ever had!" Sister Rachael predicted.

*

That afternoon, old Sister Rebecca passed out the first of six test booklets.

Liberty flew through the raw intelligence test, but could see that Ashley was sweating. The values clarification test was fun for Shawn, but Liberty was nearly in tears. The psychological profile had all three on edge, but Ashley thoroughly enjoyed the personality profile. The educational development test was familiar to all of them, but the vocational and career survey left the three young people feeling very inexperienced.

Ilika estimated that the questions he didn't answer because of his limited vocabulary would make up for the fact that his education and training had been vastly superior.

Shortly after five o'clock, the entire group dragged themselves to the cafeteria, their brains fried by the effort they had put into all the tests.

*

You guys aren't from around here, are you? nine-year-old Sarah asked with her mind as she, Rini, and Sata emerged from the petting zoo barn.

Rini froze and looked at Sarah with surprise, almost fear in his eyes. *Um . . . that's right*, he finally replied. *How could you tell?*

Sarah rolled her eyes. *Um . . . let's see . . . most of you don't speak the language very well . . . none of you know our customs . . . and I keep getting glimpses of donkeys fighting off wolves, lizards wearing jewelry, spiders in space suits, and other weird animal stuff.*

Rini turned to Sata and spoke in their native language. "She can read my thoughts, and is gonna figure us out pretty soon."

Sarah smiled, then spoke aloud. "And because of your leaky thoughts, it doesn't matter what language you use. Sister Rachael could teach you how to shield."

Sata frowned under the weight of such an important decision. After a minute gazing at llamas in a pasture, she spoke in the local language. "I need to talk to my captain and Sister Rebecca."

Sarah smiled and led them back toward the buildings.

* * *

Chapter 25: Science

After a leisurely breakfast the next morning, Sister Sheena, a large lady of about fifty, led them toward the research center.

"I understand today is Recovery Day," she said to the group as they walked along.

"Yesterday was very trying," Dario said. "Up at three, garden clean-up project, and all those tests!"

"Yes," Sheena agreed. "We put the tough stuff early in the week so the group would have less ... how do I say this? ... excess baggage when the more interesting stuff rolled around. You're down to six, I see."

"You mean it's easier from here?" Sapphire asked with relief.

"I think most people would agree with that. But there's still another project coming up, and role plays can be tough. Also, I don't know anyone who likes self-evaluations and final interviews, but they're necessary."

They arrived at the planetarium theater and entered the circular space with its dark blue carpeting and reclining seats. As they leaned back, each person had a clear view of the entire display dome over their heads, currently aglow with a pleasing mixture of pastel colors.

"As you can see," Sister Sheena said, closing the entry doors, "this is a private showing. The place will be buzzing with college kids at ten o'clock, so we have to be out by then. Preliminary questions?"

"Are you a scientist?" Ashley asked.

"Yes. My degree is in physics, but you can just as easily find me in the astronomy lab. My current research is aimed at looking for fractal patterns in the distribution of galaxies. I call it, informally, *God's Wallpaper.*"

Everyone chuckled.

"Do all members have access to the laboratories?" Shawn asked.

"Yes. Whenever I have free time, you'll usually find me in one of the labs, as opposed to a tavern or a shopping mall."

Several laughed deeply.

"Okay, let's view the program I've picked out for you. It's fairly light and simple, but will show you what the theater can do. A Nova 200 coordinates the data feeds to eight frontal, four rear, and three holographic projectors, as well as a multi-channel sound system and environmental controls that can do everything from simulate a mild earthquake to blow a warm, floral scented tropical breeze in your faces.

"Also, you will glimpse many concepts from the realms of physics, astronomy, chemistry, even biology. Some of my fractal work in physics is in there.

"Finally, and most importantly, it will give you a sense of Lyceum's mission of integrating the essential truth-seeking institutions of our world — in other words, science that leaves room for God ... or is it religion that leaves room for logic?"

With those words, the lights dimmed and the evaluation group found themselves witnessing scenes that few of them had ever imagined, beginning with the sub-atomic energy particles assembling themselves into the atoms of matter, and those becoming the molecules of the physical and biological world. All these things even Ashley knew from school, in an abstract sense, but here they were happening in mid-air, before her eyes, so close she could reach out and touch them. Of the three youth, only Liberty had seen a presentation of similar quality.

But unlike their school science lessons, the program produced at Lyceum showed several possible explanations for those parts of the process that were poorly understood, including the gods and angels themselves planning and initiating the molecular patterns.

Next, they witnessed the formation of the stars and galaxies, and saw the beautiful patterns that just might be the signatures of their creators. Watching closely, they found the same signatures in flowers and seashells, pine cones and crystals, microbes and atoms.

Several people asked questions about the show, some technical and some philosophical. Shawn was listening with part of his mind, but his heart was still marveling at the sheer beauty of God's creation, and feeling a twinge of anger that he had been guided away from it all his life.

At the group's request, Sister Sheena ran another program that was pure entertainment, with all manner of fantasy creatures frolicking and dancing to music. Ashley found herself almost standing up when a dancing, grinning wood sprite reached out a hand in her direction.

*

As ten o'clock approached, they vacated the planetarium theater just as the college students came striding down the corridor. Sister Sheena steered the evaluation group into a nearby classroom. Shawn wandered around, looking at charts on the walls, supplies for simple experiments, and interesting models. Then he remembered, with resentment, the letter from his father to his school that had exempted him from his high school science classes . . . on religious grounds.

"Scientific research at Lyceum happens on many different levels," Sister Sheena began after everyone had settled into chairs, "and in many fields. As we discussed earlier, members have just about unlimited access. Other individuals who just want to try out an idea, do a little experiment, tinker a bit, are always welcome, as long as the facilities have not been reserved for more formal activities. Schools make constant use of the facilities and resources for educational purposes. We had pre-schoolers in the chemistry lab yesterday, and I'm working with graduate students tomorrow."

Ashley smiled at the thought of toddlers with test tubes.

Shawn's concern continued to form in his mind. He wanted . . . no, he *needed* to know God's universe as it had been handed to humanity, and to no longer avoid it just because it was not, in itself, spiritual.

"And more and more," Sister Sheena was saying, "we're finding that prominent scientists choose to come to Lyceum so they can be near places of inspiration — our many lounges, shrines, chapels, gardens, nature trails . . . some even go over to the petting zoo and talk to the animals when they need a break."

All six candidates chuckled.

A picture was starting to form for Shawn, an image of himself working in the labs, assisting the scientists in their research, and maybe even doing experiments and demonstrations for school children. A smile began to brighten his face.

*

Five Nebador people and three Lyceum members sat in the conference room near Lost Forest Heliport Pad Three. Sister Rebecca wore a very serious frown.

"I know I can trust Rachael with this matter," she began. "I'm wondering if *you*, young lady, have the wisdom to handle a situation that could get many people *killed*, and possibly destroy Lyceum *completely*, if it got out . . . to anyone . . . ever."

Nine-year-old Sarah swallowed. She was pretty sure she had guessed half, maybe three-quarters of the secret Sister Rebecca was talking about. Since she was a member of a respected international service organization that hosted world leaders and world-class events all the time, she usually thought of herself as pretty grown up. Now, hearing the consequences if she, or anyone else, let the secret slip out, she felt about nine years old again.

She looked into Rebecca's eyes, then Rachael's. "I . . . um . . . want to be grown up enough. I really . . . like these people . . . and want to help . . . however I can. I know they're looking for something, but don't know what . . . or who. I could . . . stay near Rachael . . . for as long as you want . . . so she'd know if I . . . screwed up. But I won't screw up. I promise."

After a long silence, Rachael spoke. "I believe she can do it. The bond she is forming with our visitors will be her motivation. And if she ever violates this trust . . ." Rachael fell silent and looked at Sarah.

Sarah's eyes grew wide and she began to tremble. No one else ever knew what thoughts passed between them in those moments, but eventually Sarah relaxed, blinked some tears out of her eyes, and smiled.

Rachael smiled back. "All is well."

"So, I guess it's up to you, Sata," Sister Rebecca said.

Sata looked at Kibi and spoke in the language of Nebador. "I'm tempted to trust them. The risk is mostly theirs."

Kibi nodded. "We're not having much luck with the mission, and neither is . . . anyone else. This might be just the help we need."

"I don't know if it'll help us find what we're looking for," Boro began, "but I agree it's their risk, as long as we always wear mission bracelets."

Sata looked at Rini.

"Arantiloria gave us a real puzzle, something very mysterious that we're not going to figure out if we turn down *any* help, or avoid following *any* clue."

Mati nodded. "Remember, Sata, you have the final say."

Sata frowned at her, but Mati just smiled back. Then Sata took some slow breaths to give time for Arantiloria, Melorania, or anyone else to speak who knew more about these things than a twelve-year-old innkeeper's daughter.

Finally, she took a deep breath and spoke in the local language. "We noticed in your shrines and chapels that you have many different names for the people who run the universe. You call them gods, angels, and other things I don't remember. You think they look like you, maybe with bird wings or insect wings added. But they don't. They can look like anything they want. We know because we talk with them almost every day, sit in classes they teach, and do our best to carry out their missions.

"Sarah has already figured out that we're looking for something. What she, and all of you, have to understand is that we're looking for the most *important* thing on your planet right now. It's so important that the entire *universe* is waiting for us to find it . . ."

✳   ✳   ✳

Chapter 26: Crystals

"Good morning!" Brother Howard said as the evaluation group gathered the next day.

Liberty figured the man was about forty-five, and he looked extremely strong, but very gentle. He always seemed to be smiling slightly, even when he was talking — not the kind of smile that made others think he was laughing at them, just a smile of contentment. Liberty immediately liked the man.

"Six of you? Nice. Last time, we had two at this point, and we accepted one. I welcome you to phase two of your evaluation experience."

Sapphire's hand went up. "What kind of work do you do here?"

"Thank you for asking. It is a common Lyceum failing to forget to tell others about ourselves because of all our privacy ethics. I'm a stone cutter, a concrete sculptor, a zookeeper, and a healer of misplaced bones and muscles — in other words, a chiropractor."

"Thanks."

Liberty began to notice that Brother Howard never quite looked directly at the person he was talking to.

"This morning, we'll be joining the residence hall for the members' morning reflection time. This particular service will be led by a man who practices a minority religion. It's easy to lead something when all the participants believe exactly as you do. It's a much greater task to lead when diversity exists. Pay close attention to the way Brother Tim phrases things so that those present feel invited to make whatever use of the experience they wish, as opposed to feeling that they *must* believe or agree with something that they have not, on their own, chosen. And before we go in, I would like you to know that Brother Tim holds the highest diplomatic credentials. His skills as a mediator and negotiator are in demand all over the world, so he is away from the campus much of the time. I suggest you learn from him all you can this morning."

As the group headed for the door, Liberty continued to watch Brother Howard with interest. She saw him judge the distance to a certain wall based on the location of a piece of furniture, and pause to let some people pass based on the sounds they made. She realized the man was completely blind.

They found seats in the common area of the residence hall, and Bother Tim soon arrived carrying a small wooden box.

Shawn frowned and squirmed with discomfort.

Brother Tim stepped to the center of the assembled group, sat on the floor, and brought a beautiful cluster of quartz crystals out of his box. As he held it up, it caught the light and sparkled. He sat silently for a while, and all the Lyceum members became quiet and thoughtful. Most members of the evaluation group attempted to do the same.

"This magnificent work of nature lay hidden in a mountain for millions of years, covered by layers and layers of less beautiful material." He placed the cluster of shining crystals on the floor. "Likewise, in each of us there are beautiful gifts and powerful skills that lie hidden. The crystal grows slowly, deep inside the planet, adding to its substance molecule by molecule. Our gifts and skills slowly grow inside us, experience by experience, decision by decision."

Liberty found herself wondering what gifts and skills were hidden inside herself.

Brother Tim let several moments pass before he went on. "Our senses of sight, hearing, smell, taste, and touch allow us to know what is happening on the surface. This is important. Without the surface of the mountain, the crystal could not have grown deep inside. But the outer layers are temporary — they are constantly being weathered away. There comes a day when the toddler leaves his rattle behind, when the child quits playing with her dolls, when the student shelves his books, when the retiree puts away her tools, and when the dying man leaves his body behind."

Liberty closed her eyes, looking inside for the sparkling crystals that she hoped were there. She saw herself brushing a horse, and knew it was a memory from the recent past. Then she saw herself riding, as swiftly as the wind, without even a saddle. The thought scared her a little, as she had almost no skill at horseback riding. Finally, the horse leapt into the air and became a sleek helicopter, and she knew she was at the controls. With her eyes still closed, a smile appeared on her face.

"I leave you with these thoughts," Brother Tim was saying. "All the layers of your being are yours to do with as you will. The outer layers of the mountain contain much of value — soils, chemicals, ores. If unearthed too quickly, the crystals will not have grown. If left buried forever, their beauty can never shine." He held the sparkling cluster aloft again, then placed it carefully back in its box.

*

"What was *your* problem?" Liberty asked Shawn on the way back to the conference room.

"Oh ... just something I'm struggling to get over. My parents and my church taught me to dislike anyone who isn't ... you know ... clean-shaven. On the other hand, I'm supposed to automatically respect and trust a man wearing a suit and tie."

"Didn't you say," Ashley inquired, "that all the men who chased you around your home town were wearing suits and ties?"

Shawn smiled back and nodded.

After the group returned to the conference room, Brother Howard spoke. "I understand that you had an interesting example of Lyceum decision making during your very first session. Is the person who was transported by helicopter still with us?"

"Yes I am!" Sapphire said proudly.

"Good. When that situation arose, the rest of you witnessed a member of Lyceum make a decision that was small compared to the diplomatic responsibilities of someone like Brother Tim. But to at least one person, who might be a member of Lyceum soon, it was a very important decision. How do you feel now about the decision that Sister Joan made that evening?"

"I am grateful. I did not understand how it was possible at the time, and I was completely amazed when I learned her age. I have since been told that even the nine-year-old who met me could have initiated that flight. But I have also discovered that Sister Sarah is no ordinary nine-year-old."

"Yes, they are both very valuable members. But the fact that they are young is not of supreme importance here. The thing I want you all to focus on is that every member of Lyceum is empowered to make just about any decision."

"How is that possible?" Dario asked. "Isn't that decentralized management to the point of anarchy?"

"It is possible because of what you are doing right now," Brother Howard said. "The essential purpose of the evaluation process, from Lyceum's point of view, is to discover which of you are willing and able to use your intelligence, your wisdom, your energy, and your love, for service to others. Completely decentralized management *does* lead to anarchy when practiced by the average human being at this point in history. You six are far from average."

He paused to let his statements soak in.

"But let that fact go to your heads for one minute, let it become an ego trip and you are *out of here* on a fast track, whether you've been a member for an hour, a year, or a decade."

The group sat in stunned silence.

This teddy bear has teeth, Liberty thought to herself.

The room remained very quiet for a long time as the group pondered Brother Howard's words.

As Ashley, Shawn, Liberty, and Ilika walked together toward the conference center lobby, where the evaluation group was scheduled to engage in role plays, Ashley noticed that Liberty kept lagging behind. Since Ashley usually had to almost trot to keep up with the tall, long-legged girl, she knew something was wrong. When Liberty finally stopped, pretended to look at a painting on the wall, and rubbed her stomach, Ashley went to stand beside her new friend.

"What is it?" Ashley asked, thinking maybe Liberty had eaten something that didn't agree with her.

When Liberty didn't speak for several moments, Ashley looked at her. It was then that the gymnast realized her friend didn't have an upset stomach . . . she was scared to death of something.

"What *is* it, Liberty? You look like you've seen a ghost!"

In a thin voice, Liberty gasped out, "I'm gonna screw up the role plays, I just know it! I'm gonna slip and say something mean, something from the city streets. I can see it coming!"

Ashley put her arm around the shaking girl. "Does your stomach hurt?"

"Yeah. It's tied in knots, just like when I first arrived and my dad was deciding if I could stay."

"*I* know! Me, Shawn, or Ilika can volunteer to be your partner every time you're up for a role play!"

"Would you really? Oh, never mind. It probably wouldn't help . . ."

"Well, I'm certainly not going to leave you out here feeling ashamed of something that's made you strong! Every time you tell me about the streets, I feel like I've been a protected little marshmallow who wouldn't survive alone in a big city for ten minutes. If you don't go in, I won't either!"

"Me neither," Shawn and Ilika both said from behind the two girls.

Liberty turned around and stared at the gentle religious boy and the mysterious green-eyed man. "You guys are stupid!" she said, and immediately starting crying.

Ilika nudged Shawn, who clumsily put his arms around the shaking, sobbing girl. She quickly latched onto him with all her strength.

After several minutes, she relaxed and Shawn released her.

"Thank you," Liberty said, trying to dry her eyes with her sleeve. "I guess . . . we'd better get going or we'll be late."

As they strode together toward the conference center, Ashley shared her idea with Shawn and Ilika, and they agreed to do their best. They arrived only one minute late, and the session hadn't started.

Brother Randy and Sister Joan were again leading. Just as the first role plays got started, Ashley whispered into Liberty's ear, "Remember, whatever happens, be kind!"

The first two times Liberty had to engage in a role play, Ashley and Shawn were able to volunteer.

The third time, Sister Joan was pretending to have a complaint about the food, and unexpectedly got right into Liberty's face, ranting and raving. Ashley held her breath and said a prayer. She could tell Liberty was nervous, but hoped the practice with her and Shawn had helped.

"Um, I'll tell the cook. Can I get you anything else?"

"No, I don't want anything else! I just want to get out of this terrible place as fast as I can!"

Shawn closed his eyes, easily imaging the words coming from a certain member of his family.

"Well, in that case, I think you're a . . . entitled to a refund!"

Ashley breathed, and as soon as Liberty sat back down, squeezed her friend's hand tightly.

Six different people wandered into the lobby to create situations that seemed real. Shawn helped an old man get to the restroom, and Liberty surprised everyone by knowing sign language when a deaf lady asked for directions. Ashley had the challenge of asking a very handsome fourteen-year-old boy to wait until he got to the recreation center before bouncing his basketball. Ilika helped a lady who was trying to carry way too many boxes.

It was nearly dinner time when the role plays ended, and Liberty had kept her cool. All four friends slapped hands and gave each other smiles of appreciation.

"Walk with me to the Clinic?" Ashley said to Liberty after Shawn and Ilika left.

"Okay. Did you know there were going to be all those people wandering through, needing this and that kind of help?"

"No, but they were pretty easy. The leaders were the hardest!"

"You're not kidding! I had actually thought up a really good name to call Joan when she was giving me shit about the food. Sure glad I didn't say it!"

"Me too!"

They entered the clinic and plopped into a couple of comfortable chairs.

"What do you need here?" Liberty asked.

"I don't. You do," Ashley said firmly.

Liberty was too amazed at the courage of her younger friend to be angry. If it had been anyone else, in any other situation, she would have been mad as hell. But at that moment, with two days of evaluations still ahead, a little voice inside her told Liberty that this was for the best.

※

"I don't understand how you can be telepathic," Sister Rachael began, looking at Rini and Mati, "and not know how to shield your thoughts."

Sata translated, then listened to Rini and Mati for a minute. "It happened very recently, and was sort of an accident during surgery. Rini says there are classes about it, but we've just been too busy with missions. Mati says it was never a problem on . . . where we're stationed."

"You've been lucky so far," Rachael responded. "The three telepaths you've run into are respectful. The next, chances are, will rob you blind, blackmail you, publish all your dirty secrets, and laugh while you and your friends are drawn and quartered."

Sata translated as best she could, but the colorful idioms gave her trouble. Rini and Mati both blinked and squirmed with embarrassment.

Rachael began the lessons by letting the young couple listen to her thoughts as she projected them to varying degrees, then shielded them completely. She encouraged them to do their best to read her mind, just as an unethical telepath would.

When Rachael was shielding, neither Rini nor Mati had the slightest idea what she was thinking, no matter how hard they tried.

She then had them mentally share ideas with each other, and find how quietly they could do that and still hear each other. When they were down to a mental whisper, they could still hear each other well ... and so could Rachael.

"You are used to verbal speech, pushing out each idea so it can cross the distance to the listener. Forget that. Instead, form each idea and hold it close, like a tiny flame you are shielding from the wind. Then let your partner reach in and gently take it from your mind."

After half an hour of practice, they were getting to the point where Rachael had to concentrate to catch their thoughts.

"Good. Enough for today. You may still need to project for long distances, but do that consciously, only in need, knowing that others might be listening."

✳ ✳ ✳

Chapter 27: Treasure

The entire evaluation group spent the following morning in the waiting room of the medical clinic. As requested, they all brought something to read.

Liberty was called in fairly early, and spent almost an hour with nurses and doctors to determine if her stomach trouble was anything serious.

Ashley soon finished the book she was reading, so she looked over the rack of pamphlets. Most of them were routine subjects like how to brush your teeth and how not to get pregnant. Then her eyes stopped on one that piqued her curiosity — *The Lyceum Hospice Program*.

Just then, Ilika was called into the examining room.

"Shawn, look at this!" Ashley said, plopping back onto the couch with the pamphlet in hand. "People who are dying, and have some important scientific or artistic work they're trying to complete, can live right here at Lyceum, with all the labs and studios to help them finish!"

"You know someone who's dying and is working on something important?"

"Yeah!"

At that moment, Liberty returned to the waiting room. "What's up, guys?"

"Remember I was telling you about my friend Jenny who's writing a symphony?"

"Yeah . . ."

"This would be perfect for her!"

The three friends spent the next twenty minutes reading the entire pamphlet and talking about Jenny. Ashley told them about the only place Jenny could play without angering the other residents, a little outdoor porch at the nursing home. She went on to describe the young musician's only instrument, a cheap penny whistle. After discussing every aspect of Jenny and the program, none of them could think of any reason Jenny wouldn't be accepted.

Finally, Ashley was called into the examining room, so she tucked the pamphlet into her book and slapped hands with Ilika, who was just coming out.

✳

The crew of the Manessa Kwi decided it was time to do more than look and listen. They decided it was time to ask questions. It sounded pretty easy.

Sata sat down on one end of a bench. The middle-aged lady at the other end squirmed with discomfort, even though the bench was eight feet long.

Sata took a breath for courage, then spoke. "May I ask you a question?"

"Are you lost, little girl?"

Sata smiled. "No. I was wondering if you know of anyone who needs . . ."

"Where's your mother? You shouldn't be wandering around without your parents."

Sata sighed, thanked the lady for her time, and went to find Sister Rebecca, who explained that communication was only possible with most people if all social customs and rituals were handled first.

✳

Kibi tried a different method, approaching some young people about her age throwing a ball through a metal hoop in the recreation center. "Teach me how?"

"Sure!" a tall, lanky boy replied with admiring eyes.

After half an hour of instruction and practice, Kibi showed no signs of skill at basketball, but was laughing and having fun.

"Let's take a break," the tall boy announced, and when Kibi sat down on the bench with the others, her admirer sat down close beside her.

Kibi sensed his interest, felt the heat of his body, smelled his delicious male aroma, and silently promised herself that she wouldn't let things get out of hand. "I'm looking for someone, someone important who needs . . ."

"That would be me," he replied firmly. "I haven't held anyone tight for . . . at least a week!"

His friends laughed.

Kibi swallowed. "I'm looking for someone who's important to the *universe* . . ."

The boy stood up, bounced the ball, and looked at her. "What are you, some kind of freak?"

Kibi managed to hold in her tears until she found Sister Rachael, who helped her understand her mistakes.

✳

By that afternoon, Sata was ready. With clipboard in hand, she approached a couple in the heliport lobby. "Hello, I'm taking a survey for a school project. Do you have a minute?"

"Yes," the man said, "our flight doesn't leave for ten minutes."

"If you had the power to save one important person or thing, that would be lost otherwise, what would it be?"

"George Samson, coach of the Lions. He went into retirement last year, and they're gonna *lose* the championships without him. He needs to coach one more season."

Sata was pretty sure this wasn't their mission, but she made some notes.

"Instant Cake Decorator," his wife asserted. "I lost one of my attachments, and they don't make them anymore. My *mother* used Instant Cake Decorator. There should be a law about it."

Sata made more notes.

"What language is *that?*" the man asked, looking down at Sata's clipboard. She smiled. "Secret school code."

*

That evening after dinner, as the evaluation group surveyed the storeroom full of camping equipment, everyone wanted to sleep under the stars, with a large tarp along just in case of rain.

Only a month before, Shawn would have been completely lost, not having any idea what to pack. A few days in the railroad yard of his home town had brought him much wisdom about camping. He soon had his own gear packed, and several shanks of rope to help with the tarps.

When they emerged from the storeroom and announced to Sister Joan that they were ready to go, she said nothing, but only held out a large envelope. Sapphire opened it. As she examined the papers within, a smile grew on her face.

"What is it?" several others asked, all gathering around to see.

"Maps. It's a treasure hunt! I haven't done one of these in ages. The treasure is a campsite with our evening snack, breakfast, and a pile of firewood."

Ashley and Liberty sparkled with interest. The entire group spread out the maps on a table for examination.

"Okay, here's the zoo, but what's this?"

"Looks like a spider!"

"How many legs does it have?" Liberty asked, unable to see at the moment.

Sapphire looked. "Six."

"Then I bet it's the residence halls. There are six clusters, connected by covered walkways."

"Excellent deduction, Liberty," Ilika said.

She smiled at him.

"I think this foot print is a unit of measure," Dario said. "And we can determine its value if we can find two known points."

"Isn't this a fountain?" asked Sapphire.

"Yeah, the one in the Eastern Garden, I bet," Dario speculated. "That's seven foot prints from the zoo. I'll go pace off that distance," he said and dashed out the door.

"I think I know where this stream is," Shawn said. "I've seen it in the woods."

"That's definitely one of our references," Sapphire said. "Could you find it again?"

"I think so."

"But we're gonna need this distance, and this one too," Ashley said.

"But what's this?" Sapphire asked, pointing to an oval with a five-pointed asterisk at one end.

"A helicopter?" Liberty wondered aloud.

"So if that's the heliport, we can triangulate using this distance here," Ilika suggested.

"I don't think so," Shawn said. "That part of the forest is thick and almost impossible to walk through."

Dario dashed back in. "A foot print is a hundred yards!"

Ten minutes later they all felt ready to begin the hunt. After shouldering packs and helping each other to adjust straps, Shawn was in charge of the first leg of the journey, attempting to find the path and stream.

They walked behind the residence halls, beyond the petting zoo, and past the pantry and laundry buildings. The first trail they tried took them to a huge gas tank inside a fence, but no farther.

Retracing their steps, they tried another.

"Yes!" Shawn declared. "I clearly remember this gnarled old tree root!"

Ten minutes later they came to a tiny trickle of a stream passing under a little bridge.

Suddenly Liberty faintly heard the distinct sound of jet engines starting. "A helicopter getting ready to take off!"

"We need a direction to the heliport . . ." Ilika began.

"But to do that, someone will have to get up in a tall tree so they can see the chopper leave," Dario said.

Ashley raised her hand.

"Our gymnast!" Sapphire said with admiration.

Ashley looked around, and selected a tall spruce with plenty of branches. "I'll need a boost to the first branch."

"You've got it," Ilika said.

"How long do I have, Lib?"

"Two or three minutes."

Ilika lifted Ashley up, she took hold of the first branches, and began a rapid but careful climb upward.

"Relate the direction to a nearby tree," Dario suggested.

Ashley absorbed the message as she climbed.

"Rotor just started," Liberty called. "They'll be airborne in about a minute!"

Ashley climbed. The main trunk was down to a foot in diameter.

"Be careful!" Sapphire called.

Ashley silently promised. She was beginning to feel the tree sway slightly as she climbed.

"There goes the helicopter!" she faintly heard Liberty yell.

Ashley stopped climbing and looked up. She was just barely high enough, but she managed to glimpse, through the many tree branches around her, the helicopter's ascent. She quickly looked down and lined it up with a tree less than a hundred feet away. Then she closed her eyes and listened to her heart throbbing softly inside her. It was a strong heart, she knew, conditioned by more than six years of gymnastics training.

When Ashley's heart had slowed and her mind had cleared, she began the long, careful climb back down.

Ilika caught her and lowered her to the ground. She immediately found her reference tree, not far off in the woods. The group again gathered around the maps.

Sapphire pointed to the map. "So that puts our goal not down the stream, but somewhat east of the stream."

Dario blinked a few times. "But we still have to follow the stream to get the right distance from the trail."

"True, but at least we now know which way to go from there."

The next part of the journey was led by Dario, who had to pace off eleven hundred yards, and do so along a twisting little stream. They soon discovered a faint path along one side, and Liberty even found a recent shoe print.

Soon Dario stopped. "This is the place, plus or minus one percent"

"That's eleven yards. That ought to get us close enough," Sapphire said.

Shawn poked around on the far side of the stream from the rest of the group. "A tire track!"

Everyone quickly gathered to see.

"Motorcycle?"

"Lighter. Just a wheelbarrow, I think," Dario said.

Ashley laughed. "For the firewood!"

They only had to follow the wheelbarrow track about two hundred yards east, and they found the campsite, complete with ice chest, firewood, and campfire pit.

✳

Around a cheery blaze, after sharing recent memories and speculating about the remaining day of evaluations, everyone talked about what they would be doing if they didn't join Lyceum. Sapphire and Dario had jobs they would return to. Liberty said something about a school, but didn't want to elaborate. Shawn intended to get a job, and probably do some volunteer work. Ilika would go back to being the captain of a small ship. Ashley knew she would be returning to a town where she could get no further gymnastics training.

Marshmallows toasted on the ends of sticks and laughter occasionally filled the air as six hopeful hearts shared their dreams and fears in that secluded little campsite, somewhere at a place called Lyceum.

✳ ✳ ✳

Chapter 28: Complications

When the evaluation group traipsed out of the woods the next morning, they had eaten a breakfast that might have contained a pine needle or two, and their clothes smelled like smoke, but they were in good spirits and felt ready for anything.

More written tests awaited them, then a question and answer session with the entire evaluation team. Final interviews filled most of the afternoon, with at least two Lyceum members asking all the pointed questions each candidate hoped they wouldn't ask.

As evening approached, the six evaluation group members were told to dress nicely and present themselves at the banquet room an hour later.

"Let's see who can shower, change, and get there first!" Liberty challenged.

"Me!" Ashley said, and all three youth dashed for the door.

Ilika smiled and followed a little more slowly.

The three all arrived at the banquet room at close enough to the same time that Shawn suggested they call it a tie. Liberty and Ashley both agreed. They entered the room to find more than a hundred people, all formally dressed, talking, sipping drinks, and nibbling appetizers. Ilika, Dario, and Sapphire filtered in during the next quarter hour.

"A toast!" Sister Maria announced over the buzz of conversation.

Everyone quieted to listen.

"To the six brave people who put up with our ceaseless probing into their lives for a solid week, I offer heartfelt praise of their patience and commitment!"

Everyone grabbed cups and raised them into the air.

"And for the hospitality shown us by all the good people of Lyceum," Dario said, glass raised, "as we attempted to show that we were worthy of membership in this distinguished place, I offer thanks!"

"Yes!"

"For sure!"

"Absolutely!"

When the general laughing and talking resumed, Shawn and Ashley wandered away, so Liberty began to survey the room. With streamers, balloons, flowers, and tasty cuisine from all over the world on the serving tables, it was truly magnificent even to her upper-class tastes. Although she still didn't know if her future was Lyceum, or some icky reform school, enough of the pressure was off to allow her to relax.

She was sipping her punch and gazing across the room, noticing the subtle differences between Lyceum members and the six candidates, when she became aware that not everyone in the room was a member or a candidate. Three young people looked uncomfortable, and stuck close together. Liberty decided to find out something about them.

"Hi!" she said, stepping up to the group. "I'm Liberty. Do you guys live here?"

"Um . . . not . . . speak . . ." Boro muttered with a frown of concentration.

Young Sister Sarah dashed up. "They're special guests from a far-away country, and don't speak our language much, except Sata over there talking to Sister Rebecca, and Kibi around here somewhere."

Liberty glanced in the direction Sarah had pointed, and saw a stocky girl who looked no more than twelve or thirteen. When she turned back to the strange trio of young people, she suddenly felt as if they could see right into her, especially the skinny boy and girl who were standing close together.

"Why do I feel naked with you guys?" she asked.

Sarah swallowed. "They're . . . looking for someone, haven't found them yet, and are probably wondering about you. They don't bite, really!"

"Sorr . . . y . . ." Mati and Rini both said almost at once, relaxing their gazes.

Just then, Sata joined the group and looked up at the tall, black-haired girl. "Hello. I speak your language."

Liberty suddenly became embarrassed. "I'm sorry. I didn't mean to pry, I just wanted to be friendly . . ."

"We want to be friendly too!" Sata replied, then spoke a few words in the language of Nebador to the others. They all nodded and smiled.

"That's the weirdest language I've ever heard! And I can't imagine where that accent of yours is from. Who are you looking for?"

Sata took a moment to untangle Liberty's complex sentences, then decided she should only reply to the last. "We do not know. We are not sure we are looking for a person. It is someone, or something, important."

"Well . . . good luck! Everyone's sitting down, so I should go join my group." She switched to a hushed voice. "There's a guy in it I like!"

"Thank you for being friendly!" Sata said as Liberty walked away.

After a moment of silence, Sarah pointed to a table where Brother Jacob and Kibi were already sitting. As they walked, Sata shared Liberty's parting words with the other three.

I wonder who she likes, Mati pondered mentally, without much shielding.

She likes Ilika, the one with green eyes, Sarah replied with casual innocence.

Mati's and Rini's eyes opened wide, but they carefully hid their thoughts from Sarah.

✳

As Shawn savored his delicate salad of seven different greens and a fruity dressing, he pondered the mystery of why his life was unfolding as it was, instead of how his father wanted it to unfold.

Ashley felt very relaxed, almost sleepy. She took her time with her salad, and that finished, felt quite full and just wanted to try little bites of the main dishes. Luckily, the person serving their table had previously encountered the eating habits of gymnasts, and was able to create a plate that was just right.

Liberty, who had grabbed a place beside Ilika, felt quite hungry. She quickly noticed, however, that the mysterious young man at her side was eating slowly, savoring every bite, so she did the same.

The tender halibut filet, lightly covered in a tangy hollandaise sauce and sprinkled with perfectly toasted almonds, commanded almost universal praise. The succulent slices of chicken breast, layered with rich cheese and spinach, also evoked heartfelt compliments. Finally, the marinated prime rib, served with fresh creamed horseradish sauce, caused an equal sensation. Few people in the room resisted the temptation to try all three.

Rini and Mati silently discussed, as they ate, when to tell Kibi what they had just learned.

✳

The animals of the forest hardly reacted when the two shadows crept into the hidden grove, settled onto the log, and wrapped their arms around each other.

"I have about an hour before my ride gets here," Ilika whispered. "Lyceum will make their decision during the next few days."

"Since the man you're staying with has already seen the ship, we could come visit you . . ."

"If you're visiting me, you won't be working on the mission."

Kibi pouted for a moment, then realized Ilika couldn't see her, and chuckled. "You're right. But we're not having any luck."

"Me neither. It'll probably happen when we least expect it. I want you to know about something."

"Yes?" Kibi prompted lovingly.

"The tall girl in the evaluation group likes me."

Ilika felt Kibi tense up, so he held her tightly and kept talking. "I have to stay on good terms with her, but I won't let anything romantic happen. I've already nudged her and Shawn together a couple of times."

Kibi tried to breathe. "Um . . . thank you . . . I . . . trust you, just like you trusted me about . . . Toran Takil."

Ilika pulled her close, and didn't let go until, about half an hour later, his bracelet chimed.

❋ ❋ ❋

Chapter 29: New Members

The crew of the Manessa Kwi, without Ilika, settled into their daily routine of watching, listening, and asking questions. Kibi was sorely tempted to go visit Ilika, and Boro added his vote when he heard that their captain was probably fishing on a river. Sata found her courage, as the mission leader, and reminded them all that he would be back in less than a week. Rini pointed out that he had been with them for more than a year, and probably needed a vacation. Mati nodded. Kibi and Boro frowned, but soon accepted the situation with reluctant sighs.

But as the week wore on, all five crew members moved closer and closer to the same conclusion — the questions they were asking, about important people or things that might need their help, were getting them nowhere. They had no idea how to get the people of this planet to help them discover the object of their mission.

*

Sister Sarah easily found the crew by the telepathic activity between Mati and Rini. Even though they were getting good at shielding their thoughts when they were aware of the need, like when Sarah or Rachael was present and they wanted to share an intimate thought, they tended to forget when they were alone.

When Sarah approached the small covered picnic area, deep in the woods and rarely used by visitors, Kibi lay on the table gazing upward, Boro and Sata sat on a bench chatting, Rini was in a tree, and Mati lay on her belly watching some insects.

"... but if we don't ask questions," Boro was saying, "how will we know when our mission person ... thing ... whatever ... gets here? I don't think we'll know just by looking at them ... it ... will we?"

"I don't know!" Sata said with frustration. "We're supposed to be in the right place ..."

"Hi, guys!" Sarah said, strolling into the picnic area.

Rini dropped from a tree branch, Mati hopped up, and everyone gathered around.

"You are invited to eat lunch with us, and the new members will be there, including Liberty, that tall girl you met."

Kibi swallowed, but didn't let anything show on her face.

"That'll be nice," Sata said. "We could use a change. We have *no* idea what we're supposed to do next."

"I haven't heard of anything ... or anybody. But I'll keep looking and listening!"

"Thanks," Kibi said. "We should probably head for the ship and get cleaned up. It'll be good for us to *not* think about the mission for the rest of the day."

※

The two hundred or so Lyceum members currently on the campus ate their meals, when not on duty anywhere, in a section of the cafeteria separated from the public area by a low wall of planters. The Nebador crew joined Rebecca, Jacob, Rachael, and Sarah at a table where seats had been reserved. Soon, carts came rolling out of the kitchen laden with pitchers of drink and serving dishes of food. Although nothing like the banquet they had attended a week before, all the crew members enjoyed trying a little bit of everything.

Once the members and guests had served themselves, Brother Randy stood. "As the coordinator of the last evaluation group, it is my honor to present to you, Sister Ashley!"

The twelve-year-old gymnast turned red, and after nudges from several people around her, managed to stand. The room filled with clapping, and people in the cafeteria craned their necks to see what the excitement was all about.

"... Sister Liberty!"

The tall girl stood and basked in the applause, but those sitting near, including Ashley and Shawn, saw that tears were just about to roll down her cheeks.

"... Brother Shawn!"

Although he acted a bit bashful, he was obviously more used to standing up in front of people than the two girls.

"... Brother Ilika!"

The crew of the Manessa Kwi knew they had to clap and cheer for Ilika no differently than for all the other new members.

Sarah didn't notice any difference.

Rachael wasn't so easily fooled.

"... Sister Sapphire!"

※

Young Ashley Riddle had been a member of Lyceum for exactly forty-five minutes when she poked her head into the hospice center office. No one was inside, so she wandered around the spacious indoor patio and garden, with pools and fountains, lawns and carpets, benches and tables, all ringed by twenty apartments. Overhead, curving wooden beams held up a white dome pierced by six skylights.

Beside one of the pools in the garden, an elderly lady tossed bits of fish food onto the water. Then she would stop, consider a thought, and write something down in a notebook at her side. In another part of the patio, a man worked at an easel. He was not very old, perhaps fifty, but every so often he would twitch and shudder with a painful spasm. Then he would return to his painting for a few moments.

A large man backed out of one of the apartments.

"Thank you again, Clyde," an elderly male voice came from within. "I sure am sorry to have to bother you like this."

"No problem," the large man said. "That's why I'm here. Do you feel up to teaching your class this evening?"

"I wouldn't miss it even if I had to take a bed pan with me!" the voice said.

The large man chuckled. "That's the spirit! I'll see you there!"

Then he turned. "Greetings, Sister . . . Ashley?"

She nodded.

"I see purpose in your eyes. Let's go into the office." He washed his hands at a sink, then led the way and sat down at the desk.

Ashley, with her heart in her throat, described her friend Jenny, dying of cancer but hearing music, especially when she looked up at the stars, and trying desperately, with nothing but a cheap penny whistle, to play it.

Brother Clyde listened with keen interest. When she finished, he thought for a moment.

"I need to speak very honestly, Ashley," he said. "The important question we have to ask is whether this ten-year-old girl truly has something of great value to leave to the future. Most ten-year-olds have not accumulated much knowledge or wisdom. People die all the time — even ten-year-olds. We don't have the space or resources here at Lyceum for all of them."

He paused to let his words soak in. Ashley nodded.

"But as I understand it," Brother Clyde went on, "your friend has a special gift, something that she did not acquire over a lifetime of experience, but rather is receiving directly from some external source."

"Right," Ashley confirmed.

"The question is, how do we determine the quality of the music your friend is hearing and is trying to play? A variation on *Suzie Had A Little Dog* would be of little worth to the future."

Ashley swallowed and gathered her courage. "I've heard it. Not all of it, and not all of the voices together, because there's no way she could play them all at once. But I've heard three of them, and some of the fourth."

She glanced at the large adult, and realized what he needed to hear. "My parents play classical music at home all the time, and I dance to some of the best music in the world in my gymnastics floor routines. I've watched gymnasts and ballet dancers and ice skaters all my life. I know what great music is. Jenny's song is like that. It's not a little kid's tune. It's more than half an hour long, and it's deep and mysterious and wonderful. I wish I had recorded some of it, because it would make you cry, it's so beautiful, even just on a little penny whistle."

Ashley figured she had said all she could. She closed her eyes, fearing the man would now do what she had seen adults do many times — toss away the concerns and accomplishments of the young as unimportant.

"Okay," he said. "That's what we have to go on. You're a Lyceum member, you know music, and you judge the quality of the music that is being composed or transcribed by your friend to be comparable to the great music that has withstood the test of time. It sounds like we had better get moving on this."

Ashley's eyes snapped open. "You mean . . . she can come?"

Brother Clyde smiled. "It was *you* who made that decision, Ashley. Are you still comfortable with it?"

"Yes . . . I'm just . . . very happy!"

"Okay," Clyde began with a serious tone, "we have much to do." He began tapping at his computer. "I see that you have some classes already arranged. Clear your schedule, as you're now on a special project for the hospice center. Then call the nursing home and get an update on your friend's condition."

Ashley, her mind racing, grabbed a piece of scratch paper and began making a list.

"And I see that we have a non-resident member in that area. She can probably help deal with Jenny's parents. We need to find out if they're open to a benefactor situation to upgrade their daughter's care. You're the benefactor, champion athlete's home town, you know. You work on all that while I go check on the residents."

✳

Ashley, sweating and shaking nervously, took half an hour to figure out how to send messages to the gymnastics coach, the history teacher, and the kitchen coordinator, as she was supposed to wash dishes that evening.

Brother Clyde stopped by the office to see how she was doing, but said nothing and went out again.

Another half hour allowed Ashley to find the nursing home's number and make the call.

"Black Hills Convalescent Center . . ." a familiar voice answered.

"Hello, Mrs. Miller. This is Ashley Riddle. I just called to see how Jenny was doing."

"Not so good, Ashley. Her lungs aren't as strong as they used to be, and she's starting to have trouble playing her little tunes. She's working on a letter to you, but it goes slowly. Would you like to talk to her?"

"Um . . . not right now. I have to do something else, but please tell her I called, and I'll call again tonight or tomorrow."

"Okay, Honey. You take care."

"Thank you, Mrs. Miller."

Ashley put down the phone and let herself silently cry, until Brother Clyde appeared again. She quickly grabbed a tissue, dried her eyes, and related Jenny's condition.

"This is more urgent than I thought," he said. "Here's the non-resident member's contact info. You make the call, tell her everything you know, and I'll listen. She's probably at work, so you'll have video."

With shaking fingers, Ashley made the call. Suddenly there was recognition on both sides of the connection.

"Hello, Ashley. I'm very happy to hear that you became a member of Lyceum," the image on the screen said. "I'll never forget the many times I've seen you sitting on the floor searching through the gymnastics books."

"Mrs. Pearson! I thought you were the children's librarian!"

"Well, I *am* the children's librarian. I've also been a member of Lyceum for almost ten years, so you can call me Sister Laura."

Feeling a new sense of urgency, Ashley quickly told Laura all about Jenny, then added some new information that Brother Clyde had not yet heard. "She only has a mom, who rarely visits her in the nursing home. Her mom's . . . kind of . . . a simple person. I bet she won't let Jenny come here unless there's something in it for her."

"I see," Sister Laura said thoughtfully.

"If you want to talk to her, you'll probably have to buy her a meal or something."

"Hmm. Thank you for the tip, Ashley."

"And I don't think she has a phone. You'll have to call her neighbor, Susan Jones."

"Okay. I'm glad to know what I'm up against. I'll call you back in an hour or less."

The screen went blank, and while they waited, Brother Clyde told Ashley about the music studio at Lyceum, and how it could help Jenny to write and perform her music. Only about twenty minutes later, Sister Laura called back.

"Your assessment was correct, Ashley. She was extremely suspicious until I offered her a free steak dinner. She'll meet with me this evening, and I have a hunch she'll be open to the plan as long as it doesn't cost her anything."

"Thank you, Mrs. . . . I mean, Sister Laura. Brother Clyde's here helping me. We'll talk to you soon!"

"Bye, Ashley!"

"Now I think I see the situation a little more clearly," Clyde said. "Mom is gonna want a piece of the action. We'll have to be careful with this one. Sister Laura could use some help. Why don't you fly out tonight, Ashley. Take a portfolio with you, lots of pictures, a number of Lyceum vouchers, and a complete hospice program kit. Include a deluxe library case for a music disc. That ought to be inspiring to the girl, at least. I'll help you get it all ready."

Ashley's head was spinning as she experienced first hand how quickly Lyceum could go into action. She was trying to stay calm, but the part about flying home that night to help Sister Laura was almost beyond her belief.

*

The next hour was very busy for Lyceum's second-youngest member. Brother Clyde put together the portfolio while Ashley packed several changes of nice clothes. When she returned to the office, Clyde steered her to the travel desk in the main office, where she received a ticket for a flight at eight o'clock and some cash. She called her mother, who was thrilled, and promised to meet Ashley at the airport.

Before Ashley realized it, the normal dinner hour had passed. At a lone table, with members mopping the floor all around them, she and Clyde ate left-overs and talked about what Jenny's mother might want out of the deal, and how far Lyceum was willing to go. Ashley took notes, and by the time she swallowed her last bite, felt she understood the limits. Finally, Clyde gave her an envelope full of permission forms for Jenny's mother to sign.

With travel bag and portfolio in hand, Ashley dashed toward the Lost Forest Heliport, where a gleaming helicopter was warming up its engines to whisk her and about a dozen other people to the international airport.

As she dashed along the glass-walled corridor, she passed the group of five guests who didn't speak the language well, all looking rather bored. She smiled at them, but didn't have a free hand to wave, or time to stop and talk.

As Ashley, last of all, stepped onto the helicopter and found a seat, she suddenly felt a part of something much bigger than herself, something she didn't fully understand, something that seemed to have taken on a life of its own.

* * *

Chapter 30: Bad News

Kibi turned and watched the small girl, who had just become a Lyceum member, run toward the heliport lobby, where she was quickly ushered through the departure doors. "At least *she* knows where she's going."

Boro stepped beside Kibi. "Maybe . . . we're going about this wrong. Maybe we just need to relax, find something to do, and let the mission . . . you know . . . come to us."

Sata joined them. "I bet they'd let us take some classes. It would help our language skills, and keep us from being so bored."

Rini and Mati both nodded.

"See what Ilika thinks," Sata continued, glancing at Kibi, "and I'll talk to Sister Rebecca."

They all fell silent and looked at each other.

"Cafeteria?" Mati suggested.

✳

Liberty, Shawn, and Ilika spent the next few days getting used to their new schedules that included meals with the other members, chores, meetings, work assignments, and classes.

Liberty, at fifteen, had less work but more classes. She glanced at her schedule and smiled, fully intending to finish the mandatory low-level classes quickly and move into more interesting college-level subjects. The coordinator of the animal barn was happy to receive Liberty's offer to help with the horses. Finally, with an hour of free time before her first math class, she strode toward the Lost Forest Heliport with a gleam in her eyes.

Shawn didn't mind the low-level refresher courses he had to take, and smiled to himself when he saw the general science class he had requested, but his eyes opened wide when he saw his work shift, that very afternoon, as a chemistry lab technician trainee. He suddenly felt hot and sweaty, remembering how his father had steered him — no, manipulated him — away from the sciences all his life.

Ilika smiled at the two classes he had to take, both designed to improve his language skills. He had work shifts in several places on the Lyceum campus, but plenty of free time to look for the real reason he was there.

＊

That evening, as Ilika was sweeping the cafeteria floor after dinner, Liberty appeared with another broom and began helping. Ilika knew she wasn't on the schedule.

"I signed up for pilot training today!" she said excitedly. "Want to help me celebrate tonight?"

He stopped sweeping and gave her a long look. "That's wonderful, Liberty. But I have the strong hunch you'd like to . . . celebrate with someone you can . . . share affection with."

Liberty nodded with a hopeful look in her eyes.

"The problem is . . . I'm only going to be a resident member for a little while, then I'll be back on my . . . boat . . . and you know the saying about captains who have a girl at every harbor . . ."

Liberty frowned. "Oh. Yeah . . . I just left that kind of life behind and . . . don't really want to go back to it."

Ilika nodded with understanding. "It seems to me . . . you're ready for a boy who . . . will really appreciate you . . . and stick with you."

Liberty swept an already-clean spot for a moment, then stopped. "Yeah."

＊

When the Reverend Tommy Mitchell announced his intention to run for president in the upcoming national elections, many Lyceum members knew enough about him to feel somewhat less than excited. But many other members didn't realize the implications, so Shawn received nearly constant congratulations as he went from work assignments, to classes, to free-time activities. In the chemistry lab, the kitchen, and the swimming pool, smiles, waves, and thumbs up came to him from members young and old.

Shawn tried to remain modest. He thanked them for their well-wishes, assured them it would have no effect on his Lyceum membership, and went on with his life.

But by the middle of the week, he was getting sick of it. At dinner, after brushing off three supportive remarks from others at his table, Shawn suddenly dropped his fork onto his plate and stood up. The entire room sensed his serious mood and fell silent.

"If any of you think my father would make a good president, you are welcome to vote for him. Personally, I think it would be the worst thing that could ever happen to this country, and I'd rather not hear about it ever again."

Shawn sat down and stared at his plate, but had lost his appetite.

Many other members did the same.

＊

The two hooded figures kissed long and deeply in their special grove of trees. A squirrel in the branches above worked on shelling a nut.

"I've been using every free minute to read things about Shawn's father," Ilika began when they parted. "If he became president, he could, and probably would, do a number of things to move the country away from democracy and toward theocracy. This might be why we're here."

"Do you think Arantiloria ... or *someone* ... will tell us if we're on the right track?"

Ilika chuckled under his breath.

"I know," Kibi answered her own question with deep resignation. "We'll learn more by figuring it out for ourselves."

✳

A few days later, after the last flight back to Lyceum, Ashley helped Jenny off the helicopter and into a wheelchair.

"That was the most fun thing I've ever done!" Jenny squealed. "Thank you so much for bringing me here, Ashley! Do I really get to see you every day?"

The other three passengers had already departed, and the pilot and flight attendant were taking care of the helicopter. The two girls moved along the quiet glass-walled corridor, Ashley pushing, Jenny's eyes nearly bulging at the lighted gardens beyond the glass.

"Sure!" Ashley replied, "unless you're too busy recording your music. I've heard they have all kinds of instruments hooked directly to a computer, so you won't have to use your breath, and you can hear all the voices of your symphony together."

"Wow! The only life dream I've ever had was to play my music. When you're ten and dying of cancer, you don't get too many life dreams, you know."

Ashley chuckled slightly as she struggled to hold in tears.

"But even that dream always seemed just out of reach because I'd be disturbing the other residents, or I'd get out of breath, or it would be time for meds, or *something*. Now ... it almost feels like it might come true."

Ashley didn't say anything as they walked through Lyceum's main lobby, nearly empty at that hour, but she knew she was going to do everything in her power to help Jenny with her dream.

✳   ✳   ✳

Chapter 31: The Plan

Nearly all eyes at Lyceum carefully watched the presidential campaign of the Reverend Tommy Mitchell. Shawn's thoughts on the matter had given them all, even the least politically-aware, plenty of motivation to keep an eye on that particular candidate.

Within a week, it was clear that Reverend Mitchell was going to use every opportunity to further his campaign. His weekly sermons, already known for their lack of spiritual themes, shifted from church politics to national politics. His talks at revival meetings fired up the people as they always did, but for a new purpose.

None of this would have been of great concern, as charismatic religious leaders often tried for the presidency, and always failed. However, this time the candidate's political speeches started to include the name *Lyceum*, and it wasn't for the purpose of thanking the international service organization for accepting his son as a member.

Assignments quickly went out to non-resident members in all the cities where the reverend had scheduled events, and reports flowed back within hours. Lyceum had a big problem.

✳

Both Shawn and Liberty were asked to attend the next meeting of the Lyceum Council, which was devoted largely to that problem.

Sister Rebecca began, her weathered, angular features accented by her gray hair. "We all appreciate the warning Brother Shawn gave us about his father, but . . ."

"But we completely missed the *real* threat," Liberty interrupted. "He knows he can't become president. He's just going to use his campaign to get back at his son, and destroy Lyceum in the process."

Liberty's words jabbed deep into Shawn's heart. She was talking about his father. But he also knew, underneath the emotions he was feeling, that she was very close to correct.

"You do have a way of getting right to the point, Sister Liberty," the elderly member who had been speaking said. "And I honor that quality in you. That is one of the reasons you are here. The other is because Shawn needs a very good friend right now."

Liberty sat blinking, absorbing the idea that Shawn needed her.

"It's going to be hard for me to sit here and listen to everyone talking about my father," Shawn said, his voice revealing his inner conflict.

"We understand," a tall, white-haired man said in a comforting tone. "Even though it will be hard, can you do it? Can you . . . *will* you help us with your insights about the man who is attacking Lyceum, the man who just happens to also be your father?"

Liberty moved closer to Shawn and took his hand in hers.

Shawn took a deep breath. "I'll . . . try very hard. I don't like what he's doing either."

"Thank you, Brother Shawn," the man said. "And we'll be with you every moment, even if you need to step out of the process at times. And I assure you that we'll deal only with the problem, and do nothing to hurt your father in a personal, vengeful way."

"I understand," Shawn said. "And I'm sorry I didn't realize sooner he'd do something like this. Liberty's right. It was obvious, but I didn't want to see it."

❋

The fifteen council members and two guests spent the next three hours discussing every aspect of the problem. After the council adjourned, everyone spent the rest of the afternoon at their regular activities while pondering what they had heard. Liberty discovered, at a computer, that Sister Rebecca had already found a substitute for her work shift in the horse barn, so she went to help Shawn in the gardens.

Between his slumped shoulders and some things he mumbled, Liberty knew he was carrying a huge burden of guilt. She asked questions as they trimmed plants and raked leaves, and by dinnertime, Shawn had pulled himself up to his full height and decided he was the one responsible for solving the problem. He just didn't know how.

When the Lyceum Council reconvened that evening, most of the councilors were of the same opinion, not because the problem was Shawn's fault, but simply because he was the one who could best solve it.

Shawn listened carefully as councilor after councilor agreed with the notion that Shawn would have to confront his father, publicly, at one of his upcoming televised speeches where thousands of people would be present, and millions more watching from their homes.

The thought would have scared him to death, except that it would also deal with his guilt. He couldn't imagine living one more day at Lyceum unless he did everything humanly possible to put this mess behind them for good.

Liberty held Shawn's hand tightly in hers.

"It will be the hardest thing I've ever done," he began, "standing up there alone to confront my father. But . . . I know I have to do it."

"No one envies the task you must do," Sister Rebecca said, "but you will be far from alone. There will be security people to protect you, and your friend Liberty will be at your side . . ."

Liberty nodded vigorously and looked at Shawn with admiring eyes.

"There will be additional Lyceum people throughout the audience for psychological purposes. I'm sure Rachael and Sarah will make good use of their talents. A number of technicians will be necessary, and I believe you have some other friends from your evaluation group . . ."

"Ashley and Ilika," Shawn mumbled.

"I can easily see a team of twenty or thirty Lyceum members at the event. No, Shawn, you will not be alone."

Shawn brightened. "Thank you. But I still have to be the one to speak to my father. I hope I'll know what to say . . ."

Sister Maria stood. "That is where the still, small voice inside you comes into play, Shawn, and the legions of angels who will be with you, watching and listening. If your father is going to hurt others with lies and twisted theology, his indwelling spirit and his guardian angel are going to be very unhappy with him. Stick with the truth, and you will have help beyond your imagination!"

Shawn smiled as Sister Maria sat down. Then he became aware of Liberty at his side, holding one of his hands in both of hers. He looked into her moist eyes, saw tenderness and love, and immediately began crying as she wrapped her arms around him.

✳   ✳   ✳

Chapter 32: Precautions

When the crew of the Manessa Kwi returned to the ship, on the very day that Brother Jacob gave them a list of Lyceum classes they could take, Arantiloria greeted them from the middle of the large oval table.

"We know what the mission is!" Boro announced excitedly.

Their seldom-seen training supervisor said nothing.

"We want to be at that political rally when Shawn confronts his father, who's trying to destroy Lyceum," Sata explained.

The purple-haired girl on the table continued to sit silently.

Kibi frowned. "We were thinking we could . . . you know . . . help protect Shawn with our . . . mission bracelets . . . maybe . . . um . . . maybe not?"

Arantiloria looked at each of them for a long moment as they found seats around the table. The silent tension in the room became thick as she swiveled from one to another without moving her arms or legs. Finally she floated to the steward's console so she could face them all.

"There could be great harm done if you helped protect *anyone* in that situation, other than yourselves, so there is no point in going. Lyceum can take care of itself, I assure you."

"Oh," Sata whispered.

Boro looked defiant for a moment, then relaxed.

Kibi sighed.

Mati and Rini looked at each other. *You were right*, Rini said silently.

"But of much greater importance, and the reason I am here, has to do with the list of classes you were given today."

Sata, with a wrinkled brow, pulled it from her pocket and unfolded it.

"It is very important to the mission that Rini does not take any of those classes, nor attempt to become fluent in the language, nor otherwise mentally distract himself."

Rini raised his eyebrows. "Can you tell me . . . why?"

"I do not know yet."

"That started way back on the star station," Kibi began, "when you had new training for everyone but Rini, didn't it?"

Arantiloria nodded. "Sometimes it is necessary to be . . . empty."

"Maybe . . . that will tell us something about the mission," Boro pondered aloud. "Or at least . . . some things that the mission *isn't*."

The training specialist just smiled.

✳

Liberty awoke one morning to find an extra work shift listed on her computer screen. Since she was supposed to be spending lots of time with Shawn, she frowned. Then she noticed it was only one hour, one time, so she sighed and wrote a note to Shawn explaining that she couldn't meet him for breakfast. She promised to make it up to him.

She lay back down and stretched her arms over her head. A smile crept onto her face, and she glowed with happiness because she was, for the first time in her life, loving a boy who appreciated every moment they spent together, and who truly needed her companionship and affection.

She sat back up and looked at the computer screen again. She had no idea where the Northeast Retreat Center was, but a cart of food would be ready to take there in less than an hour. She shrugged and hopped out of bed.

To Liberty's slight annoyance, no one had time to show her the way. They handed her a map and went back to their work.

At least the cart didn't look too heavy. Liberty drained a glass of milk and headed out along the paved walkways.

A quarter hour later, she was surprised by a man in a suit blocking her path. She frowned while he spoke into a microphone, then he asked if she had any weapons.

"No, but I'll bring one next time, now that I know there are goons in these woods."

The man nodded with a slight smile and waved her along.

Liberty didn't stop frowning until she came to the building of yellow logs and large glass windows, and saw her father leaning on the deck railing grinning down at her.

After bounding up the steps, Liberty embraced him and they headed inside, already chatting, leaving one of the men to unload the food cart.

"Sorry about all the secrecy," he apologized as they sat down to a hearty breakfast. "It's absolutely essential that no one finds out I'm visiting Lyceum, or that you're living here. I've been meeting with Brother Jacob to make sure there's no way your membership can become public knowledge. We're even watching the four people who weren't accepted from your evaluation group."

"But, Daddy, why?"

"Because my work on the nuclear peace treaty is causing death threats from several groups, and if they can't get to me, they'll come after you. So I'm going to ask you to put up with some inconveniences for a while . . ."

✳

Liberty was not seen by Shawn, or anyone else, until dinner time. Members arrived at the cafeteria only to find a sign directing them to a large conference room. A muscular man at the door checked each person's I.D. card.

Finally the doors were closed.

Brother Jacob stood. He gestured to a tall girl, sitting next to Shawn, of about fifteen years, who wore her short, blond hair slightly curled. "This is Sister Chelsea. Any reference to her previous name, if you happen to know it, could easily cause her death. The reasons for this will be made known when it is safe to do so. Enjoy your dinner."

Only a few members, all fairly new, attempted to pump those sitting near for further information. They received looks so stern that they didn't dare speak again for the rest of the meal.

*

When Ilika approached the hidden grove in the forest that evening, he was making more noise than usual, and Kibi sensed he was excited about something. A large four-legged animal, rubbing against a tree nearby, snorted a warning. Ilika slowed down and proceeded more carefully.

After a quick kiss, Ilika sighed. "I'm not sure whether to think this is good news, or bad news. We have another mission possibility."

Kibi listened as Ilika described the precautions about Liberty, who her father was, and what senate bills he was working on.

"So . . . do you think we might be here to protect Liberty — I mean Chelsea — or her father? And if her father, how are we supposed to do that from Lyceum? The senate's a long way from here . . ."

"No idea. Because of where we were placed, we'll have to assume L . . . Chelsea, but remain open to the other possibility during one of his visits. And, of course, there's still Shawn. Ironically, those two have become *very* close. I think she liked him from the beginning, but held back because of his religious background . . . until I brushed her off."

"I'll be more comfortable around her now that she found what she needed somewhere else."

Ilika nodded. "I can't really learn any more about the threat she faces, as the members have been told all they need to know. I'd like you and Sata to sit down with the Lyceum leadership and offer your services to help protect her and her father. They'll assume you learned of it through mysterious Nebador channels."

Kibi giggled under her breath and nodded.

*

"Brother Chad made me a penny whistle — he calls it a recorder — that I don't even have to blow into," Jenny chatted non-stop as Ashley pushed her along the carpeted corridor toward the music studio, "and we've recorded Voice One three times! He's teaching me how to use the editing computer when I'm tired of playing. I never thought it would be so tricky! Each time I play, the computer finds places that aren't quite the same as the last time, and I have to decide which is right. I'm starting to be able to fix them myself while he does other things."

While Jenny talked, Ashley just smiled, holding in tears of joy for her friend.

"Greetings, Jenny, and Sister Ashley," Brother Chad said as they entered the studio. "Are you ready to record Voice Two?"

Jenny nodded while smiling.

"Can you stay, Ashley? Jenny loves an audience."

"For about half an hour, then I have a dance class, but I'll be back to take Jenny to lunch with the members."

"Fantastic!" Chad said, setting up Jenny's instrument. "Do you remember Voice Two, Jenny?"

"Remember it? I heard it again last night while I was out under the stars, then *dreamed* the whole thing, every note, and woke up humming it!"

The two girls laughed and snickered together as Brother Chad got his computer ready.

✳   ✳   ✳

Chapter 33: Confrontation

Shawn awoke in Liberty's arms, as he had for the last several mornings. It was the only thing keeping him from screaming and running into the woods to hide and never come out again.

Liberty stirred, then kissed his shoulder.

"What did I do to deserve . . ." he began, struggling to find the right word. ". . . this?"

"Let me think," she replied, snuggling close. "You're cute . . . you like triple chocolate ice cream . . . you need me, and no one ever has before. It feels *wonderful* . . . and . . . um . . . when I offered, you accepted, in your own shy little way. Oh, did I mention that you're cute?"

He smiled self-consciously. "I've never thought of myself as cute before. It wasn't really a value in my family."

Liberty chuckled. "Would you rather be cute, and have me love you, or politically powerful, and have your hired goons chase your enemies around . . ."

Shawn sighed.

"Oh, and you're *nothing* like your father, or I wouldn't be within a *mile* of you, much less in your bed."

"Actually, this is your bed."

"Is it?" she said, glancing around. "You're right."

"My father would call this a sin."

"Can you see how that fits into his political agenda? If you can control people's basic needs, you've got them by the . . . you know."

Shawn blushed. After a long silence, he replied, "I see your point."

"So . . ." Liberty began, stretching. "What do you wanna do today? As I remember, we don't have any classes or work shifts . . ."

"That because I'm *supposed* to fly a thousand miles, with thirty other members, and confront my *father* at his televised rally."

"I'll be at your side, Ashley and Ilika will be close, Lyceum's muscle men will be all around you, and you'll have a microphone your father can't turn off. But *you* have to do the talking. Can you do it?"

Shawn took a deep breath. "I have no idea. I'm just gonna go . . . and try."

*

Shawn numbed himself for a long day of traveling by helicopter, airliner, and bus. Once they arrived at the small conference center Lyceum had rented, a short walk from the indoor stadium where Reverend Mitchell would be speaking two days later, everyone had work to do — everyone except Shawn and Liberty.

He understood the need for others to take care of all the logistics and technical arrangements. He knew he wouldn't be able to contribute a coherent thought even if he tried. But he craved some distraction from his anxious brooding and worrying.

Liberty anticipated his need, so right after dinner she stuffed him into a taxi and they were soon sipping soft drinks and tapping their feet to the music at a teen dance club.

*

As soon as Shawn and Liberty were gone, Ashley, Ilika, and Sarah gathered when Sister Rachael announced a meeting of the primary support team. Someone slid a plate of cookies onto the table.

"We're going to try to do this without anyone getting hurt," Rachael began, snagging a cookie. "Um . . . Chelsea, and you three, will be right with Shawn for support, but remember that none of you can fill his shoes if he freezes. He will have the best chance of finding his words if he *must*.

"Around you will be the security people . . ." she continued, gesturing toward a group of twelve large men, at another table, studying diagrams of the stadium. "I will be a little ways away, as I will not be paying attention to Shawn, but rather to everyone else. My psych team will be sprinkled throughout the stadium . . ."

*

After all the meetings were over, and Ilika had helped with dinner clean-up, he slipped out into the warm night. A small park nearby provided him with darkness and cover. He slid his mission bracelet from above his elbow.

"Hello, Manessa."

"Hello, Ilika."

"Any news?"

"I am still in the hanger of Pad Three. The crew is still trying to find the object of the mission. Arantiloria has been in and out. Mati is the only one on the bridge right now."

"Hi, Mati."

"Ilika! I was just doing some piloting simulations so I don't forget how."

"As soon as Boro gains a little more confidence, you two will alternate often."

"Good. By the way, Aran says your mission bracelet will be inactive day after tomorrow. What does that mean?"

Ilika was silent for a moment. "It means I'm in the wrong place."

"Want us to come get you? It would just take a minute."

"Um . . . no. That would look suspicious. I'll finish what I started, and maybe I can help somehow, even though it's not the mission. Besides, knowing I'm in the wrong place doesn't mean I have any idea where the *right* place is."

Mati laughed with understanding.

*

Shawn and Liberty stood together, arms around each other, wind blowing their hair back. A huge bullet left a gun barrel and moved slowly toward them. With no time to think, Ilika leapt into the path of the bullet, but an arm, faster than sight, grabbed him and pulled him back. A purple-haired girl grinned at him.

*

"You okay, Ilika?"

Ilika struggled with his sheets for a moment, then relaxed and blinked. In the dim light of early morning, Ashley's face looked down at him.

"I was stretching," she explained, "and heard you tossing and turning and saying *no* to someone."

"Heavy dream. The kind that isn't fun, but contains important stuff anyway."

"I get that kind before every gymnastics meet."

Ilika rose and busied himself helping with breakfast for the entire group. Warm sweet rolls and beverages were soon calling others out of their beds. The technical team was clearly excited, as this was their day to get everything set up, including Shawn's special microphone.

Liberty had a day of fun planned for Shawn, as they knew his father would be speaking in other cities until that evening. They ate together at a small table, chatting and laughing as they looked at tourist brochures.

For everyone else, the day passed slowly. Whenever there was no meal to help prepare, or meeting to attend, Ilika pondered the mystery of why it was proving so difficult to figure out the details of their mission.

*

Despite everything Liberty could do for Shawn, all evening and all night long, he staggered into the common room the next morning like he was going to his own funeral.

"How did you sleep?" Sister Rachael asked while carrying a bowl of fruit.

"This is all my fault! How can everybody be so nice to me?"

"Brother Shawn, you are NOT your father, never were, and never will be. God gave us all free will. Your fellow Lyceum members know it. Even your father's religion knows it, although it is conveniently forgotten sometimes. Are you smart enough to keep your guilty feeling from interfering with the work we must do today, work that is necessary to save Lyceum from huge political and legal problems?"

Liberty caught up with Shawn and slipped a protective arm around him, then looked into his face with all the tenderness she could muster.

Shawn breathed deeply and tried to relax. "You're right. I guess . . . if my father wasn't attacking Lyceum . . . some other religious . . . um . . . fanatic . . . would be. I'm sorry. I'm just not used to being treated so . . . so much like an adult."

Rachael smiled. "You should have seen what Sarah went through when she became a member at seven, and then found out she had all the rights and most of the responsibilities of any other member!"

Lyceum's youngest member looked up from buttering sweet rolls.

Sister Rachael walked toward a table where the technical team was eating, leaving Shawn and Liberty to get their breakfast.

✳

An hour later, Shawn was given a thin device to put in his shirt pocket, and soon the entire team filed out of the building and began the short walk to the stadium.

At several points along the way, they split into smaller and smaller groups, each taking a slightly different route. By the time they arrived, they were in groups of no more than five, groups which seemed, to any observer, to not know each other.

The stadium held about ten thousand people, and it was expected to be filled to capacity by the event. As Shawn entered, he could see the television cameras in the media alcoves, and the platform where his father would speak, elegantly decorated with draperies and flowers.

The seats very near the speaker's platform were already filled, and Shawn was glad, feeling the need for as much distance from his father as possible. He felt Liberty tug his hand, and realized he had no idea where to go. They followed the security team, dressed in very casual clothes to disguise their purpose, up a stairway. He glimpsed Sarah ahead of them, and Ashley and Ilika behind. The group moved into an area of empty seats at about the same level as the speaker's platform. Shawn struggled with himself for a moment, his legs almost moving to seats at a lower level against his will.

A soft but strong hand pulled him along a row, Liberty took a seat, and he took the next. Ashley got the next seat, then Ilika. The large men in the row in front all looked familiar.

Another twenty minutes passed as everyone found seats. A choir began to sing, and the Lyceum technical team leader, seated just behind Shawn, used a small hand-held device to adjust a piece of equipment hidden amongst the other fixtures on the ceiling. Sarah, next to him, watched his progress while she listened, with her ears and her mind, to the many emotions in the huge room.

Sister Rachael looked around with keen eyes. She saw several policemen, but knew they would stay near the doors unless violence erupted. The private security people, however, were everywhere, but luckily showed no awareness of Shawn's presence. Sarah silently informed her that the equipment was ready.

✳

The Reverend Tommy Mitchell walked out onto his platform and began to speak.

"My fellow citizens, let us pray."

Pride welled up inside Shawn. His father, a famous and respected religious leader, was masterfully leading the opening prayer, just as Shawn had heard him do so many times before. Ten thousand people had their heads bowed, and unknown millions more watched from their homes. The prayer avoided any words that would offend anyone and cause the reverend to lose votes. Shawn was deeply impressed.

During the next twenty minutes, Reverend Mitchell spoke eloquently on topics that were always popular. Shawn was transfixed, and completely forgot why he was there. He was even beginning to feel like he was back in his father's good graces. What, he tried to remember, were the names of those seminaries his father wanted him to consider?

But Sister Rachael, and most other Lyceum members, observed a carefully planned progression of topics, starting with the nature of Good, moving on to the nature of Evil, shifting to specific categories of Evil, and even now beginning to focus on specific Evils. He had only one more step to make, the small leap to talking about evil places, and it would begin. They listened intently.

He made the last transition slowly, carefully, and hardly anyone in the stadium was aware that he wasn't still talking about wonderful things. When he finally did take that last step, he did it in a most subtle and clever manner, starting with an evil place that everyone could agree on.

"Fellow citizens, we live in a free society. I wouldn't want it any other way. But occasionally places of such obvious evil spring up, no one can deny that they *must* not be tolerated. The factories where chemical and biological weapons are still being created, those are evil places!"

Murmurs of agreement ran through the stadium.

"The abortion clinics around the world where babies are killed every minute of every day!"

The agreement of voices was not universal, but the majority made itself heard.

"And, my fellow citizens, a place called Lyceum where adults and even children do the Devil's work by building shrines and chapels to false gods, by worshipping *science* instead of God, and supporting its immoral activities!"

Shawn saw red. His heart pounded as he sat glaring at his father. He had expected to take this moment calmly, but now he bristled. His father was talking about Liberty and Ashley, Brother Jacob and Sister Rachael. Shawn jumped to his feet.

Someone nearby pressed two buttons, and suddenly Shawn was lit up in a shaft of warm light. He could hear himself breathing, and knew his microphone had been activated. He spoke, slowly and seriously, and ten thousand people and a dozen television cameras turned to look at him.

"You are speaking ill of my home, father. I'd like to answer those charges."

The Reverend Tommy Mitchell turned his head slowly and looked at Shawn with an icy stare. The entire stadium was silent, waiting for the reverend to respond, but all he did was make some hand signals to an assistant behind him.

The assistant spoke into his headset, and a technician in the control room worked fervently at a control panel behind a glass window. Several lights went off and on, but the spotlight remained on Shawn. The technician spread his arms and shrugged.

The reverend made more hand signals, this time in front of him where everyone could see, and security guards began to converge on Shawn's position from several directions. The Lyceum security team waited until they were almost upon him, then suddenly stood and locked arms. The reverend's men were forced to either stop short or start a fight. Without further instructions, they chose to stop.

"Let him talk!" someone yelled from across the arena.

"He's your son!" someone else said.

"We want to hear him!" a third voice said.

Shawn's heart pounded. He recognized at least two of the voices who had just spoken, but he was breathing too fast to smile or laugh. Words started coming to his mind.

"I was moved by your prayer, and the first part of your talk, Father. It was excellent. Why did you have to stoop to fabricating lies about a respected international service organization that does nothing but good in the world?"

The reverend's men stepped back a little, as they had received no further instructions, and the Lyceum security team took a lower profile so Shawn could be seen.

"Talk to us, Reverend!" someone yelled.

"Yeah!" several other voices echoed.

"Then why didn't you stay in that evil place?" the reverend finally burst out, "where even the children enact *pagan* rituals!"

Shawn could feel every hair on his body standing on end, every muscle tightening. But words kept coming, so he spoke them, loudly and clearly.

"Yes, father, it so happens that I'm friends with the youngest two members of Lyceum. Sarah's so-called *pagan* ritual is called BALLET DANCING! Ashley does GYMNASTICS!"

Ashley blushed as a rumble of laughter ran through the audience.

Shawn caught the mood of the audience and ran with it. "But Sarah doesn't do ballet dancing *all* the time. Often she can he found in the gardens feeding the GOLDFISH!"

Sarah grinned. The entire stadium was now talking and laughing.

The reverend's amplified voice cut through and silenced everyone. "You will *never* be welcome in our church again! You are not worthy to call yourself a man of God!"

Shawn's face suddenly became burning hot, and he knew what he had to say.

"On the other hand, you, father, will always be welcome at Lyceum. And ALL of you out there are welcome. I invite you to come and see for yourselves. Walk in our gardens, worship in our chapels and shrines, stay in our lodge, play in our gym or pool. Look for the Devil anywhere you want. Yes, you will find people with different skin colors. You will find people who speak different languages. You will even find people who have different names for God. But you will not find the Devil unless you bring him with you!"

The entire audience was roaring now, and the Reverend Tommy Mitchell would tolerate no more. He made a sweeping motion and then a chopping sign to the technician, who turned and went all the way to the very back of the control room, found the largest lever, and with two hands, pulled it.

✳

Within a second the huge stadium was pitch dark. Two seconds after that, people began screaming.

In the dim glow of emergency lights, Ilika could see the security team trying to resist the stampede of people from the seats above, but without complete success. He saw Liberty fiercely guarding Shawn, and he glimpsed Ashley bravely face a group of screaming, bolting teenagers.

A moment later, a large man crashed into Ilika, he felt himself falling, and saw no more.

✳

Manessa immediately knew when Ilika lost consciousness. In a viewing lounge near the recreation center, where the crew had been watching the rally, five mission bracelets screamed. Less than a minute later, Kibi was the first one into the ship, with the rest right on her heels.

"Manessa, emergency departure!" Kibi commanded.

"I'm sorry, Kibi, but I cannot do that."

"Says *who?*" Kibi questioned, breathing fast.

"Arantiloria."

"Arantiloria, get your purple-haired carcass in here!" Kibi nearly screamed.

When the training specialist appeared a second later, she couldn't decide whether to frown or smile.

"Ilika's hurt!" Kibi gasped between breaths.

"I know that, Kibi. How, exactly, do you intend to help him? He's inside a building filled with people, and police and rescue workers are arriving. Many people are hurt much worse, and three have already died. How will a deep-space response ship aid the situation?"

Kibi, red-faced, glared at her training supervisor and tried to catch her breath, but couldn't find any words to speak.

"I see what you're saying," Sata said in the silence that lingered. "If we went, we'd just cause more fear and confusion."

Boro nodded.

Mati frowned. "But what if Ilika needs medical care these people can't provide?"

"I will watch over him, I promise," Arantiloria said in a soothing voice, "and if he needs the care only a star station can give, Manessa will be notified immediately."

Kibi struggled to regain her breath and composure.

"To be the best commander you can be," the training specialist continued, "you need to do something right now, don't you, Kibi?"

Kibi breathed several more times before speaking. "Yeah. Boro, you're in command. I just wanna curl up and cry."

Boro accepted with a nod.

Mati put her arms around Kibi. "You can cry all you need to, and one of us will be with you every minute."

✴ ✴ ✴

Chapter 34: Friendship

Two days later, the Lyceum team made their way home from the last televised rally of Reverend Tommy Mitchell's presidential campaign. With five people dead, seventy-nine injured, and the local prosecutor preparing to file charges, there would be no more rallies, and no more campaign.

Shawn, only scraped and bruised, helped Liberty off the helicopter, careful not to bump her right arm that rested in a sling. Ilika came next, the side of his head still red and a little swollen. Ashley came behind, watching to make sure Ilika was steady on his feet.

Kibi, behind others in the heliport lobby, had to fight all her instincts to avoid rushing forward and embracing Ilika. When she felt tears coming, she quickly strode away down the corridor and back into the Manessa Kwi. Sata followed her to the lower deck and sat with her while she cried and fumed with frustration.

*

After a long nap and a check-up at the clinic, Ilika activated his bracelet light as soon as he entered the woods. Kibi quickly met him, and together they walked slowly to their secret grove.

"This is the second time you've . . ."

She silenced him with her lips on his, gently at first, until she was sure it wasn't causing him any pain. Finally she looked at him in the faint twilight. "I didn't like the idea of being separated from you when this mission started, and I like it less with each passing day. When are we going to do what we came to do, and go home?"

Ilika chuckled slightly. "If I had to guess, I'd say . . . when we least expect it."

Kibi moaned. "I was afraid of that."

She listened while Ilika recounted every detail of the trip, and concluded with his opinion that no one, mortal or spiritual, could have devised a better outcome than the natural consequences of the Reverend Mitchell's own actions.

Kibi grinned in the darkness. "Hopefully Shawn will feel more grown-up now. I had some growing up to do myself."

"Thanks for not blowing my cover."

"Me and purple-hair had some words, and she had to *promise* me she'd keep two eyes on you."

"She did, and told me that if I didn't get better very quickly, you'd be on your way, by foot if necessary."

Kibi nodded and laughed.

＊

The warm days of summer passed slowly as the members of Lyceum resumed their routine tasks and projects. Shawn was very proud to return the dedication Liberty had shown him, helping her with anything she needed, including writing for her classes and cleaning her room. They were rarely apart, except during work shifts. Liberty learned to brush horses and donkeys with her left hand, and continued her piloting theory classes, but couldn't begin flight training.

＊

Ashley did well in all her classes and work assignments, spent many long hours in the gym training for the World Championships the following year, and gave every remaining minute to her friend Jenny. One morning, she arrived at the recording studio a few minutes late.

"Now that I've heard all seven voices," Brother Chad was saying, "I'm starting to get a sense of how important this symphony is. Hi, Ashley. But there's no way anyone but *you* can get it all scored properly."

Jenny smiled at Ashley, who pulled a chair close.

"Shall we start by cleaning up a few places in Voice Seven that didn't feel right?"

"Yes, please!"

They all gathered around the large display screen of the editing computer. Brother Chad had the computer play a few bars. "Any problems there?"

"Sounds okay to me," Jenny said.

"Me too," Chad said.

Ashley just smiled, knowing when music sounded good, but not why.

The computer played a few more bars.

"I was wondering about this area here . . ." Chad began.

"Yeah. Something's wrong. It's too slow. Um . . . all those notes in bars thirty-five to thirty-seven should be quarter notes."

"Yes, I was thinking something like that too," he said, tapping in the changes.

The computer replayed it, and Jenny nodded with satisfaction.

The process continued for the next forty-five minutes, then they took a break. Ashley hugged Jenny and headed for gymnastics. Jenny and Chad munched on cookies while listening to the cleaned-up version of Voice Seven.

When it ended, Jenny had a contented look on her face. All seven voices, in isolation from each other, had now been recorded, to the best of her ability. That felt very, very good.

"Now comes the hard part," Brother Chad admitted with a serious tone. "Do you know how far into the symphony all seven voices are in perfect sync, in my opinion?"

"How far?"

"Five bars."

Jenny looked sad.

"Yes, we have a lot of work to do." He caused the musical notations for all seven voices to be displayed together, one on top of the other. Then he had the computer play the five bars he felt were properly aligned. "Do you like what you hear so far?"

"Gosh. I've never heard it all together before."

"So we're going to have to use your musical insight and my musical knowledge."

Jenny frowned. "I *think* it's right so far . . ."

Then he had the computer play the next five bars. The corresponding notes turned blue on the screen.

"Something's wrong in bar seven!" she declared.

"You can hear it too? Remember our agreement — you always have to tell me what you think before I make any suggestions."

"Um . . . I think it's Voice Five. It's slipping behind."

"Do I shorten this note?" Chad asked.

"No. Take out the rest at the end of bar four."

He did, and the ten bars replayed.

"Wow . . ." Chad breathed as he looked at Jenny with wide eyes and a big smile.

Jenny was smiling too. Her life dream was starting to come true. She was going to hear all the voices of her music played together . . . if she lived long enough to make the necessary corrections.

They continued working until Jenny was exhausted from the mental effort and could no longer think.

"Let's end with a final playback, and we'll start tomorrow by making any needed corrections in this part before moving on."

Jenny listened. She couldn't believe she had played the music she was hearing. In a sense she hadn't. Only the computer, or seven musicians, could play it all together. And yet all of the voices came from her — or *through* her. She knew with certainty that she had not composed the music, although she couldn't say who had.

"There's something in about the middle that bothers me a little."

"Sleep on it. We'll look at it tomorrow."

*

A few days later, at dinner, while passing the big bowl of mashed potatoes, Liberty asked Ashley if she had time to go on a walk that evening. Shawn was at work somewhere, and Liberty felt the need for a little girl-to-girl time.

Ashley frowned slightly, but somehow sensed that she needed to be there for Liberty, at least on this occasion. She quickly let the frown melt. "That would be fun, Chelsea! I could use a break from other things, too."

Ashley didn't reveal that she'd have to skip a class.

✳

An hour later, Sarah was in her room alternately gazing out the window and drawing little dancers on a sheet of paper. She hoped they would be good enough to use on the poster for the upcoming Junior Dance Festival.

Sarah drew another dancer, this time a boy ballet dancer. She thought that was only fair, as the festival would include both girls and boys. Then her pencil stopped moving, her eyes glazed over, and her skin became cold and sweaty. A face came into focus, a man's face almost completely hidden behind a bush, and then a black metal thing in front of the face, a gun, lifted up to his eye level. Her heart pounded, and suddenly she saw Liberty and Ashley walking in one of the gardens, and knew the gun was pointed at Liberty.

CHELSEA, DUCK! she screamed with her mind with more force than she had ever used in sending a telepathic message.

Liberty didn't receive a thought she could ponder at her leisure. It was more like the impact of a hammer, and she could do nothing but drop to the ground and clutch her head in pain.

At the same moment, Ashley heard the whizzing sound of something fly by at high speed, then the *ping* of it hitting a stone fountain nearby.

RUN, CHELSEA, RUN! the next thought screamed inside her head. With nothing but raw instinct guiding her, Liberty jumped up and ran.

Ashley was right beside her. "Someone shot at us!" The winding path took them toward the residence hall. "Let's get inside!"

Liberty's half-healed arm began throbbing with pain, but unlike Ashley, she didn't have the spare breath to say anything.

Together they ran along the path and soon burst into the small parking lot beside the residence hall. They kept running, side by side, and were about halfway across the lot when Ashley focused on a man in a suit standing right beside the door. Ashley didn't recognize him, but saw him pull something out from under his coat and raise it to his eye level.

No one points a gun at my friend! she said to herself, and immediately used the only weapon she had.

Liberty, just beginning to wonder who the man was, saw Ashley suddenly double her speed. Then she saw the gun and screamed, "ASHLEY!"

But Ashley had already launched herself into the air just a few yards away from the stranger and was curling herself into a tumbling mass of fury. Liberty saw Ashley collide with the man, heard the gun go off, and saw them both fly through the large window. The sound of shattering glass filled the air. Liberty kept running, but tears quickly filled her eyes and she could barely see.

By the time Liberty got inside the residence hall a few seconds later, everything had come to rest. Glass was everywhere, the man lay still with his head at a funny angle, and Ashley was sprawled on the floor with glass under her, glass on top of her, and a pool of blood rapidly forming around her.

Liberty gasped for air and tried to scream for help, but nothing would come out of her mouth. She managed to see a fire alarm through her tears, dashed to it, and pulled with all her might until lights started flashing and an alarm began to scream. Then she ran to her friend.

Ashley lay still, with blood pouring from her face and neck and arms. With every heartbeat, more of the precious red liquid came flowing out. Liberty knew she had to stop the blood. Somehow she had to keep her friend from bleeding to death, and she had nothing to work with but her own hands, and they were shaking. Tears made it hard to see, and she couldn't keep her breath from coming in desperate gasps. But none of that mattered. Liberty forced herself to focus on the problem, picked the two worst gashes, and placed her trembling hands over them, ignoring the pain in her right arm. The blood seemed to slow, but there were many other cuts still letting Ashley's life flow into the carpet beneath her. "Help!" Liberty screamed, but still couldn't make much sound come out. "Help!"

Seconds later, others ran into the room and helped put pressure on Ashley's many cuts. Liberty couldn't remember ever feeling so relieved, but knew that even if bullets were flying at her, she was not going to leave Ashley's side.

※　※　※

Chapter 35: Understanding

When Ashley first awoke, she didn't immediately open her eyes. An instinct told her to take it slowly, just as she did in the gym, after coming in from the cold, during warm-ups and stretching.

She knew she was in a comfortable bed. Some machine nearby was humming and beeping softly. A loudspeaker somewhere called a doctor to the operating room.

Carefully opening her eyes, Ashley saw a nurse sitting beside the bed looking at the beeping machine and taking notes on a clipboard.

"Hi, there! How do you feel?"

"Meat slicer . . . I was the meat."

The nurse chuckled. "Don't try to move, as you've got lots of bandages, and you'll need help for a while. There are some people in the waiting room, if you feel like visitors . . ."

"Sure."

Ashley's mother was the first one in the door, but her legs gave out when she beheld her daughter completely wrapped in bandages, save for two eyes peering out. Luckily, Ashley's father caught her.

While her father helped her mother into a chair, Brother Jacob, Sister Rachael, Sarah, Liberty, and Ilika all gathered around the bed.

"Hi, guys!" Ashley said in greeting.

They all waved and said embarrassing things about Ashley's courage, and expressed wishes for her quick recovery. Liberty, however, remained silent, clearly fighting back tears.

Finally, when everyone else had had plenty of time to speak, Liberty cleared her throat. "Um . . . I haven't done this yet because I wanted you to hear it, Ashley." She turned and knelt on the floor in front of Ashley's mother and father. "It happened because . . . someone was trying to kill me . . . and Ashley saved my life. Please, if you're mad at anybody, you should be mad at me. And if there's anything I can ever do for her . . . or for you . . . I'll do it . . . no matter what it takes."

They were deeply touched. The woman just wiped at her eyes, so her husband spoke. "We raised Ashley to always do the right thing, even when that required a personal sacrifice. It looks like . . ." He paused to deal with mixed feelings. "It looks like we succeeded."

Liberty hung her head, until Ashley's mother reached out and touched her on the shoulder.

At that moment, a nurse entered. "There's a sheriff here to interview Ashley. I told him he had to keep it short and simple."

"You feel up to it, Ashley?" Brother Jacob asked.

"Sure. I even feel ready for a good workout in the gym!"

Everyone chuckled nervously with cringes of pain at the thought.

*

"We've examined the scene, and we've already interviewed everyone else, so I just have a few quick questions to complete my investigation."

Brother Jacob sat down nearby.

"When you were running beside Chelsea toward the door, what made you decide the man standing there was a danger?"

"He was aiming a gun at Chelsea."

"Were you sure it was a gun?"

"I was as sure as I could be."

He wrote in his notebook for a moment. "I have to ask this next question, even though I can find out from public records. Have you ever killed anyone before, Ashley?"

Ashley glanced at Sister Rachael.

"You only have to answer if you want to, Ashley."

Ashley looked troubled. "I don't mind answering. No, I haven't. But . . . did I kill someone this time?"

Brother Jacob answered. "The man broke his neck when he went through the window, Ashley. However, what you did is not a crime, because you were defending yourself and another person."

Ashley wasn't listening. She was crying softly and wishing she could curl up in a little ball and hide somewhere. She had never imagined, in her wildest dreams, that she would ever kill someone with her gymnastics skills.

As soon as the sheriff stepped back, Sarah came over to the side of the bed and took Ashley's hand. "I've never been tested like that . . . but I hope that if I ever am, I make the right choice . . . like you did."

Ashley's father joined Sarah. "Honey, your mother and I also feel that you made the right decision. Imagine how terrible you'd feel right now if you had stood by and watched your friend die."

"I'd feel ten times as bad!" Ashley wailed.

"Yes, you did the right thing," her mother said, finally gaining the courage to come close.

Ashley looked at her parents. "I hope and pray I made the right choice."

The sheriff was about to leave when Liberty stood up. "Sir, I need to add something to my statement."

"Of course, Chelsea."

"When you asked me if I knew who would want to kill me, I wasn't thinking very deeply. I was just thinking about myself."

"And you have a new idea?"

"Yes. You see, the name *Chelsea* is just for cover. My real name is Liberty Buchanan, and I'm Senator Michael Buchanan's daughter."

Everyone in the room could see the wheels turning in the sheriff's head.

"Okay. Now I'm beginning to see what might be going on here. So . . . the attempt on your life, Liberty, may have been an effort to influence your father."

Liberty nodded.

"And since it appears there were two men," the sheriff went on, "and one is still unaccounted for . . ."

"We're not going to let her out of our sight," Brother Jacob promised.

"Good. Way out there in the woods, there's not much the department can do."

"We understand," Sister Rachael said.

"Thank you for the additional information, Liberty . . . Chelsea," the sheriff said. He shook hands with several people, and then left with a wrinkled brow.

✳

The evening was warm and buggy, so Kibi tapped a code into her bracelet and the insects kept their distance.

News that a Lyceum member had been badly hurt, while saving another from an attempt on her life, had circulated all over the campus. Unfortunately for the crew of the Manessa Kwi, Lyceum members were very good at keeping secrets, so little more could be learned. Ilika shared the whole story.

Kibi burst out laughing.

Ilika looked at her askance.

"I'm sorry," Kibi said between chuckles and gasps. "I'm not laughing at Ashley or Chelsea. I'm laughing at us!"

Ilika joined in the humor of the situation.

"What *is* it about this mission?" she begged to know. "We just *cannot* seem to ever be in the right place at the right time!"

"I can only make a guess," Ilika began, smiling in the dark, "but it may not be worth anything because . . . I haven't had much more training at these kinds of missions than the rest of you."

"Please, make your best guess before I tear out my last remaining strand of hair!"

Ilika laughed, knowing Kibi's head was as bushy as ever. "We're used to being the most important part of a mission. When we take cargo or transport passengers somewhere, we're the only ship doing it. But this mission is different. Many other beings are involved, and the situation is very complex, with the outcome unknown to anyone, except maybe ... you know ... Melorania or Kerloran."

"Okay, I think I'm starting to see. We have *some* part to play, somewhere, sometime, but no one knows when our cue will come."

"Right. And we're in training to tell the difference between things that *are* related to the mission, and things that *aren't*. People get murdered, and people get cut up by glass, all the time. It really pulled at my heart because I went through the whole evaluation process with those two, and now they're my friends. Shawn too. But ..."

"But they're not the mission!" Kibi finished. "None of them are doing anything that's ... how did Arantiloria put it? ... that's of enduring value for the universe."

✳ ✳ ✳

Chapter 36: A Helping Hand

Liberty's life was in shambles.

Even with pain killers, her arm ached almost constantly, especially at night as she lay awake beside Shawn. Her squirming and fuming often woke him, and he'd kiss her and wrap his body around her, putting her to sleep for another hour or so, until the pain woke her again.

Her work shifts were reduced to a little helping in the office, she couldn't concentrate in her classes, and her pilot training was on hold until she could once again grip a helicopter's cyclic control with a firm and steady hand.

Shawn's tenderness kept her sane. Visiting Ashley in the hospital kept her distracted.

At other times she wandered the Lyceum campus, trying to figure out how she fit into the huge events swirling around her. The body guards were respectful, giving her as much freedom as possible, and staying out of sight whenever they could. Her father had promised to visit as soon as he was able, and she looked forward to telling him all her thoughts and questions, and listening to his wisdom.

After watching a flight depart for the international airport, Liberty wandered into the Pad Two hanger, dark and silent until she turned on the lights. Lyceum's oldest helicopter perched on the floor, like a sleeping raven, facing the big door. Years ago, she knew, it had been their transport craft, but it only held six passengers, and their two newer birds each seated twenty. She would get to fly it someday, when she was comfortable in the little two-seat trainer.

She nearly jumped out of her skin when suddenly Sister Nancy burst through the door and began doing the fastest pre-flight inspection on record. Several people came behind, flung open the helicopter's passenger door, and began tossing equipment bags and med kits inside.

"Emergency start in thirty seconds!" Nancy yelled as she punched the hanger door control.

Liberty stepped back out of the way, wondering what was happening, but quite sure no one had time to tell her.

Nancy hopped into the pilot's seat, completed the start-up procedure from memory, and the twin jet engines roared to life about when she had promised.

By this time, several other Lyceum members were present, some handing additional equipment to the team in the passenger area, others connecting the towing tractor at the front of the aircraft.

Nancy hopped back out even as the tractor began pulling the aircraft outside. She looked around at all the people present, cursed, then looked at Liberty. "Chelsea, in the co-pilot's seat! I need a pair of eyes on radar!"

Liberty swallowed but didn't hesitate. By the time the helicopter was on the pad and the towing tractor was moving away, both Nancy and Liberty were in their seats.

While the rotor began to turn and everyone on the ground scattered to safety, Nancy taught Liberty how to use the radar console in one minute flat with a stream of verbal instructions.

Liberty's mind raced as she touched controls and struggled to remember everything else. The device was just warming up as Nancy pulled the collective lever and the large helicopter took to the air.

*

Sister Rebecca stood just inside the hanger, watching with pride as more than a dozen Lyceum members, all trained in helicopter air or ground operations, worked together smoothly in the heat of an actual emergency.

Sata appeared at her side. "Anything . . . we can do to help?"

The Lyceum elder looked at the twelve-year-old mission leader from another world, considered the situation for about two more seconds, then spoke. "Someone very important to the future of our planet is on a small jet plane. An engine blew up just as they were crossing the mountains. Other things are falling apart — too many things. It looks like sabotage. No official rescue operation can act fast enough to make a difference. Our helicopter may get there in time, but a rescue will be tricky and dangerous. If you can help, and you are willing, please do so."

Sata blinked once, then tapped a code into her bracelet that would bring all crew members to the Manessa Kwi as fast as their legs could carry them.

*

Boro was the first one into the ship after pressing the hanger door control. He remembered that he was in command, looked at the command chair, then stopped and frowned. The emergency departure code was only used for real emergencies. Someone needed to be at the helm who knew what they were doing, and the same at engineering. He knew Ilika wasn't involved in the emergency, as Boro had just seen their captain vacuuming carpets near the cafeteria.

Kibi flew through the hatch.

"You're in command," Boro asserted as he sat down at engineering.

Sata dashed in, took the navigators seat, and began looking for the radio frequency Sister Rebecca had given her.

Rini jumped in and brought his station to life.

Mati arrived last, saw that the ship needed a pilot, and provided one.

Arantiloria appeared at the steward's station.

Kibi glanced behind her. "Thanks."

"Ship secure, hatch closed," the purple-haired training specialist reported.

"Take us out, Mati," Kibi began, "while Sata tells us what we're doing."

Mati didn't have to say a word. She glanced at her display, saw anti-mass drive and maneuvering thrusters ready, ion drive warming, charts from here to the mountains, and a weather map. She studied the current weather as she reached for her flight control.

✳

"Recalibrate and wide-scan," Sister Nancy commanded as she pushed the helicopter at full power over the first mountain ridge.

Liberty could feel beads of sweat tingling her skin as she tapped at the radar controls.

"The pilot reports they're in the river gorge heading north," a voice came over the radio. "I know that canyon, and there's no way out except right down to the bottom where it empties out into the lowlands, and it gets pretty twisty before that point."

"That's where they'll have trouble," Nancy replied. "I'm switching to the emergency channel now."

"Nothing on radar yet," Liberty reported. "Who are we rescuing?"

Sister Nancy was silent for a long moment, torn between telling Liberty now, and letting her find out at a more critical time.

"Your father. And I need you calm, cool, and collected in one minute flat."

Suddenly Liberty's fingers were shaking too much to operate the radar, and her eyes quickly became too wet to see the screen. *Please be okay, Daddy. Please, if there's a god up there somewhere, please let my daddy be okay.*

Then she remembered Shawn's arms holding her at night, and she somehow found the courage to clench her shaking fingers and wipe her tears onto her sleeve.

"Radar contact!" Liberty nearly screamed a few moments later. "Bearing eighty-six, elevation . . . minus two."

"Damn!" Nancy spat. "There's no way they can get out of the canyon before the curves." She pressed her transmit button. "This is rescue zulu three-seven-eight to aircraft in distress. What's your status?"

The first few words were spoken in a foreign language, but the pilot quickly realized his mistake. "One engine only, oil losing. Please, where we can land?"

✳

As Sata shared everything she knew, Mati quickly took them to four thousand meters so they could look down on the situation.

"But I have to admit," Sata added with a wrinkled brow as she spun around and looked at Kibi, "just because Sister Rebecca thought Senator Buchanan was important, doesn't make it our mission."

Kibi took on a thoughtful expression. "It doesn't even mean she's *right*. He could be ... you know ... just important to *her*, or something she believes in."

The commander didn't see the training specialist smile.

After sending a weather update to all stations, Rini swiveled his chair. "Or ... she could be right, but that doesn't mean saving him is the best thing to do."

Mati frowned, touched the position-lock symbol, and leaned back. "But we don't have enough information to know, one way or the other ..."

Boro cleared his throat. "But someone's right here who probably *does* know," he said, turning slowly until he was looking at the steward's station.

The rest of the crew also looked at Arantiloria.

She looked back with sparkling eyes that made them all nearly dizzy. "*Now* I see why Melorania likes you guys so much, and scheduled you for advanced training so soon. You learn quickly, and your strong bonds allow you to think collectively."

Kibi frowned slightly. "Thanks, but unless you know something we don't, we're gonna rescue Senator Buchanan as a favor to Lyceum, to Sister Rebecca and Liberty, even though it may not be our mission ..."

"But it so happens," the training specialist interrupted, "that *any* interference in the current life-path of Senator Buchanan would be very bad for the political development of this planet."

All five crew members shrank into their seats with glum faces.

"But ... this planet *would* be better-off if Liberty Buchanan survived this flight, which, without your help, will not be the case."

"Now *that's* something we can sink our teeth into!" Boro asserted, turned to his console, and made sure every engine Mati might need was ready.

*

"Aircraft in distress, prepare for in-flight evacuation," Sister Nancy ordered.

"I no understand."

Nancy sighed. "Slow down, full flaps, get your rear cabin door open, and get ready to grab rescue ladders!"

"Okay."

During the next minute, with Nancy pushing the helicopter to its limits and beyond, it finally began to catch up with the crippled jet, whose one working engine was starting to smoke. Suddenly the jet's rear door opened and was immediately torn off by the wind.

Just then the canyon curved sharply and both pilots were forced to bank.

"Damn!" Nancy cursed. "We're in the curves. It's gonna take a miracle. Get ready back there, I may only have one shot ..."

The rescue team in the back of the helicopter slid open their door and prepared to toss out rope ladders.

The small jet followed another curve in the canyon, but before it had leveled out, its remaining engine burst into flames.

"No!" Nancy screamed. "Five hundred feet and dropping fast. One chance. Here it comes!"

She drove the helicopter over the jet's tail section.

Rope ladders came tumbling down.

A rocky cliff loomed directly ahead and the jet's pilot tried desperately to bank his aircraft, but his stall alarm was already screaming and his wings wouldn't respond.

Nancy saw the cliff and jerked back on her cyclic control. The helicopter started shaking violently and a moment later was dropping like a rock.

The last thing Liberty saw was the little jet slamming into the rock wall and bursting into flames. Then the helicopter suddenly gained several thousand feet in a heartbeat and everything went black.

✳

"I hope they had inertia canceling," Mati said after lifting the helicopter to a safe altitude.

Before she finished speaking, broken rotor blades and other parts came raining down from above the Manessa Kwi.

"I . . . don't . . . think . . . so," Boro muttered slowly.

"Let's get whatever's left of it back to Lyceum," Kibi said, "and see if we saved *anyone*. No ion drive, low-inertia flight."

Mati and Boro nodded. Sata quickly plotted a course that would keep them below the ridge lines as much as possible.

"You okay grappling those struts for that distance, Manessa?" Kibi asked.

"Yes."

Kibi glanced behind her.

Arantiloria smiled.

✳   ✳   ✳

Chapter 37: Coming Home

When Sister Nancy awoke, she was already in a stretcher and was about to be whisked away to the clinic. She demanded they stop so she could learn what had happened to Liberty and the rescue team.

Overhearing, Sister Rachael came near and looked down at the trembling pilot. "All alive and well, except for some bumps and bruises. Like you, they all experienced acceleration black-out, so the docs are going to do some tests and keep a close watch for a couple of days."

Nancy thanked the older member with her eyes, then turned her head to look at the helicopter. Its battered fuselage, broken rotor, and missing tail somewhat resembled a dead chicken. "Vortex ring state — we were falling. How did we survive?"

Sister Rachael raised her eyebrows. "Guardian angels?"

"You mean our friends on Pad Three?"

Rachael nodded.

*

Late that evening, Kibi slipped through the darkness to find Ilika waiting in their secret grove. They shared a deep kiss before either spoke. She carefully felt his head, and found the swelling almost gone.

"For eight wonderful minutes," Kibi began with a mixture of humor and frustration, "we thought we had discovered the mission. Then purple-hair had to ruin it with, you know, reality."

Ilika laughed. "She has a nick-name for you, too, and it's also about your hair."

"What!"

"You'll have to ask her. But believe me, she's deeply impressed by you, is very glad we're together, and likes the whole crew, especially after today."

Kibi glowed for a moment. "But we didn't save that senator, Chelsea's father, and we broke the helicopter."

"And saved six lives."

"Well ... yeah ..." Kibi said as she squirmed. Then she spoke more firmly, with one word coming from her native language. "But what's the damn mission?"

*

The following day, Liberty was still under observation, not to mention grieving for her father, and Shawn was at her side constantly.

That left Ilika, of Ashley's friends, to pick her up at the hospital.

Ashley, with several bandages still covering parts of her face and neck, spoke little on the flight back to Lyceum. Ilika sat beside her in companionable silence, then carried her suitcase to her room.

As soon as he was gone, she hurried to the hospice center, where she found a doctor at Jenny's bedside.

"Hi, Ashley!" Jenny whispered. "I heard you got a bunch of cuts."

"Yeah. They'll heal, but no gymnastics for me for a while! What happened to you?"

Jenny looked at the doctor.

"Hello, Ashley, I'm Brother Kenneth. Jenny has already given me permission to tell you everything. Her immune system is failing, and she has pneumonia, one of the more difficult strains, so we've had to fill her with antibiotics."

"Will that ... allow her to work on her music?"

"Maybe a little, for short sessions, with lots of support from the clinic, good nutrition, and you at her side. But she tells me there's another problem." He looked at Jenny.

"I'm starting to hear it, all of it, all the time, and I can't separate out the voices anymore. It's like ... wherever it's coming from, they've decided time's up, and if I haven't done something with it by now, I never will."

✳ ✳ ✳

Chapter 38: Angels

At breakfast the next morning, someone sitting near Ilika mumbled that Ashley seemed to be deeply troubled by something, but wouldn't talk about it. The member glanced at him, knowing they were friends.

In Ilika's language class, the gymnastics coach, also a non-native speaker, whispered in confidence that Ashley had wandered by the gym and looked terrible. He assured Ilika he wasn't referring to her cuts and bandages.

In the kitchen, where Ilika was slicing celery and carrots just before lunch, young Sarah appeared, opposite his cutting board, with a worried expression. "Ashley's in the dumps, won't talk to me, and I can't read her. Whatever it is, she's keeping it bottled up inside. And Chelsea and Shawn are, you know, just into each other right now."

Ilika nodded, finished his work, grabbed a slice of bread, and headed for the door to the residence hall.

No response came to his repeated knocks upon Ashley's door.

He strode to the gym.

There had been no sign of Ashley since her brief appearance hours before.

Ilika stood in the recreation center lobby and sighed, then realized who he needed to ask.

He was glad to find Shawn in the clinic waiting room. Liberty came out a few minutes later.

"I'm off observation! And I can get rid of the cast and sling in another week."

Ilika smiled. "I've had acceleration black-out before, *and* a broken arm, but luckily not at the same time. By the way, I can't find Ashley in any of the usual places."

"Have you tried the hospice center? Room fifteen."

Ilika frowned.

"*She's* not dying," Shawn said quickly. "It's a friend from her hometown."

Ilika breathed deeply, thanked the young couple, and strode out of the clinic.

Ilika found the door ajar, so he knocked, then slipped in when Ashley waved.

The girl in bed looked peaceful but weak. Ilika sensed she was not fighting her approaching fate.

"Jenny, this is Ilika, a very nice man from my evaluation group."

"Hi," Jenny whispered without any strength or joy.

"Chelsea liked him before she found out he wasn't interested. It's a good thing, because she and Shawn are *so* perfect for each other."

Jenny nodded.

"Jenny, can I borrow Ashley for a few minutes? I need to talk to her about something important."

"Sure," she whispered. "I feel like a nap."

Ashley kissed Jenny on the forehead, then went out with Ilika, leaving the door ajar. She spotted the nurse-on-duty, gave her an update of Jenny's mood, and promised to be back soon.

"Take as long as you need, Ashley."

Ashley nodded, but Ilika could sense that she intended to return soon. They strolled into a nearby garden.

"Lots of people are worried about you, and I've been elected to make sure you're okay, and getting whatever support you need."

Ashley half-smiled. "I'm okay. I mean . . . I know my face is all torn up, and I can't do any gymnastics for a *long* time, and my best friend is dying with her only dream slipping away, but . . . you know . . . I'll survive."

Ilika was silent for a long moment. "Somehow . . . you need to let people take care of *you*, now and then, or you won't have anything to give to your dying friend."

"I know. It's just . . . I was taught that when God puts an important task in your face, you don't run away from it. You jump in and do it . . . and finish it . . . whatever it takes. And . . . I really believe that. It just . . . feels right."

"I know . . . and I agree."

"But . . . I *can't* finish this one, even though it's the most important thing I've ever been asked to do."

Ilika frowned with confusion. "From what I hear, you're giving nearly all your time to Jenny. Is there any hope of recovery, or even giving her a little more time?"

Ashley looked up at the sky. "No."

"What more can you expect of yourself?"

Ashley sighed. "You don't understand. I'd like to go back and be with Jenny now." She started to take a step.

"So what if you *can* finish this task that God has given you, but it requires someone else's help, and you're too stubborn to ask for that help? Are you willing to admit that to Jenny?"

Ashley froze and started silently crying where she stood. "I've . . . never liked . . . leaning on anyone else. It's . . . part of being a gymnast. You have to . . . build your own strength . . . your own skill . . . you can't rely on others . . ."

"But what if God has decided this task is worthy of a team effort?"

Ashley wiped her face with her fingers, slowly and carefully between bandages. She slowly sighed, then looked at Ilika again. "Jenny has a beautiful piece of music, a symphony, that she's been hearing from . . . she doesn't know where, but she hears it best when she can look up at the stars. I brought her here so she could record it, and Brother Chad in the music studio was helping her, but she's only about three-quarters done, and now she doesn't have the strength, and she can't hear the seven voices separately anymore. How could you, or anyone else, *possibly* help with that?"

Ilika didn't answer, but his eyes were open wide. After a moment of thought, he said, "Let's go back to Jenny's room."

Jenny awoke when Ashley touched her hand. Ilika knelt at Ashley's side.

"Did you have a nice nap?" Ashley asked.

Jenny nodded weakly. "Thanks for waking me. I don't need much sleep." Then she looked at Ilika.

He smiled, took one more deep breath, and touched his shirt several times just above his left elbow. "Manessa, I need to talk to Arantiloria."

Neither Jenny nor Ashley had time to be confused, for suddenly a female with purple hair appeared at the foot of Jenny's bed.

Jenny thought the new arrival might be about her own age.

Ashley recognized deep wisdom and experience, like Sister Rebecca, maybe older.

Both could see that the visitor wasn't standing or kneeling, but just floating, sometimes right over Jenny's feet.

"Are you an angel?" Jenny asked.

"Yes," Arantiloria replied. "And you're a musician!"

Jenny grinned.

"I think this is why we are here," Ilika said to his training supervisor. "We need to take Jenny to a star station for medical treatment so she can finish her symphony."

Arantiloria looked at him. "No. It's Jenny's time to rest, to have no further mortal pressures or deadlines, and to join the universe as spirit."

Ilika looked confused.

"You have, my dear monkey mammal, everything you need, on your ship, to allow Jenny's symphony to be completed."

Ashley was silently following the conversation with big, round eyes.

"But the medical supplies on Manessa are not adequate for . . ." He stopped, and his face changed expression several times. "Not . . . in the supplies on the ship . . . in the crew!"

Arantiloria nodded.

Ilika quickly tapped another code into his hidden bracelet. In the minutes that followed, the purple-haired angel hummed passages from Jenny's music. Ashley recognized them and smiled.

Suddenly the entire crew of the Manessa Kwi filed into the room and gathered around Jenny's bed. A nurse came in also, with a worried look, but stayed near the door.

"Are you all angels, too?" Jenny asked.

Sata, barely holding in tears, shook her head. "Just angels' helpers, like Ilika."

The nurse continued to listen as Ilika explained the situation to his crew, then she slipped out the door.

Mati looked at the dying girl intently. "You need . . . someone . . . who can help you . . . carry your music . . ." She paused to remember the correct word in the local language. ". . . to Heaven."

Jenny swallowed. "It's all jumbled up now, and starting to fade. I don't know if I can remember it much longer."

Mati looked at Rini and their eyes and minds locked. His heart pounded in his throat as they wordlessly shared their mutual realization of why Rini hadn't been allowed to fill his mind with classes and other distractions. Mati scooted over so Rini could kneel closer to Jenny.

Jenny looked at Rini. "You *must* be an angel, you are so handsome!" she said with a sudden burst of strength, both of voice and spirit.

"No, I'm just a boy, but I think . . . I'm here because of you. I think . . . there is a large empty space inside me . . . . . . so I can carry your music . . . to the stars . . . if you want me to . . ."

He glanced at Arantiloria, and she nodded.

At that moment, the nurse returned with Doctor Kenneth, Sister Rebecca, Brother Jacob, Rachael, Sarah, Chad from the music studio, Nancy the pilot, Liberty, and Shawn. They all found places to silently lean against the walls.

Arantiloria floated onto Jenny's bed. "With all these good people as witnesses, are you ready, Jenny, to entrust your beautiful symphony to this helper of mine, so that your music may be played and enjoyed in Heaven?"

Jenny looked at Rini again. "Yes," she whispered with little strength remaining.

"Then your life work is done, and done well."

With those words, Arantiloria became a barely-seen purple cloud that drifted over Jenny, then stretched itself toward Rini.

Rini couldn't help but close his eyes as melodies, harmonies, and rhythms began to fill his mind. He shuddered at the sheer volume of information that made up a symphony, and the vast depth of life experience that came with it, all necessary, he sensed, to correctly interpret the music.

Mati held onto his hand and his mind, and was deeply honored that she could be *his* helper at that moment, in addition to a deep-space response ship pilot and engineer.

*

Eventually, the purple cloud faded from sight, Rini and Mati opened their eyes, and Jenny whispered, "Thank you."

Then she died.

✳ ✳ ✳

Chapter 39: Mission Accomplished

In the silence that followed, tears flowed down Ashley's bandaged cheeks when she felt her dear friend's hand go limp.

Even on his knees, Rini started wobbling and Mati had to grab him so he wouldn't fall over.

Shawn bowed his head, and Liberty squeezed his hand tightly.

Sata snuggled against Boro and started crying softly.

Brother Chad sighed and rubbed his eyes.

Ilika reached for Kibi, and they held each other while watching for anyone else who needed their support.

Sarah knelt at the end of Jenny's bed and reached out to stroke the motionless feet.

Doctor Kenneth came forward and the others made room. He silently took vital signs, looked at his watch, and returned to his place.

The nurse's eyes continued to nearly bulge out of her head at what she had just witnessed.

A couple of hours later, in a small conference room with the door closed, Sister Rebecca and Brother Jacob both scanned the *six* crew members of the mysterious ship parked in one of their hangers.

"Generally, I don't care for under-cover agents," Rebecca said with stern eyes, looking right at Ilika.

"I understand," Ilika said, feeling a bit like a guilty child.

"They're usually from some government agency, fishing for any taxes we haven't paid, or anything else politically incorrect."

Ilika nodded.

"But considering where you're from . . ." She stopped and grinned.

Ilika grinned back.

"We are honored to have someone from . . . what did you call it?"

Sata knew the answer. "We're not allowed to use names you don't already know."

Ilika and Kibi both nodded.

Rebecca grinned again. "You can't blame me for trying."

The entire crew smiled.

"We are honored to have an angel's helper — is that okay? — as a member of Lyceum."

Ilika nodded.

At that moment, a knock was heard.

"That will be one of two people I asked to join us," Rebecca said as Jacob opened the door slightly.

"Come in, Brother Chad," he said, pulling it open wider.

The audio technician entered a bit shyly, still feeling the loss of his favorite musician. He stood at the head of the table, fidgeting with a small box. "Um ... this contains all the voices of Jenny's symphony, recorded separately, and the little bit of synchronizing we were able to do. I put it in several formats so hopefully you can read one of them." He reached out with the box, but wasn't sure who to give it to.

Ilika and Kibi looked at Sata.

Sata pointed to Rini.

Rini received the box like a great treasure.

Another soft knock was heard.

Jacob looked, and opened the door for Ashley. Although her bandages were fresh, her eyes remained red from crying.

"Although you will get as much time as you need to grieve," Rebecca began, "as I understand it, no one in the world, including her mother, was closer to Jenny than you, Sister Ashley."

Ashley squirmed, still not used to the title, and very unsure she deserved it.

"Since you cannot, at this time, follow your athletic profession, nor most of your work assignments, will you do us the honor of helping to plan Jenny's funeral?"

Ashley nodded slowly and took a deep breath. "I'd go crazy if I didn't find something to do. The hardest part ... will be getting Jenny's mom on a plane. She's ... very large and ... almost disabled. Maybe Sister Laura, a librarian there, can help. And I bet some of the nursing home staff will come ..."

*

After a quiet meal in the cafeteria, Ilika and his crew made their way back to the Manessa Kwi.

Mati held Rini's hand constantly, as he was so distracted by the music playing in his head, and whatever else he was seeing and hearing, that he could barely walk without stumbling and falling.

They all felt more comfortable when the hatch was closed. Rini managed to get into a chair at the big table, but couldn't keep his feet from tapping and his head from swaying with the melodies and rhythms that filled his mind.

"I'm . . . curious . . ." Sata began with a sparkle in her eyes, looking at Ilika. "How long have you known? The rest of us have been tearing out our hair . . ."

Ilika chuckled slightly. "Only about two minutes before I called Manessa, and most of that was spent getting back to Jenny's room."

"You're forgiven," the mission leader announced with a smile.

Ilika nodded his head in thanks, then spoke to the air. "Arantiloria, you have any thoughts on what needs to happen next?"

She materialized on the galley counter. "Sata knows."

After a quick roll of her eyes, which the training specialist pretended not to see, Sata spoke. "We need to get Rini somewhere he can finish Jenny's music."

Ilika looked around the table. Rini was completely lost in his head, and Mati, at his side, appeared supportive but slightly annoyed. Boro was solid and ready for action, as always. Kibi looked back at her lover like a hungry cat, ready to pounce, only held back by the needs of the moment.

"Satamia?" Ilika questioned, looking at Arantiloria.

"Just as a transfer point, then he'll go on to Kerusemia where the symphony will be prepared."

Ilika raised his eyebrows. "Rini, you and Mati will get to see the local universe capital before the rest of the crew. It makes a star station look like a little supply dome."

"What about . . . the rest of us?" Sata asked with concern.

"We'll finish our business here, then arrive in time for the first performance. Kibi and Boro, please transport Rini and Mati to Satamia. You can be back by dinner time."

Kibi thought. "Okay, Boro can cover helm and engineering, I can do the rest. We'll be back *before* dinner time."

✳

Since Ilika was a member of Lyceum *and* the captain of the Manessa Kwi, the crew was invited to eat with the members for the remainder of their stay.

At the dinner table, Liberty looked back and forth from Ilika to Kibi, but was obviously happy with the way things had turned out. Shawn, at her side, was equally happy.

For the next several days, Ashley busied herself with the funeral planning. Sister Laura made all the arrangements for getting Jenny's mother to the funeral, and never told Ashley the expenses involved. Young Sister Sarah was at Ashley's side almost constantly, helping the wounded gymnast in every way she could.

Ashley was amazed — and deeply bothered — that three hundred and forty people wanted to come to Jenny's funeral, when the dying girl had rarely received a visitor in the nursing home, other than Ashley herself.

Sister Rachael listened to the young gymnast's frustrations, and explained that it was often so with great artists.

Knowing that Rachael's paintings hung in galleries and museums, Ashley was comforted that her deceased friend might now have the same status.

Ilika and his partial crew wrapped up the classes they were taking, and met each day to talk about the many things they had learned from the mission. Kibi was especially glad to have her lover back in their cabin at night.

Ilika was glad to be back, too.

*

Upon arriving at Lyceum, Jenny's mother was invited to speak at her daughter's funeral. She immediately declined, but during breakfast on the day of the funeral, Sister Rachael overheard her mumbling to herself, seemingly pondering what words to say. Rachael quickly sent a message to Ashley to be ready for the possibility.

When the hour of the funeral arrived, most of the members of Lyceum, eight hospice center residents, eleven nurses and doctors from Jenny's home town, twenty-seven random people who had somehow heard about it, four special visitors from far away, and one mother, all made their way solemnly to the Lyceum Temple.

As they came down the aisles and could see into the open casket, they beheld no sickly invalid, but a beautiful girl just approaching the flowering of her youth, with golden shoulder-length hair and a full pink dress with accents of white lace. Flowers were tucked in around her and many more filled vases nearby. Only one thing seemed strange — one of Jenny's arms lay upon her chest, its hand empty.

As everyone found seats, Jenny's mother looked around in confusion. "Why are all these people here?"

"They all came to pay their respects to your daughter," Sister Rachael said. "Some knew her. Many have heard about her unfinished musical symphony. We're reserving time if you decide you'd like to speak . . ."

"Oh . . . no . . . I wouldn't know what to say."

A quiet passage from one of the voices of Jenny's song opened the funeral, with the laughter of children at play superimposed. After a minute, the audio faded into the background, and a nurse from Jenny's home town stood and spoke. She shared words of remembrance from her heart, and from several other nurses who could not attend.

A section of another musical voice preceded Brother Kenneth's time. He talked about how she had been willing to take any medicine, as long as she could work on her music. He spoke of how the musical voices of her symphony became tangled in her mind, and how she fought it for several days, to get a little more work done, before finally giving up.

Another melody played as lasers created musical notes that danced on the edge of the casket and finally floated away, higher and higher, until they disappeared somewhere above the highest balcony of the temple. Brother Chad stood. He had much to say about the creative power the world had lost when Jenny passed away, and he invited the listeners to imagine the many beautiful symphonies that would have been written if Jenny had been able to stay with them. He ended by describing the presence that now haunted the music studio, a presence that, at least for him, would never be forgotten.

Everyone listened to the melody line of Ashley's favorite part. The young gymnast finally had all her bandages off, but the scars that remained were visible to all, even with make-up. She talked about the things Jenny liked to do other than work on her music, such as take walks in any kind of weather, and watch any movie at least once.

When Ashley finished speaking, she seemed lost in thought for a moment, then blinked and took something small and slender from inside the podium. She held up Jenny's first instrument for all to see, a cheap penny whistle, then placed it in Jenny's hand in the casket.

Tears started dripping down Ashley's scarred cheeks, so she hurried up an aisle, but as she was passing the second row of seats, something made her stop. She looked around, and her eyes met two other very sad eyes. Not knowing why, her hand reached out, and the large lady stood, stumbled past Sister Rachael and others, and was soon standing in the aisle with Ashley, crying deeply and embracing the gymnast.

Somehow, through her own feelings, Ashley saw an opportunity and took it. She slowly guided the grieving mother to the podium. During the next ten minutes, neither spoke to the audience as the other speakers had, but rather shared with each other fond memories of Jenny. The grieving mother spoke of the unbearable quiet of her house after Jenny went to the nursing home. The funeral guests perched on the edge of their seats, listening to the private and intimate conversation, and few faces remained dry.

Finally, they both fell silent, and Ashley guided the woman back to her seat.

Melodies from Jenny's music played again, and Sister Sarah led several young ballet dancers, who pranced around Jenny's casket even as bearers approached and lifted their burden.

Jenny's mother slowly walked hand-in-hand with Sister Rachael toward the cemetery, and most of the other guests followed.

Finally, after everyone else had left the temple, Ashley's own feelings caught up with her, and she sank onto the floor and cried like a baby. A few moments later, she felt arms around her, and looked up to see Ilika, with Kibi, Boro, and Sata right behind him.

✳   ✳   ✳

Chapter 40: A Far-Distant Place

After a quiet, leisurely breakfast the following morning with the members of Lyceum, Ilika and his crew wandered back to the ship. Without a word, they all began checking supply levels and running diagnostics. Sata selected the flight plan that would take them home.

Arantiloria appeared, cross-legged, in the middle of the large table.

"Hi, purple-hair," Kibi said in greeting from the watch station.

The training specialist laughed. "Leaving so soon?"

Ilika, looking at fuel levels with Boro, frowned slightly. "This mission hasn't been long enough?"

Arantiloria laughed again. "You're almost done. The first performance of Jenny's symphony is tomorrow, Nebador time. How many Lyceum members were present at Jenny's death?"

Ilika stepped up to the steward's station, thinking. "Twelve ... no, thirteen."

"And how many passenger seats do you have?"

Ilika grinned. "Room for one more!"

Arantiloria nodded.

Sata came up from the bridge with wide eyes. "I bet you had to ask Melorania herself to get *that* approved!"

"No, Sata, I had to go a *lot* higher than Melorania ... but she put in a good word for me. It just so happens that this planet is due for a nudge forward."

"You have anyone in mind for the fourteenth seat?" Ilika asked the training specialist.

"No. You can let Lyceum decide."

Ilika looked at Sata. "Sounds like a job for the mission leader."

"Tell them, eyes and ears only," Arantiloria added, "no recording devices."

Sata nodded and strode through the hatch.

✴

All of the invited guests were called to an emergency meeting, including Brother Malcolm, a simple, quiet man who worked in the kitchen and the gardens, and who had been selected randomly to fill the extra seat. Sister Rebecca would only say that they were invited to the first performance, perhaps the only performance, of Jenny's symphony. It was somewhere far away, and they would journey there in the same ship that had recently saved six members from certain death. The ship was preparing to depart, and they had one minute to decide.

All of them nodded, some with huge grins, others with hearts in their throats. Minutes later, they were hurrying toward Lost Forest Heliport Pad Three. Few of them had seen the outside of the Manessa Kwi, none the inside.

Arantiloria disappeared before the first few approached the hatch.

Shawn's mind had been swirling ever since Jenny's death, trying to figure out the relationship between their visitors and the figures of religious history he had studied and worshipped all his life. As he stepped, with fear and trembling, up the ramp and into the mysterious ship, only Liberty's firm hand kept him from feeling dizzy.

Liberty knew little of religious history, but was very aware that this little ship had recently plucked her from the clutches of Death with such determination that the helicopter, which she had once thought of as powerful, had been broken to pieces.

The moment Sister Rebecca stepped into the ship, she sensed that she was somewhere else, far from Lyceum. She knew she was seeing, with her old eyes, and touching, with her wrinkled skin, the real thing, of which Lyceum was just a pale shadow.

Sister Marsha, the hospice center nurse, stood at the base of the ramp trying to breathe. Something about these people, and everything they did, went against her deepest values. For some reason, they seemed to accept, even celebrate, Jenny's death. To her, every illness, and certainly every death, was a terrible event to be avoided at all costs.

Brother Kenneth appeared at her side and offered his hand.

She didn't accept his hand, but held her breath and forced her legs to take her up the ramp.

Sister Rachael the artist followed young Sarah into the ship, and was immediately enthralled by the harmonious colors, elegant curving lines, and rich, comforting textures. Everything, from the simplest control panel to the strongest structural beam, was gracefully integrated. Nothing was fake, nothing for show, and yet everything was beautiful. She grinned like a child in a candy store.

When Ashley, last of all, arrived at the ship, Brother Malcolm was still at the bottom of the ramp, shuffling his feet and looking at the floor. She held out her hand to him, he grinned and took it, and together they went aboard.

Kibi, standing beside a glowing panel, gestured to the remaining two seats, both in the front row beside Sarah.

The steward spent a few minutes helping with inertia straps and passing out little pillows, then stepped back to look over her passengers. They were much better behaved than her ship full of young reptiles about a year before.

Seeing that no one seemed to need anything else, she strode down the ramp, walked all the way around the ship, and pressed the hanger door control.

Back inside, she took her station seat, closed the hatch, and spoke softly in the language of Nebador. "Manessa, is Arantiloria my star transit guardian?"

"No, she does not have that ability, but one is here who does."

"Ship and passengers secure for departure," she announced to her captain on the bridge.

Sister Nancy had not piloted, nor even flown in any aircraft, since the failed attempt to rescue Senator Buchanan. She knew she had to wait at least until the shaking inside her stopped. She wasn't absolutely sure she would ever again hold the cyclic and collective controls of a helicopter.

But after a little nervousness at the thought of journeying to some unknown far-distant place, she was beginning to relax, and was comforted knowing they were attending the first performance of a symphony written by a little girl she had seen, with her own eyes, in life and death.

Also, Nancy was fascinated by the mysterious ship that had remained hidden at Lyceum for several months, only coming out once to save her life. From where she was now sitting, she could see the large young man who must be the pilot. He had the quietness and intensity that Nancy had seen many times, in others and in herself, that came from knowing the journey would rest on his shoulders, more than on anyone else's.

Nancy was thrilled as she watched the large screen, first as they snaked through the trees, following back roads, then as they pitched up, instantly gained speed, and rapidly left the clouds and sky behind to reveal the star-studded blackness of space. But she was confused, for a moment, when she became irresistibly sleepy.

She must have nodded off, as the next thing she saw on the screen was a vast and beautiful array of gleaming jewels floating in space, some clustered close together, some attached to others with glowing threads, and a few off by themselves but still part of the same grand design.

When Sarah awoke and beheld the glowing local universe capital, she instinctively reached out her hand to whomever was near, and found Ashley's hand.

They grinned at each other, then turned back to the screen.

Small and large ships came and went, but they did so like flower petals floating on the breeze, not like cars in traffic or people bustling along a sidewalk.

Each glowing jewel was a different size and shape, some as big as a large building, others more the size of a mountain. When the ship came near one of them, Sarah could see huge windows of many shapes, with movement inside, but little of it, maybe none of it, appeared to be . . . people.

Sarah squeezed Ashley's hand, and was comforted when Ashley did the same. She could hear the crew speaking softly among themselves in a language she had never heard, except a few times at Lyceum when they thought no one was listening.

From where she was sitting, Sarah could see part of the small screen in front of Sata, who seemed to be speaking to the person on the screen. Sarah rubbed her eyes, but when she looked again, the green bird on the screen was still there.

At that moment, the ship entered a tunnel, and the sparkling walls and gleaming windows of the local universe capital of Kerusemia could no longer be seen.

✳   ✳   ✳

Chapter 41: First Performance

Brother Malcolm would rather die than be the first one to step through the hatch into this magnificent and frightening place, so he shuffled toward the toilet room as soon as the shaggy-haired lady released his seat belt.

A tall, golden-haired man stood just outside the hatch, greeting each guest with a warm handclasp or a slight bow. Sister Rebecca took his hand and felt comforted in body, mind, and soul. Liberty blushed when she looked into his penetrating eyes. Marsha steeled herself for the encounter, and offered neither hand nor eye contact.

When Brother Malcolm finally peeked out of the toilet room, all the other Lyceum members were gone, and the shaggy-haired lady was waiting for him. He swallowed and shuffled toward the hatch. Last place was safest, he knew.

At the bottom of the ramp, the golden-haired man bowed deeply to Brother Malcolm, put his arm around the simple Lyceum member, and together they made their way along the boarding tunnel.

※

Kibi, standing at her console, let out a deep sigh. "In a way, reptiles are easier."

Ilika swiveled his chair and grinned. "With our own kind, many levels of cultural and emotional concerns come into play. You did better than I would have!"

Sata and Boro, just finishing the shut-down procedures at navigation and helm, turned and smiled.

"I was . . . wondering about quarantine . . ." Boro began thoughtfully.

Sata shook her head. "Lyceum's planet is pre-approved, and we haven't been anywhere else."

Boro nodded.

"Let's go hear Jenny's music, shall we?" the captain proposed.

*

Beyond the boarding tunnel, a dimly-lit passage brought them directly to the visitors' box, a room with a few dozen comfortable seats that looked over a low railing into a vast indoor theater. Row upon row of spectators were getting settled, and a large circular stage, currently empty, filled the bottom of the huge space. A ring of water encircled the stage, with heads bobbing and flippers splashing. Little bridges spanned the water at several points.

Elegant tables along the sides of the visitors' box offered finger foods and beverages, and several Lyceum members were filling plates. The tall, golden-haired man stayed with Brother Malcolm, holding his plate while the simple man selected food and drink with a child-like grin.

Suddenly Ashley stood before Ilika. "This arena . . . theater . . . whatever . . . is full of birds and lizards and dolphins and . . . I don't know what else!"

Ilika smiled. "Is it?"

Kibi and Sata, both within earshot, suppressed the urge to snicker, but couldn't help smiling.

Sister Rebecca decided to rescue Ilika. "You didn't think humans were top-dogs in the universe, just because we are on *our* planet, did you, Ashley?"

"Well . . . actually . . . I . . ."

Rebecca grinned and interrupted. "Rachael and Sarah are at the railing, seeing how many different kinds they can spot. I bet they'd love some help."

Ashley's scarred face twisted in thought. "I . . . guess I should . . . take another look . . ."

Ilika and Sister Rebecca looked at each other and exchanged silent laughter.

*

Over the next quarter hour, hundreds of musicians set up their instruments on the circular stage, leaving a large open space in the middle, and aisles between their sections.

Sarah and Ashley bounced up and down with excitement when they finally spotted a few humans in the audience, and one or two among the musicians.

Eventually, everyone in the visitors' box was seated with food, drink, or both.

The lighting in the vast theater, from unseen sources, slowly dimmed. The entire audience fell silent, thousands of hearts beating in anticipation.

The musicians created the opening phrase of Jenny's symphony, first one voice, then three, then seven, all played in perfect harmony for the first time.

Shafts of light found two large fanators circling, each with a slender monkey mammal riding. The birds moved their huge wings to the rhythm, turned and banked to the musical phrases, then back-winged, almost face to face, just above the center of the stage as the symphony's first exciting crescendo ended. The musicians rested, and the large birds touched the floor with strong feet.

A tiny white light hurried through the air to catch up.

Rini and Mati slid from the birds' backs and bowed to them.

The fanators bowed in return and walked up the aisles into the audience.

Brother Chad, basking in the memory of the music he had just heard, leaned back with a contented smile on his face. Shawn wore a puzzled expression. Marsha stared with intense, judgmental eyes.

Mati, standing beside Rini in the center of the circular stage, looked around at the thousands and thousands of Nebador citizens, and just as many sparkling points of light of many different colors, and filled her lungs with the rich air of the local universe capital. "The monkey-mammal girl who discovered the beautiful music you will hear today had no other path she could follow in her mortal life."

The tiny white light settled onto Mati's shoulder, who glanced at it, then continued. "Jenny accepted that situation gracefully, far more gracefully than I once accepted a similar fate."

Sata translated for the Lyceum members in the visitors' box.

Mati giggled when the little white light swirled around her several times. "On this mission, in addition to my usual piloting and engineering jobs, I had to keep this freckled boy, whom I love dearly, from falling over his own feet while he brought Jenny's music to Kerusemia."

The white spec of light jumped to Rini and danced in the air in front of him as he stood chuckling, unable to speak for a long moment.

Eventually the light settled onto his shoulder, allowing him to think. "My little brain barely held all that wonderful music!"

The audience roared with laughter and other sounds of humor and sympathy.

"Now that the music has been completely recorded, scored, analyzed, synchronized, taken apart and put back together, I can relax and try to remember what my name is, how to do my job, stuff like that."

As the audience howled and Sata translated, Sarah and Ashley grinned at each other.

"The only sad part," Rini went on, holding in a smile, "is that Jenny cannot be present to hear her symphony performed for the first time."

The tiny white light started bouncing against Rini's head, trying to get his attention.

Rini smiled and pretended not to notice while the entire theater filled with cackling, honking, and happy roaring once more.

The visitors from Lyceum looked confused. With a huff, Sister Marsha flopped backwards into her seat and crossed her arms, frowning.

The lighting of the vast theater dimmed again.

*

The symphony began once more, this time quietly, with a subtle, tentative feeling. Soft horns carried the melody, while strings created a background as dancers came down the aisles with flowing arms or wings.

The little white light bounced to the rhythm and swayed to the melody, sometimes around Mati and Rini, who had taken seats in the front row of the audience, sometimes around the dancers, sometimes all by itself.

Brother Malcolm stood and did a clumsy dance for a moment, then sat back down and looked around to see if anyone was mad at him.

When the second theme began, the horns and strings teamed up on three of the voices, and reptiles, suddenly illuminated by unseen lights, brought in a strong rhythm with drums of many sizes. Sparkling points of light flowed into the air from somewhere high above, pulsing to the music, a different group for each musical voice, a different color for each tone.

The tiny white light seemed overwhelmed for a moment, and hid behind Mati. After a moment, it carefully crept up to her shoulder.

Shawn was trembling and sweating. None of this looked like he had been taught to expect. He glanced at Liberty, who appeared ready to hop up and dance with Malcolm.

The first bridge in the music was so intricate that the horns and drums rested and a section of insects began tapping on their keyboards, legs moving almost faster than eyes could follow. Rich sounds, that no simple instrument could make, filled the theater as birds took to the air and wove a pattern that somehow complemented the music perfectly.

The little light on Mati's shoulder found it's courage and floated up to join the birds, quickly picking up the pattern.

Shawn breathed deeply, held Liberty's hand tightly, and tried to focus on the beauty before him, instead of the theological analysis in his head.

When Sister Marsha saw who — or rather what — was playing the keyboard instruments, she closed her eyes and concentrated on keeping her stomach under control.

The next theme began suddenly, and several furry horn players stood to pick up the melody. The lone white light was ready for the transition when the birds departed and many colorful shapes, made of pure light, began to dance in the air and on every surface. It chased the dancing lights, mimicking the shapes they made, dashing from avian to equine, insect to ursine.

Then the little light entered the visitors' box and quickly traced a shape, for each person, in the air before them — a diamond or spiral, circle or triangle. But when it came to Ashley, it stayed much longer, and soon the young gymnast had an elaborate snowflake, made of light, etched into her memory forever.

Sarah watched and giggled with delight.

Brother Kenneth saw that Marsha was in distress, so he reached over and touched her hand. She jerked it back and opened her eyes, then silently reconsidered, grabbed his hand, and held on for dear life.

When the first musical transition came, the audience was almost startled as the entire theater went completely dark for several heartbeats.

For a moment, the little white light was alone, until it dashed into the sound box of a reptile's stringed instrument, causing him to hiss with laughter.

Soon, a shaft of light revealed a green bird dancing with strong movements in the center of the stage, a single wind instrument took up the haunting melody, an energetic blue avian joined the dance, a stringed instrument added a bold harmony, a red bird leapt into the dance, and a powerful drum completed the ensemble.

Emerging from it's hiding place, the little light spun itself into the air with delight.

Sister Nancy, so comfortable with machines large and small, decided in that moment that she was going to add something new to her life — music, dance, painting — she wasn't sure exactly what, but something.

The next musical bridge was majestic and triumphant, and all the musicians created a rich sound as hundreds of colored lights filled the air again, pulsing brightly to the rhythm.

But the orchestra did not resolve the tension it created, until suddenly a single feathered horn player stood in a shaft of light as the rest of the stage darkened. In its clear voice it began the next theme, while the other musicians, still in near-darkness, took up the quieter voices.

The white spec of light hovered for a long moment, transfixed by the horn player.

Brother Chad always enjoyed hearing this theme, so relaxing and comforting. For the first time since the symphony started, he turned his head and looked around. Thousands of creatures of every size and shape were sitting or perching with rapt attention, listening to the same music he had attempted to record in Lyceum's little studio. His heart throbbed in his chest at the realization that he had been a small part of something so great and wonderful.

Ashley was grinning, and felt nearly overwhelmed with happiness. She had never, in her wildest dreams, imagined that more than a few people would ever want to hear Jenny's music. With few exceptions, only old people listened to symphonies.

Marsha's mind raced. She had admitted to no one, and barely even to herself, that she was attracted to the handsome doctor beside her. Now that he was holding her hand, she could not stop deep feelings from welling up inside her. Somehow the music was making every cell in her body throb with a yearning to know life on all levels, and no longer hide from it just because . . . there might be germs or side effects.

Seemingly in anticipation, the little white glow dashed back to the comfort of Rini's shoulder.

The part of the symphony began that Brother Chad called *The War of the Worlds*. Probably the most complex passage of Jenny's song, it brought the bone-scraping tension to a peak. The musicians provided everything from the shrillest whistles in Voice Two, to the throbbing drumbeats of Voice Seven, while lights of many shapes and colors dashed around the theater, colliding, recoiling, tangling and untangling.

When the musical tension reached its climax, suddenly equines and tall giraffadea came thundering down all the aisles, and the little white light again dashed for the safety of a stringed instrument's sound box.

Ashley frowned slightly, as she had never been comfortable with this part of the song. Brother Chad had assured her that it was important, in order to emphasize the beauty of the themes that followed.

And indeed, nearly half an hour into the symphony, Ashley's favorite parts began. All the stringed instruments created flowing, undulating melodies and cool, quiet harmonies. A variety of different musicians executed the section Ashley called *The Playground*. Its frolicking tunes and laughing rhythms reminded her of the times, years before, when Jenny had been able to play with her in the park.

The tiny white glow was out again, bouncing and spinning joyfully, sometimes forcing musicians and dancers to pause, laugh or grin, then re-find their place in music or movement.

Brother Chad knew the symphony was nearing its end when the part he called *Thunder* began, booming and crashing, with tiny, delicate melodies appearing just in time to be purposefully drowned out.

Then all the themes from the entire symphony returned, as if to say farewell. Countless balls of colored light glimmered, dancers filled the aisles and the stage, birds filled the air, and everyone sat wide-eyed, remembering their favorite parts. Suddenly all the voices came together in a completely satisfying chord that made all the listeners feel they were bursting out of deep water and into air, or out of a dark and frightening cave into daylight. All the musicians stood to enrich the ending with the power of their instruments.

Brother Kenneth squeezed Marsha's hand tightly, and they exchanged smiles.

Ashley and Sarah embraced each other.

Shawn and Liberty kissed deeply.

Malcolm stood and did another little dance.

Finally the beautiful chord faded, all the musicians and dancers bowed, and the audience roared with applause, whistles, honks, stomping feet, squeaks and splashes, and many other joyful noises of appreciation.

The little white light settled into Mati's lap, completely exhausted.

✳   ✳   ✳

Chapter 42: Farewell to Lyceum

As the birds, mammals, reptiles, and other creatures filed out of the vast theater, the visiting Lyceum members sat quietly, most of them slowly becoming aware that they had just witnessed something greater than *anything* that had ever happened on their little planet.

The older ones, and Brother Chad, pondered the beauty and grandeur of the music and dance they had beheld with their own ears and eyes.

Kenneth and Marsha continued to hold hands, and even though they wouldn't claim to understand what they had just seen and heard, they knew, looking into each other's eyes, that something wonderful had just begun between them.

The young ones all sat with thoughtful expressions, sometimes frowns, slowly realizing they had glimpsed things that didn't fit into their previous assumptions about the universe.

Malcolm was tired and ready to go home.

The quiet was broken when Mati and Rini, laughing and chatting, entered the visitors' box from the rear and immediately grabbed plates and began picking over the goodies on the tables.

The other members of the crew rose and joined them, happy to be all together again. That prompted Ashley, Sarah, Shawn, and Liberty to do the same. Soon everyone was milling about, nibbling on finger foods or sipping fruit juices.

Several Lyceum members put questions to the tall, golden-haired man, or to Ilika and his crew.

In reply, they received only smiles.

As Boro munched on some tasty snacks and listened to others talking, he noticed that none of the Lyceum people ever mentioned the thousands of colored lights, or the little white light.

*

The return journey to the Lost Forest Heliport was quick and easy, piloted by Mati, with Rini glad to be back at his watch station. Night had settled over the land, and the pathway lights sparkled in every garden.

After saying good night to their thoughtful passengers, the crew settled around the table. Ilika quickly made six mugs of tea.

"That little white light," Boro began, "that was Jenny, wasn't it?"

Mati and Rini both nodded while sipping tea.

"Too bad we couldn't bring her back with us," Kibi said.

Ilika laughed. "She has another path now."

Mati nodded. "Coming to that performance was a special deal, only possible because . . . you know . . . she wrote it."

Rini chuckled. "Even though she was brand new there, it just *wouldn't* have been fair to not let her attend."

Boro took a moment to compose his question. "Ilika . . . why couldn't they see . . . Jenny and the other spirits?"

Their captain took a slow breath before he answered. "By living and working in Nebador, we are being changed, Boro. We are gaining abilities that are extremely rare among people who live on planets. I think Rebecca, Rachael, Sarah, and maybe Malcolm, caught some glimpses. Lyceum is the natural gathering place of the gifted and talented on this planet. Even so, Arantiloria had to help them see the little gifts of light that Jenny gave them."

Everyone fell silent as they sipped tea and pondered Ilika's words, the sights and sounds of Jenny's symphony, and their first visit to Kerusemia, the local universe capital.

Eventually Boro yawned. "Can we go home now . . . I mean . . . maybe after a good night's sleep?"

"No," Sata replied.

Everyone looked at her.

"I noticed on my console on the way back, something's been added to the mission. We have to pick someone up in three and a half days. I haven't looked up the coordinates, but it's on this continent."

Kibi looked at Ilika.

He shrugged. "I wouldn't mind three more days at Lyceum."

"Swimming pool!" Boro declared.

"Gardens!" Rini chose.

"Library!" Sata added.

"Right now, I'm sleepy," Kibi announced.

"I'm with *her*," Ilika said.

Mati laughed and started collecting empty mugs.

*

The crew of the Manessa Kwi didn't awaken in time to have breakfast with the members of Lyceum, but eventually made their way along the carpeted, glass-walled corridors toward the cafeteria.

They were almost to the main lobby when a familiar face approached, going in the opposite direction, with a small duffle bag over one shoulder.

Make-up hid most of her scars.

"Hi, Ilika!" Ashley greeted. "Hi, everybody!"

The crew gathered around her. "Where are you headed?" Boro asked to make conversation.

"I *finally* don't have any medical check-ups for an entire *week*, so I'm going home to visit my parents and friends, see how Jenny's mom is doing, stuff like that."

"We have to go in three days," Ilika informed her.

Ashley's face became sad. "So . . . this could be the last time I see you guys."

She set down her travel bag and hugged each of them, Ilika last and longest. When she finally stood alone again, her face was wet and her make-up ruined. "Please come back and visit when you can."

"We will," Ilika assured, "but it might be a while."

"Our missions are getting harder . . . and longer," Sata shared.

Ashley nodded, picked up her bag, and continued on toward the heliport.

Kibi took Ilika's hand and squeezed it. "She's a strong one."

"Yes," he agreed, watching Ashley walk with confidence into the crowded lobby of the recreation center. "Shall we . . . go find some breakfast?"

*

The following day, Ilika and Kibi were strolling, hand in hand, along one of the trails through the woods, when two people appeared ahead, jogging toward them.

Kibi grinned.

Liberty, in the lead, began walking to slow her breathing. Shawn did the same at her side.

"We hear . . . you guys are . . . leaving soon," Shawn said between gasps of air.

"Yes, in two days," Ilika confirmed.

They all found tree roots or rocks to perch on.

"This girl is so good for me," Shawn began. "Can you believe . . . I have *never* gone running, or camping, or anything else challenging, with my dad."

Ilika chuckled. "Your dad doesn't seem like the kind of person who likes challenges."

"He likes to be in *control!*" Shawn verified.

Kibi blinked. "I heard he might go to prison."

Shawn nodded. "I wouldn't wish that on anyone, but . . . I think it might be good for him."

After a moment of silence, Liberty spoke for the first time. "Thank you, Kibi."

"Um . . . you're welcome . . . for what?"

The taller girl smiled. "For loving Ilika, so I'd realize that Shawn was the best possible boy for me."

Kibi nodded with sparkling eyes.

"When the evaluation week first started, and I saw that Shawn was, you know, all goody-goody, studying religion and stuff, I didn't think that would work for me, even though he's cute."

Shawn blushed.

"But the more I got to know Lyceum, and started seeing larger purposes in my life, then Shawn's big break with his father, *my* father being killed, and finally Jenny's music and that trip . . . it all started to fit together."

"We were just talking about that," Shawn began, "before we went jogging. We know we can never just *tell* people about that trip, and the musical performance, and all those . . . different kinds of people . . . without it sounding like complete fiction . . . or getting us thrown in the loony bin . . ."

Liberty laughed. "But it'll really help us to spot when someone . . ."

"Like my father," Shawn interjected with a grin.

". . . is, you know, full of . . ." She paused and looked at Shawn.

"Bullshit," Shawn finished.

Ilika and Kibi both howled with laughter.

✳

At lunch with the Lyceum members, on the crew's last full day without any mission responsibilities, Mati and Rini heard a voice in their minds. *Me and Rachael are getting together in the Cedar Garden for some . . . you know . . . telepathy time. Want to join us?*

They both looked toward the source of the message. Sarah was just one table over, and was looking at them, but her lips weren't moving, other than to chew a bite of her sandwich.

The couple mentally nodded to each other, then projected their answer to Sarah.

Sarah continued chewing as she reached for the mustard jar.

✳

Sarah and I meet once a week to talk about whatever's going on — I'm her mentor, every Lyceum member has one — and we usually do it completely unshielded, but you two are welcome to keep your minds on the public level.

Yeah, Rini began, *there are things we're not supposed to share. People on planets like this have been misunderstanding glimpses they get of . . . the universe . . . since the beginning of time!*

So . . . Sarah pondered for the other three to hear, *why were we able to go to that huge, beautiful theater to hear Jenny's song?*

Mati thought for a moment. *Even though glimpses of star stations and local universe capitals easily lead to confusion, they're important to the growth of every planet with people. We once parked our ship somewhere the priests would see it because Mel . . . the one in charge . . . knew those people needed to see how bad their priests were.*

They tried to burn the ship, Rini explained, *but to Manessa, it was like warming her toes at a campfire.*

The other three laughed.

So can you give us any advice, Rachael began, *about what we should or shouldn't do with our glimpse of the universe, to avoid confusion and misunderstanding?*

Rini and Mati pondered the question for a long minute, sharing some thoughts just between them. Eventually they nodded at each other.

Try to think of it, and remember it, as a personal experience, Rini said, *not as something you should tell the world about.*

It's okay to let it inspire you, Mati added, *but you're on thin ice if you write some holy book about it, or start a new religion or political party . . .*

✳

That evening, Boro and Sata were exploring Lyceum corridors and lobbies they had not yet seen, when they came to an open door.

Sata read the sign on the wall. "Recording Studio."

They peeked in.

Brother Chad sat in a chair, tapping at a computer keyboard. A large display screen showed musical notes as they were written on that planet. "That's five," he mumbled to himself. "About a million to go."

"Hi," Sata said softly.

He looked. "Come in, come in! I was just entering my most recent revelation."

"Are you writing a . . . song?" Boro asked, coming close.

"No, no, this is Jenny's symphony. As soon as we got back, I started wondering if maybe I could get it properly synchronized so it can be played here someday. And in a dream that night, I saw a little section of the score. It was the first time I've dashed to the studio in my pajamas!"

Sata and Boro chuckled.

"I'm getting one or two more bits each day, sometimes when I'm awake. This one came while I was washing dishes. At this rate, getting Jenny's symphony all properly scored is going to take years, maybe the rest of my life."

Boro blinked. "Wow."

"It'll be worth it. It's the . . . most important thing . . . I've ever been able to do. And when I get chunks of it in shape, I'll have the others, who were there, listen to it to help me spot problems."

Sata remembered the reptiles they had helped to resettle on a jungle planet, and Silmula Sorafax telling the crew they'd be involved with that project for the rest of their lives.

✳ ✳ ✳

Chapter 43: The Gift

After their last meal with the members of Lyceum, a fancy breakfast with every imaginable delicacy, the crew of the Manessa Kwi wandered slowly back toward the ship. They took their time, savoring one last look at the beautiful architecture, the wide variety of interesting artworks on display, the inviting gardens and ponds, and the cozy corridors and lounges.

As they had many times before, they passed through the main lobby, the recreation center, and finally the heliport lobby, before arriving at the hanger for Pad Three. Kibi used her Lyceum bracelet, for the last time, to unlock the door.

Party horns and poppers immediately caused their hearts to race, and after a moment, grins replaced surprised looks on Ilika and his crew.

Most of the Lyceum members who had journeyed to the local universe capital stood in a half-circle around a small table. Something, about half a meter high, remained hidden under a white cloth.

The crew of the Manessa Kwi completed the circle with sparkling eyes and curious faces.

As soon as everyone fell silent, Sister Rebecca took a slow, deep breath. "We are glad you had to stay three more days, as our gift was not quite finished until yesterday!"

Ilika smiled and looked into her gentle, old eyes.

"Perhaps," she went on, "if I wanted to be politically correct, I would say that this gift is from all the people of this planet, as a gesture of friendship and respect."

A moment of silence lingered, until Sata broke it with one word in the local language. "But . . ."

Rebecca looked at her. "Your civilization must truly be amazing if your upbringing could produce someone with such penetrating intelligence and wisdom in a person so young."

Sata blushed. "Actually . . . my parents are medieval innkeepers. But my new civilization has tested and trained me — and all of us — in ways you wouldn't believe."

Kibi and Boro nodded vigorously. The rest just smiled.

"However that may be," Sister Rebecca continued, "I think all of you, on both sides of this circle, know, as well as I do, that I would be lying if I gave this gift on behalf of this entire planet, whose primary activities are economic oppression and tribal warfare."

Ilika chuckled. "It is like that, in one way or another, on almost every planet."

"Comforting, but not a good excuse," Brother Jacob said softly.

Rebecca looked at Sister Nancy.

"This gift," the pilot said, stepping to the table, "represents our promise that Lyceum will remain open to you and your people, for as long as we can defend it from the forces that would tear it down."

"And even if Lyceum does fall," Brother Chad said, stepping to the other side of the table, "this gift is our thanks for saving Jenny's music, and allowing us to hear and see it performed, an experience none of us will ever forget."

They lifted the cloth to reveal a small replica of the sculptured globe in Lyceum's main lobby, this one made of glass and accented with sparkling gemstones and precious metals.

"Wow," Rini breathed. "Very . . . pretty!"

Sata smiled. "It will go in the museum on the nearest star station, and people from all over the local universe will come to see it."

The Lyceum members smiled with pride, and several couldn't hold back tears of happiness.

✳

The gift was packed into a sturdy box with plenty of padding. Kibi and Boro secured it behind the passenger area.

Hugs, handshakes, and parting words were shared, until Sister Rebecca hobbled, with Chad's help, toward the corridor. The other Lyceum members followed, except Nancy, who stood by the hanger door controls.

Kibi walked around the ship to check for obstacles, then stood on the ramp and nodded to Nancy.

The huge door began to slowly rise.

The ramp and hatch vanished, and a minute later, the golden ship soundlessly began to hover and its landing struts retracted.

Nancy watched as the mysterious craft slipped outside, gained a little altitude, and began to wind its way silently through the trees.

Brother Malcolm appeared at her side. "I hope they come back soon."

"That would be nice, Malcolm, but I don't think so. I think our little world has given all it can to the greater universe for . . . who knows how long."

Malcolm looked at the ground and shuffled his feet.

Nancy pressed the *close* button, wondering if she would have the honor of living long enough to see the next time a ship landed on Pad Three.

*

"Where am I going?" Boro asked in the language of Nebador from the helm.

"Flight plan on channel five," Sata said, "and we'll be just about on time."

Boro looked it over.

"Still no idea who we're picking up?" Ilika asked from the command chair.

Sata shook her head, without turning around, while making a selection on her console. "No other Nebador ships on the planet, and no active missions listed."

Ilika turned to look at Kibi, and they exchanged shrugs.

"It's only six hundred kilometers," Boro noted. "Ion one, please, Mati."

"Ion one, full inertia canceling, warmed and ready."

"Weather and local traffic on channel four," Rini said. "Nothing but some lenticular clouds over the mountains, and an airplane at twenty-two thousand meters."

"A little more distance from Lyceum," Ilika requested, "then the pick-up point is your flight objective."

Boro nodded, and started following a dirt road through the forest.

*

Ashley grinned when the trail brought her through an oak grove and she saw the Manessa Kwi perched in the clearing beyond.

Rini and Mati sat side by side in the open hatch, Ilika was at the bottom of the ramp, Boro was hanging by his arms from a low tree branch nearby, and Kibi was seated on the ground, examining some little insect.

"What are *you* guys doing here?" Ashley asked with complete innocence as she approached.

Kibi looked up. "We don't know. What are *you* doing here?"

The gymnast plopped onto the ground near Kibi. Overhearing, Sata emerged from the ship, Boro dropped to the ground, and everyone gathered around.

"I've been having dreams about these hills for three nights!" Ashley announced. "I used to come up here with my mom and dad when I was a little kid."

"Anything . . . happen in your dreams?" Ilika asked.

"No. I'd always wake up when I got to that oak grove," she replied, pointing behind her.

Rini grinned with understanding.

"How are your parents, and Jenny's mom?" Sata asked.

Ashley's expression darkened a bit, and she started pulling dry grass in front of her. "Um . . . Jenny's mom is acting like her death was somehow my fault. *My* mom avoids looking at me whenever she can find a reason not to. My dad's okay, be we were never very close. I'm adopted, you know."

"Did you get to visit your friends?" Mati asked with a slight tilt of her head.

Ashley looked at her for a moment. "You mean the friends who aren't my friends anymore because I have scars on my face and I'm not doing gymnastics right now?"

Mati frowned.

"That's cold," Boro said. "Are you going back to Lyceum soon?"

Ashley brightened. "I have a ticket for day after tomorrow!"

A long moment of silence stretched as no one could think of anything to say.

"I . . . think I know . . . what this part of our mission is about," Ilika began slowly and tentatively. "Any information to the contrary, Arantiloria?"

"Who's Aran . . . whatever?" Ashley asked.

"Our training supervisor," Kibi revealed. "Jenny's angel."

Sata raised her eyebrows. "Is that enough time, Ilika?"

"Yes, that's plenty."

Ashley looked completely confused.

"Ashley," Ilika began, "we're here to offer you a ride."

"To Lyceum?"

Rini shook his head.

Mati smiled with understanding. "To a beautiful place called Satamia Star Station."

Boro suddenly opened his mouth. *"Now* I see why we had to pick her up *here!* If she disappeared from Lyceum, it would cause them trouble."

Ilika nodded. "Ashley, your education, your religious background, your gymnastics training, and your own temperament and values choices . . . have all prepared you for this moment, but there will still be many, many surprises ahead . . ."

Rini and Mati both nodded.

". . . and vast amounts of knowledge you must study and learn . . ."

Kibi and Sata grinned.

". . . and you must make your decision here and now. If you are coming with us, you must disappear, today, without anyone here, or at Lyceum, having the slightest knowledge of what happened to you."

Ilika fell silent, and Ashley sat thoughtfully, rolling the situation around in her head. She looked at the oak trees and the blue sky. By turning her head, she could see part of her hometown in the valley below.

"You can only step onto this path of your own free will," Ilika added.

After another minute, Ashley slipped off her little day pack and opened it. "I was wondering why I grabbed these this morning. Now I know." She smiled as she held up her diary, a stuffed animal none of the crew members could name, and a little wooden box of sea shells and other treasures.

Ashley looked at each of the six people from somewhere in the stars, then turned her head and glanced at her hometown one last time.

When she turned back, she looked at her new friends with sparkling eyes and a big grin.

✳   ✳   ✳   ✳   ✳

Buna's Search

by Shadow Buffalo-walker

This story takes place after Buna and Misa bid farewell to Ilika and the others near the swamp in *Book Three: Selection.*

Misa and I didn't mind walking to the capital city with Neti and Toli. I knew our paths would go different ways very soon. Neti kept saying things about us all sticking together. I could tell Misa didn't like the idea, and I didn't like it either. My guts told me we should split up right then, but I didn't say anything just to be nice to Neti. Then Toli got all dorky at the city gate and it cost us more to get in because of it. I should have listened to my guts.

By the time we got to the marketplace, I was glad Neti wanted to get a room at the inn before doing anything else. Toli was like a little puppy and did everything she said. Misa and I waved good-bye. When they were gone, we both laughed our heads off and took Tera to a stable. The bakery still had some tarts so we got a bunch and sat down on a log to eat our dinner.

"Boots!" Misa said. "I'm gonna get boots!"

We stayed at the witch's house for three days and Misa got her boots. I'm glad we didn't stay any longer because the religious orders were getting weird. I kept seeing things I could spend my money on, but then I thought about how I had to drag everything around while I looked for Noni. I could either buy stuff, and a wagon, and horses to pull it, or I could look for Noni. I decided to look for Noni.

*

We visited the old shack and the corral. I think Tera remembered it, but didn't like it when I put her inside and closed the gate. She was glad when we left the next day.

Farmer Keni sold us bread and cheese. Kora remembered me, and said she was happy there and had forgotten all about reading and writing and stuff. While we were there a boy came down the road, and they ran up to the goat pen together. Misa smiled. I think she likes boys.

After that we went into the hills and all the way down to the hot springs. I showed Misa the little camp by the stream, and the sandy place where Noni camped once, but we didn't find Noni anywhere. Misa loved the hot springs, and so did I. She asked if we could stay there forever. A part of me almost wanted to say yes.

We traveled north to Lumber Town, and some other little towns. Misa asked everywhere about her parents, but never found them. Lumber Town had one little store made of new logs and boards, but no inn yet. No one was trying to rebuild her old burned house.

Winter was coming and snow started falling around Lumber Town so we headed south. We visited the house with good people where all the refugees had gone, and they gave us dinner after we carried firewood, but all the people we remembered were gone.

At the little fishing village called Fish, we had fish stew one more time, and camped in the trees, but didn't go onto the beach south of there. I told Misa why it was so dangerous. She shrugged and wanted to go that way, and if we didn't have Tera, I probably would have said ok. I remembered how hard it was to keep Tera under control when she was scared.

On the road south, I saw some sheep for sale by an old shepherd who was gonna live with his son. It was really tempting. I asked if he knew Noni, and he did, but hadn't seen her in months.

When we got to Port Town, I told Misa about all the thieves, and she spotted them as soon as we walked into town. I was glad I hadn't bought any new clothes, and Misa's boots already looked old, so they didn't bother us.

We stayed with the baker all winter. Misa and Kit were like two peas in a pod, and she didn't care that he could hardly talk. He could laugh and play, and that was all that mattered. He showed her his mother's grave. After he curled up to take a nap, I pulled Misa away and showed her the cave by the beach.

I asked all around Port Town if anyone had seen Noni. One sheep shearer remembered her, but hadn't seen her since last spring.

All winter we worked for the baker, and on our days off we walked to little towns and farms and asked about Noni. Sometimes people knew her, but hadn't seen her in a long time.

The next summer we walked all over the kingdom, except the mountains where Noni couldn't go with her wagon and flock. No one in the eastern part of the kingdom knew her, and thought it was weird that a girl would be a shepherdess without a man. One person in the middle of the kingdom remembered her, but hadn't seen her in years.

Even in the western part, people were starting to forget her. I figured out that no one had seen her since about when I first met her. I started to wonder if maybe she was just a spirit that had floated away into the clouds after me and Ilika's other students had said good-bye and gone down to the hot springs. That now seemed a long time ago.

✳

Misa was getting very tired of looking. She kept talking about Port Town, and the baker and his family, and Kit, and the hot springs.

I sighed and felt in my guts that it was time to let go of Noni.

We returned to Port Town, bought a wagon, twelve sheep, and lots of boards and nails. Misa asked Kit if he wanted to join us. He was confused for a while, but said yes when we told him we were gonna stay near Port Town and visit it often.

We took everything up the green valley and built a little house by the hot springs. The sheep loved the grass and started having babies.

I had forgotten all about Noni when one day, in the middle of summer, a shepherd's wagon pulled by a donkey came wobbling along the trail to the hot springs followed by ninety-three sheep.

✳   ✳   ✳

About the Authors

Born in the Mojave Desert, J. Z. Colby now lives and writes deep in a forest of the Pacific Northwest.

He has studied many subjects, formally and informally, including psychology, philosophy, education, and performing arts, but remains a generalist. His primary profession as a mental health counselor, specializing with families and young adults, gives him many stories of personal growth, and the motivation to develop his team of young critiquers and readers.

All his life, he has been drawn toward a broad understanding of human nature, especially those physical, emotional, mental, and spiritual situations in which our capacity to function seems to reach its limits. He finds fascinating those few individuals who can transcend the limits of our common human nature and the dictates of our cultures.

In his spare time, he flies helicopters and airplanes.

He may be contacted at the email address listed on the internet site www.nebador.com.

Shadow Buffalo-walker is completely comfortable on a moon-lit night with coyotes yapping, wolves howling, and buffalo stomping, but has little use for cities and other man-made things. She learned more at the feet of an old native-American woman than in school, but admits that schools are probably necessary for those who want to fit into the human world. For her, it's too late — she has seen the other side, and will spend her life with at least one foot there. The publication of *Buna's Search* was her best 18th birthday gift.

www.ingramcontent.com/pod-product-compliance
Lightning Source LLC
Chambersburg PA
CBHW031336170626
46807CB00002B/726